MW01631697

SEIZURE

SEIZURE

A Novel By

Peter Black

Skean Dhu Press
Cambridge, Massachusetts

Skean Dhu Press
Cambridge, MA 02139
Skeandhupress.com

Publisher's Note: This is a work of fiction. Names, characters, places, and incidents are a product of the author's imagination. Locales and public names are sometimes used for atmospheric purposes. Any resemblance to actual people, living or dead, or to businesses, companies, events, institutions, or locales is completely coincidental.

Cover and text design by Mayapriya Long, Bookwrights
Printed in the United States of America

Seizure/PeterBlack.—1st ed.

ISBN 978-1-952683-00-8 paperback
ISBN 978-1-952683-01-5 hardcover
ISBN 978-1-952683-02-2 ebook

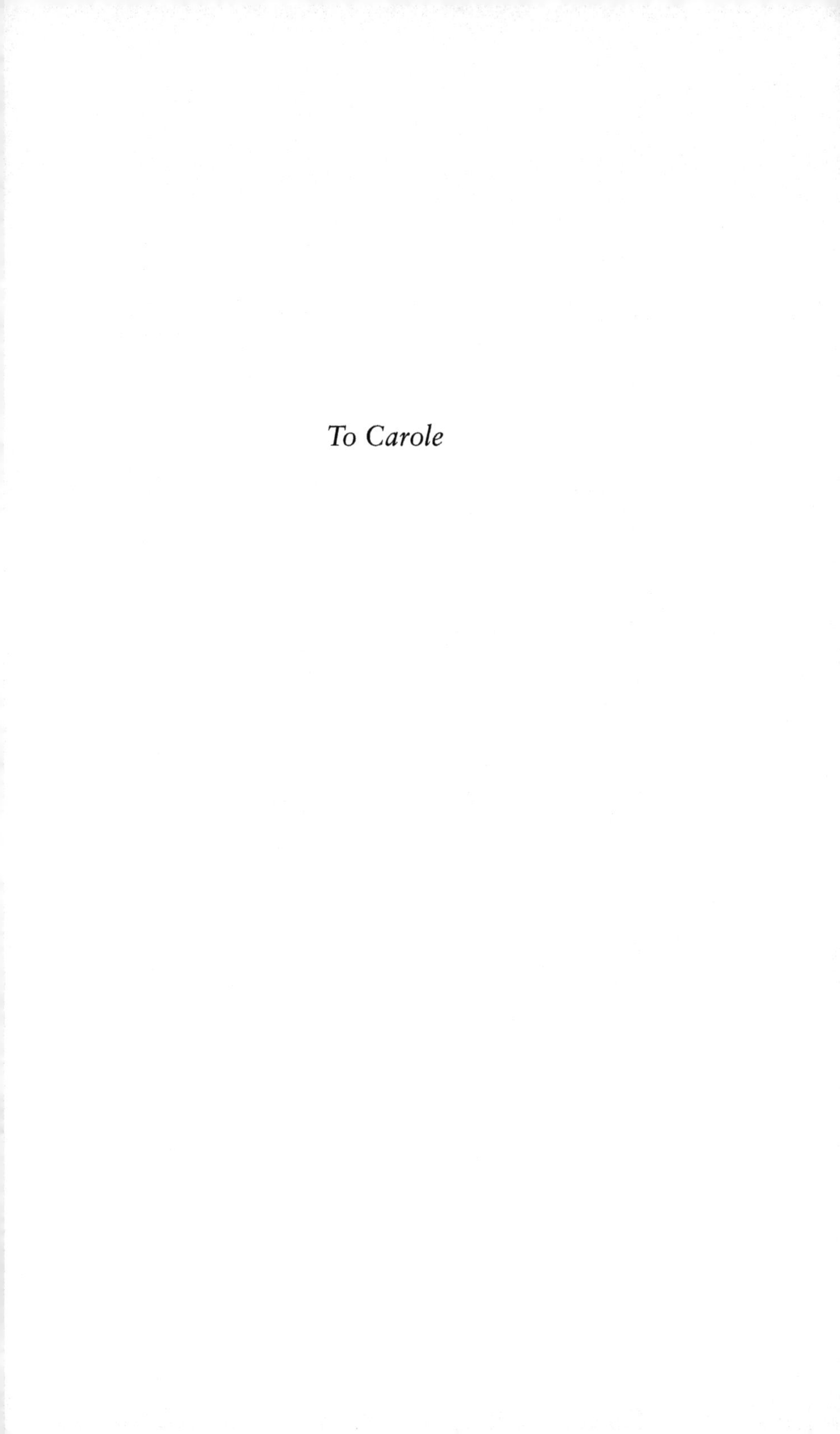

To Carole

Siping
Huadian
Tumen
Vladivostok
RUSSIA
Nakhodka
CHINA
Khasan
Musan
Najin
Badaojing
Tonghua
Ch'ongjin
Hyesan
Ji'an
Manp'o
Kanggye
Kimch'aek
NORTH KOREA
Dandong
Sinuiju
Kusong
Yongbyon
Hanhung
P'yongyang
Wonsan
Sea of Japan
Namp'o
Sariwon
Changyon
P'yonggang
Haeju
Ch'orwon
Munsan
Ch'unch'on
Ongjin
Kangnung
SOUTH KOREA
Inch'on
Seoul
Wonju
Ulung-do
Suwon
Ch'onan
Ch'ongju
Andong
Taejon
P'ohang
Yellow Sea
Kunsan
Taegu
Chonju
Ulsan
Kwanju
Masan
Busan
Mokp'o
Yosu
Hiroshima
JAPAN
Korea Strait
Kitakyushu

PART 1

CHAPTER ONE

PYONGYANG, NORTH KOREA

FEBRUARY 14

Four MiG-29 jets roared in formation above Kim-Il Sung Square.

Thousands of citizens in the stands roared back.

Generalissimo Day ignited.

Rocket launchers lumbered onto the parade grounds, shaking the earth with their twenty-ton Hwasong-14 missile payloads. Heavy artillery and T-72s tanks pounded past the reviewing stand. Platoons of soldiers goose-stepped with razor-sharp precision. The Women's Corps displayed spectacular synchronization.

On the reviewing stand, Dr. Ahn Junsu rejoiced in his recent appointment as personal physician to the Supreme Leader. With a smile, he glanced over to check on his patient four feet in front of him.

And froze.

Not because of the frigid air or acrid diesel fumes or pandemonium erupting from the spectators.

Because of a laugh.

A hollow, unpleasant laugh. A laugh completely out of place. A laugh that was accompanied by turning of the Supreme Leader's head to the right and staring for five seconds.

Ahn knew that laugh. He stood transfixed, watching the parade, but not paying attention. With a pounding heart and churning gut, he was reliving a memory.

Early in his career he was assigned to an institution for children. A three-year-old boy in that place laughed just like the Supreme Leader. Three months later, that boy died in Ahn's arms convulsing with a massive seizure impossible to stop.

Ahn could not forget the terror in the boy's eyes, the continuous twitching and shaking, the foaming mouth, the final agonizing breath, his own helplessness.

He witnessed the autopsy. The child had a mass deep in his brain, a rare benign tumor called a hypothalamic hamartoma. That was what had made him laugh in such a twisted way. That weird laughter was in fact a seizure, and it could establish the diagnosis of a hamartoma with near certainty.

Ahn's own breathing came in short bursts as he considered the implications of his knowledge. He scanned the other people on the reviewing stand: chief of staff General Kung, heads of the armed forces, other Party officials. No one appeared to have noticed anything unusual.

The Supreme Leader himself seemed oblivious to the event. He looked over at General Kung with a frown. "Two men are out of step. Karl Marx Brigade, fourth line left. They bring shame to my country."

"I'll take care of it," Kung said. He barked into his cell

phone, then returned. "They'll be rotting in a re-education camp tomorrow."

Ahn knew Kung should be the person to tell about his concerns, but the general filled him with fear. A large, muscular frame, six-centimeter forehead scar, and piercing black eyes personified terror. And Kung seemed to wield enormous power in the country.

Ahn sucked in his breath and headed toward the general. "Excuse me, sir," he said, thin body quaking as he adjusted his thick glasses.

"No," Kung said, and turned away.

Ahn breathed relief. He had more time to prepare what he would say.

But what would he say? That his new and only patient, the leader of the country, might have a hypothalamic hamartoma? That the laughing spells could progress to generalized convulsions and death?

A doctor who dared to suggest that the Supreme Leader had epilepsy would disappear without a trace.

And who was he, Ahn Junsu, to make such a snap diagnosis?

Ahn felt sweat drip down his back despite the February chill. In his gut he knew that his patient, Supreme Commander of the Korean People's Army, Marshal of the Democratic People's Republic of Korea, First Chairman of the National Defense Commission, and Chairman of the Worker's Party, had a serious problem.

And so did he.

CHAPTER TWO

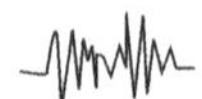

BOSTON, MASSACHUSETTS

FEBRUARY 14

Seven thousand miles across the globe, Dr. Duncan MacGregor also faced a problem with a hypothalamic hamartoma.

As a neurosurgeon at Boston's Harbor Hospital, he had refined techniques for operating on this tumor beyond anyone else in the world.

Now he had to respond to a surgical trainee's plea for help dealing with one.

Dr. Julia Pedroza burst through the OR doorway as MacGregor finished a case. "Mac," she said, eyes widened by fear, "can you come with me to OR eleven? Now?"

MacGregor rushed to keep up with her. "The patient Dr. Knight and I were operating on just had a cardiac arrest. She's a fifty-year-old woman with a hypothalamic hamartoma."

Mac stopped. "Knight? He won't let me help."

"Just come. Please."

Julia stepped into Knight's OR as the cardiac arrest team

poured through the opposite door. They pumped on the patient's chest, injected drugs, drew blood specimens. Their leader shouted orders that competed with clanging alarms. Nurses rushed back and forth around surgical and resuscitation equipment. The intermittent crack of the defibrillator electrified the atmosphere.

"What happened exactly?" Mac asked Julia, shouting to be heard.

"We were dissecting around the hamartoma when the patient's heart stopped."

"In the hypothalamus behind the mass?"

"Yes."

"I know what's going on."

"And?"

"And I need to look at the surgical field."

"Give me a minute," Julia said, and headed for the center of the room, where Michael Knight stood arguing with the code team leader.

"Hypothalamic hamartoma. A tumor that causes laughing seizures," Knight was shouting.

The code team leader seemed unperturbed by the aggressive tone. "Can those seizures cause cardiac arrest?"

"How should I know? That's for a cardiologist to answer, not a surgeon," Knight said with a scowl.

"Was there anything in the surgery that could cause the heart to stop?"

"Hell no," Knight said with a dismissive gesture. "This is the anesthesiologist's fault."

Julia interrupted and said something Mac could not hear.

The code team leader turned to Knight. "Dr. MacGregor just joined us. I want him to look at the operative area."

Knight's eyes became slits as he looked toward the door where Mac stood. "MacGregor? How did he get here? No way he's going to scrub on my case. We don't need a surgical consultant. We need a more competent code team."

"The hospital puts me in charge during a cardiac arrest," the team leader said. "I'm officially asking Dr. MacGregor to inspect the surgical field. No insult to you. This patient will die if we don't change our strategy. Please move aside."

Knight retreated to the edge of the room, clenching and unclenching his fists.

Mac had already put on a new gown and gloves and moved to the surgeon's chair. Despite his calm exterior, his heart was pumping furiously. The patient's life depended on the next few minutes.

He was grateful that the scrub nurse had been trained by him and the instrument set was exactly the one he had established for use in this kind of surgery. Although the adrenaline pumped, he knew he had a team he could count on.

He adjusted the operating microscope to his personal optical settings. With a small dissector, he nudged the tumor forward, probing gently. "I know it's got to be here," he muttered, turning the microscope's magnification up as high as possible. The nurse mopped sweat from his forehead.

The code team leader called out, "Eight minutes of cardiac inactivity. Another minute and we'll start to get brain damage."

Mac knew the center in the hypothalamus that controlled heart activity lay just behind the tumor, yet he saw no obvious bleeding that might cause pressure on that critical area.

A small cleft in the brain behind the tumor caught his eye. He inserted a microscopic probe and teased the edges apart. The slit opened wider, revealing a red surface previously hidden. Could be just a fleck of blood, but perhaps...

He touched the tip of a tiny metal suction to the red base. The instrument had a hole on its shaft that normally vented the suction. He covered that hole and felt the suction kick in, pulling a blob onto the tip of the catheter. As he drew the suction catheter from the field, a blood clot the size of a pea hung from the tip, held in place by the continuing negative pressure.

"A clot hidden behind the tumor," he said with an exhalation of breath. "This is what I was looking for."

He dropped the red ball onto the scrub nurse's specimen dish, then washed the brain it had come from with a small squirt of sterile saline. The brain surface glistened smooth and white at first, then displayed a rivulet of blood. Only then did he notice a tiny arteriole pumping blood into the cavity he had just evacuated.

"Is that bleeder the cause of the clot?" Julia spoke for the first time since Mac had started.

Mac nodded. "Easy to miss, but deadly in this location."

He squeezed tiny cautery forceps against the walls of the pumping arteriole. The red stream stopped.

The anesthesiologist, who had been hand ventilating the patient, called out. "We're starting to get a heart rhythm."

Mac turned his attention back to the tumor, determined to remove it while he was there. He slid his tiny dissector along the margin between it and the normal brain, using the sense of touch to distinguish the abnormal tissue from the soft brain that enveloped it. The mass began to lift away.

"Blood pressure sixty systolic," the code leader said.

After a few more minutes of dissection under high magnification, Mac lifted the entire hamartoma from the brain with microscopic tumor forceps. "Hard to imagine such a small lump could give so much trouble," he said and handed it to the scrub nurse. He inspected the surgical site to be sure there was no residual bleeding.

The anesthetist sang out, "Blood pressure one ten over sixty, pulse ninety."

"Are we done?" Julia asked.

"For now," Mac said. "My only worry is that the patient may have brain damage from the clot or the arrest. We won't know for a few days."

He paused, realized the room was silent except for the regular heart rate beep and the sigh of the ventilator. Everyone was staring at him.

The cardiac arrest team, looking from Mac to the monitors and shaking their heads, picked up their equipment and filed out of the room.

Mac also headed for the door, where the code team leader intercepted him. "What just happened?"

"Bleeding behind the tumor," Mac said. "In this part of the brain, even a small clot can stop the heart by pressing on vital centers."

"Will the patient wake up?"

"Don't know. The tumor is out. Best to close and find out how she is. Of course, that's Dr. Knight's decision." He looked toward Knight, who was glaring at him from the corner.

On his way home later that day, Mac found Julia in the surgeon's lounge.

"How's our patient?" he asked.

"She's awake and doesn't show cardiac damage. We'll check enzymes and watch her EKG for seventy-two hours, but I think she'll be OK."

"Nice to have luck," Mac said.

"Not luck. *You.*" Julia beamed.

"I have one request. Could you keep my name out of the official reports? Let Dr. Knight take credit for finding the clot and removing the hamartoma."

"I can try, but the operating room is a small village. People will know what happened no matter what the record says."

Knight interrupted them, bursting through the door of the lounge. "I've been looking for you," he said to Mac. "Julia, can you step out?"

"I hear your patient is OK," Mac said, trying to calm Knight's apparent agitation as Julia exited. "Good job."

"You think you can just walk into another surgeon's OR and start operating?" Knight asked through clenched teeth. "You had no right to take over my case."

"The leader of the code team asked me to consult."

"Because you were in the room. Who told you about the cardiac arrest?"

"Word travels fast," Mac said.

"You don't have to tell me. We'll find out at the complications conference next week," Knight growled. "The precedent of one surgeon barging into the OR of another can't be tolerated."

He stomped out of the lounge.

Julia returned, shaking her head. "Dr. Knight needs to calm down a little. He really looks pissed. You should go home and enjoy what's left of Valentine's Day. Forget him."

Mac felt his stomach clench. "Valentine's Day?" He checked his watch. "Jesus, it's eight thirty. I was supposed to take Lauren out. And pick up flowers!"

"I'm so sorry. My fault. Can I do anything to help?"

"Too late, I think." He headed for the garage without changing out of his scrubs. The car would warm up a lot more quickly than his wife would.

CHAPTER THREE

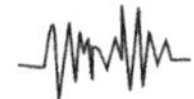

PYONGYANG, NORTH KOREA

FEBRUARY 15

In the Democratic People's Republic of Korea, Dr. Ahn spent the night tossing and turning on his sleeping mat on his floor. Neither his medical training nor his upbringing had prepared him for the situation he now faced.

He belonged to the "loyal" stratum of North Korean citizens because his grandfather had participated in the revolution. He would never be counted in the "wavering" or "hostile" classes. His ancestry automatically gave him upper-class status that less fortunate members of his generation would never attain.

Despite this, he knew he could be eliminated in a moment. Suggesting that the Supreme Leader had a brain tumor would be a death move.

The sound of knocking at the door rousted him to wakefulness.

"Comrade Ahn, you must come to the meeting," the voice of his *immimban* leader bellowed. "It starts in ten minutes."

He looked at his recycled army watch. Six a.m.

Attendance at the neighborhood Communist Party gathering was mandatory. He jumped from the mat, shivered when he felt the draft from the empty window frame, and removed the overcoat he had worn to bed. He grabbed his only shirt, tucked it into the pants he had also worn to bed, and slipped shoes over his thin cotton socks. He wrapped the overcoat around him again.

No time to wash his face or empty his bladder. That would require going down the hall to the communal bathroom. He could take care of those necessities when he got to work.

By ten after six he was at his apartment door ready to leave for the day. He turned back to be sure he had left nothing troublesome for the police should they inspect his room while he was away.

Empty table and chair, tidy mat and sheet, a radio permanently set to government channels, a small dresser with underwear, and pictures of the three Great Leaders of his country as the only wall decoration. His flat would pass muster. He raced down the dark stairway to the meeting hall across the street.

The boss, a woman, was calling the roll as Ahn arrived. She had short, cropped hair and wore the plain gray clothes of Party members. Most of the other men and women of the *imminban*, the neighborhood citizens group, were already there.

"We will start by describing lapses any of you have noted in your dedication to our Supreme Leader this week," the cell leader began. A few citizens confessed to moments when their loyalty had wavered, but none of the transgressions seemed to be egregious.

She continued. "What about lapses you have noted in those around you? Vigilance is required of every citizen in our great republic. It is what allows our democracy to be so strong." A few accusations were made, with no opportunity for the accused to respond even if he or she were sitting right beside the accuser. The organizer jotted some notes but did not say or do anything as these recriminations passed back and forth. Ahn's name was not mentioned.

"Now the weekly bulletin." Her weathered hands turned on a radio, which crackled out a few rousing sentences by the Supreme Leader. Ahn knew he could hear the same remarks from the loudspeakers at every street corner if he missed them here, so he let his mind wander.

An amazing state, where honesty and community are fostered so extensively. No wonder the country is so successful. He knew that everywhere in Pyongyang similar weekly meetings provided opportunities to proclaim loyalty.

He seemed so fortunate. At age thirty-two, he had been appointed personal physician to the Supreme Leader. He had been able to move out of his parents' house, though he could not reveal his real job to anyone. To his neighbors, he tried to be a cooperative citizen.

He had never faced accusations of disloyalty or been charged by the police in their midnight raids. For him, the Party way was the only way. He had stood out in the Youth organization and had proudly accepted the coveted invitation to join the Korean Worker's Party.

Despite his unwavering loyalty, he now felt uneasy about his future for the first time since his appointment. He knew the previous physician to the Supreme Leader had disappeared overnight. Had that man been murdered for something he knew or said?

And there were worse things than just disappearing quietly. Two men had recently been convicted of publishing pornography. They had been strapped to the muzzles of anti-aircraft guns and, with full television coverage, had been blown to bits, fully alive, by the firing of multiple shells. The cameras showed bits of bone, hair, brain, blood showering down on the crowd. Suffering a public disgrace was worse than death itself.

Ahn squirmed with the conflict. He decided he needed to seek another opinion. No physicians in the DPRK had more expertise than he, as specialists were forbidden in the medical system. The only person he knew that might help was his cousin David Ko.

Dr. Ko lived in South Korea, working as a neurosurgeon at the Seoul National Hospital. Their families had split after the 1953 Accord that divided Korea into North and South.

Ahn knew Ko only by reputation and realized that communicating with him would be a problem. He could not use official channels because that would show weakness. He decided the medical library was his only hope.

He arrived at Pyongyang Medical University library just as it was opening the next morning.

The library was a sparse, windowless room with a green linoleum floor and three wooden desks. One forlorn bookshelf held a few Korean medical textbooks. There were no journals on the shelves and there were no textbooks in English. Although there were three computers, only one appeared to have active internet capability. That computer and phone line were guarded by the so-called medical librarian.

Anyone who interacted with the thickset woman who occupied that position knew her job was to prevent internet access, not facilitate it. Ahn called her Comrade B for "Blockade." He had never seen her smile.

"I need to use the official telephone to call a colleague at Seoul National Hospital," Ahn began.

"Exactly why do you want to speak with someone in South Korea?" Comrade B asked, her voice suspicious and accusatory. Her face, free of makeup and scarred with the ravages of acne, was as gray as her worker's clothes.

"One of my patients may have a serious neurological problem."

"Do you understand this will be your only call allowed for the next three months?" she asked as she checked off a box beside his name in her logbook.

"I understand. It is vital that I speak with Dr. Ko now."

"Sign here. Include your official identification number."

She pushed a worn ledger toward Ahn, who instinctively touched the plastic card hanging from his neck chain and wrote down the number, a number which characterized him more than his name.

"What is the telephone number you wish to call?"

Ahn scribbled it on a card.

She dialed.

He reached for the phone, but she waved him off.

"No response." she said after several rings. "We're done."

Ahn dropped his shoulders along with the corners of his mouth. "Could we please try again? Maybe leave a number? It's really important." He showed his pass for the Ryongsong Palace to emphasize that he had status.

She looked closely at the pass, then dialed again. The tone reverberated three times. As she was putting the receiver back on the cradle, Ahn heard a click. "Dr. Ko is answering," he said and reached for the phone.

She passed the receiver with a sigh of resignation and sat with her eyes focused on him.

"David?" he asked, ready to burst with the problem's description.

"...will get back to you as soon as I can," he heard the machine say.

"Dr. Ko, this is Dr. Ahn Junsu from Pyongyang. Please call as soon as you can. The number is..."

His gaze darted to find the number but could see no evidence of one. Comrade B snatched the phone, spat a number into the receiver, and hung up.

For ten minutes, Ahn drummed his fingers, trying not to look at the telephone or the glowering woman who guarded it. How could she make it so clear she resented his presence or the presence of anyone else who would violate her library by entering it?

The jangle of the bell interrupted his musings. Comrade B remained motionless despite the ringing. Ahn pointed to the telephone and made the sign of picking it up. After eight beeps, her hand moved slowly toward the receiver.

"This is the medical library of Pyongyang Medical University," she said after she had picked it up and held it for a few seconds.

"Hold," she barked. She punched the hold button as Ahn reached for the receiver, afraid that the call would disconnect. "Your allotted time is three minutes," she growled before letting him have the precious device.

Ahn could hear almost nothing through the crackling and spotty line. "David," he asked as the connection opened. "Dr. Ko?"

"Yes," the voice was distant, almost incomprehensible. "Who is this?"

The librarian showed three fingers and bent one of them. The timer was running. "Your cousin Dr. Ahn Junsu. I have an urgent medical question."

"Junsu? I haven't heard from you in years. How is your medical work? Family?"

"All OK, but I have limited time to talk. I have a patient who has episodes of laughter that are inappropriate and humorless. Something like this." He forced himself to laugh without smiling or suggesting that anything was funny, then added, "The patient seems otherwise OK."

"When does this happen?"

"I've only seen it once."

Silence on the line, then Ko answered. "It's probably a hypothalamic hamartoma."

"Could it be anything else?"

"Not likely."

"Is it likely to progress?"

"Absolutely. Your patient may end up with generalized seizures."

Comrade B began to reach for the phone. Ahn turned away. "How could I make the diagnosis for sure?"

"A three-tesla MRI scan with thin section slices of the hypothalamus."

"And while I have you on the line, what's the best treatment if that is what we're dealing with?"

"Surgery by an expert neurosurgeon. The world expert is at Harbor Hospital in Boston—"

Comrade B severed the connection. Ahn shook his head in protest. "That was only one minute."

"It's the time you are allowed," she said, returning the phone to its cradle. Ahn knew better than to argue, especially if he ever wanted to make another call. He left without comment or question. Besides, his next meeting would make this one look like afternoon tea.

CHAPTER FOUR

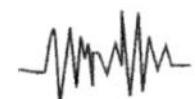

PYONGYANG, NORTH KOREA

FEBRUARY 15

Ahn commuted by train every day to his office in the Ryongsong Residence. Not really a residence—a sprawling complex of buildings and tunnels on the outskirts of Pyongyang. The nerve center of the DPRK, housing the Supreme Leader and his family, it also provided offices for senior government officials.

Usually Ahn could expect a quiet day in his windowless underground office. Today he had to leave it to meet with General Kung, and his heart pounded as he anticipated the upcoming encounter. Ahn tried to avoid direct contact with Kung as much as possible.

The visit to the library had delayed Ahn. He wove through mid-day pedestrian and bicycle traffic as he walked to the central train station, then navigated to a far corner of the station. He ignored the "No Admittance" sign, passed through two security checkpoints guarded by fully armed soldiers, emptied his pockets and showed his official ID. He mounted a train with no destination label.

The car had three fellow travelers who sat in silence for the eleven-kilometer trip from the center of the city to the compound. At the outskirts of the city, the train dipped below ground level into the extensive rail system that criss-crossed under the residence.

Protected by cement, steel, and lead from any bombardment including potential nuclear blast, a complete underground government and transportation system had been built by the Supreme Leader's father. Above it the palace grounds stretched for almost five square miles, guarded by military units and surrounded by electric fences and mine fields. The subterranean city contained all the facilities required to remain under siege for months.

Ahn dismounted in the underground station and headed for the operations center, General Kung's office complex.

Like its occupant, the office suite was large and harsh. Ahn had visited it only a few times since beginning his job. His heart rate still increased whenever he crossed the threshold. General Kung tipped the scales at twice the weight of most Koreans. Muscle rather than fat made up his bulk, maintained by a vigorous exercise schedule.

As Ahn entered the office, the general sat at a simple wooden desk writing. His black hair was cropped short. His forehead scar wasn't throbbing. Good, but those gimlet eyes and scowling lips still made him terrifying.

He did not invite Ahn to sit. "What issue is so important that you must see me on short notice?" he asked without looking up.

"I believe our Supreme Leader may have a neurological problem."

"What kind?"

"Laughing seizures."

"What the hell are laughing seizures?"

"Episodes of laughter at inappropriate times."

Kung stared at Ahn. "The leader of this country can laugh whenever he damn well pleases. Who are you to decide the laughter is inappropriate? Go back to your textbooks."

"It's not the laughter that's the problem."

Kung put down his pen. "Then what is?"

"These symptoms may point to a tumor in the center of his brain."

Kung sprang to a fully erect position and glared at Ahn. "I remind you that the last personal physician disappeared because he called the Supreme Leader obese and tried to get him to diet. Even the suggestion of a seizure would be treason unless it is proven. Why do you have the audacity to think this?"

"I have witnessed an episode and you may have seen one too. The issue is whether he has the condition they usually represent."

"Which is what again?"

"A benign mass in the part of the brain called the hypothalamus—a hypothalamic hamartoma."

"Why do you think that's what he has? Medicine is not an exact science. Everything has more than one explanation."

"I've communicated with another doctor, a neurosurgeon, who agrees with me about the diagnosis."

"You what?" Kung stood. "You discussed this with someone else?" His eyes narrowed and fists clenched.

"Not the specifics, of course. But the concept." Ahn shrank back.

"Who did you talk with?"

"I prefer not to say."

"I remind you that your life and your family's life can be snuffed out like this." Kung snapped his fingers.

Ahn looked at the floor. "I consulted with my cousin David Ko at Seoul National Hospital."

"Did you speak with anyone else?"

"Absolutely not."

"You should have conferred with me first. Why did you feel it necessary to reach out to South Korea? Was there no one in the DPRK who could help?"

"No one deals with this in our country. I wanted to be sure I had not missed anything before I came to you. I wanted an independent opinion from an expert."

Kung shuffled the papers in front of him. "What are the consequences of a problem like this if it is left untended?"

"Our Supreme Leader could have a shaking seizure accompanied by loss of urine and bowel control and foaming at the mouth. You can imagine what effect that would have if it occurred in an official meeting."

"How likely is that?"

"Impossible to say."

"Not a good enough answer, Comrade. Fifty-fifty chance, one in a million?"

"Maybe one in a thousand."

Kung contemplated something on his desk. After several seconds he looked up at Ahn again. His eyes were narrow slits and his tone menaced.

"What would it take to know for certain?" he asked. "To know whether we are dealing with what you think?"

"An MRI scanner that has a three-tesla magnet."

"Do we have such a scanner in Pyongyang?"

"No. He would have to go somewhere else."

Kung looked at his own bridged fingers. "He's not going anywhere."

He sat again, leaned forward on his elbows. "You will do nothing about this. Understand? Nothing. And you will say nothing. I order you to attend whenever our Supreme Leader appears in groups larger than one. You will carry the means to stop a seizure immediately if it begins. That is all you are going to do now."

"Can I start medication?"

"Not if you tell him it's to prevent epileptic fits."

"But I may not be able to stop a seizure once it starts." Ahn looked worried.

"Dismissed." Kung returned to his papers.

Ahn backed away, still facing Kung to show respect. He was not surprised by this response, and he realized that if the Supreme Leader had a seizure in public, it would probably prove fatal. For the doctor, not the patient.

CHAPTER FIVE

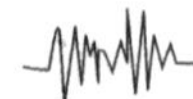

BOSTON

FEBRUARY 15

The morning after Valentine's Day, the atmosphere in the MacGregor household approached the chilly temperature outside. Lauren said nothing as she drank her coffee. Eleven-year-old Maggie stared into her reading book. Seven-year-old Peter played with his x-box controller.

Mac broke the silence by suggesting a skating expedition on the Frog Pond rink of the Boston Common that evening. The children responded with an enthusiastic "yes." Lauren agreed. *Maybe I can make up for missing Valentine's Day after all*, Mac thought.

By six p.m., darkness had descended on the city. Mac felt like a novice as he wobbled around the open-air rink with Lauren clutching his right arm. They tried to keep pace with their children, but Peter rocketed ahead, eager to show off his skills. Maggie reprised her figure skating classes as she ice-danced along, executing pirouettes and en-point moves. The children skated circles around their parents.

Despite frozen feet and a numb nose, Mac enjoyed every minute. Children's laughter rose into the evening sky. The air entered his nostrils crisp and clean. Christmas lights made the Boston Common, in Maggie's words, "a winter wonderland."

A speeding teenager raced by, spraying them with ice shards and almost knocking Mac over.

"Seniors' night is Tuesday," the youth shouted. He turned and skated backward, taunting Mac with "come here" hand movements. He then laughed and tore off, weaving in and out of the other skaters' pathways.

"That's the kind of kid who could really cause damage if he hit somebody," Mac said to Peter. "I hope you never do that."

"I can't skate that fast," Peter said and took off in a racer's crouch.

"Wait a minute; that's not what I meant!" Mac shouted after him, then turned to Lauren. "Let's rest. The children don't need our support."

They sat shivering on a bench, watching their offspring zip around the ice. Mac unlaced his skates and slipped back into his winter boots. "Impressive how good the kids are," he said. "I have to admit I never really got this skating thing down."

"It's part of their winter sports curriculum," Lauren said as she slid closer and looked directly at him. Her tone softened. "This was a nice idea, Mac. I'm sorry I was so upset about last night. I was frustrated because I had been looking forward both to dinner and a concert for our Valentine's Day. The performance was great, but not the same without you."

"I'm the one who should apologize," Mac said. "Julia Pedroza asked me to help with an emergency. The surgeon she was assisting got into trouble operating on a hypothalamic hamartoma."

"But those tumors are your specialty. Why would anyone else decide to do surgery on one?"

He shrugged his shoulders.

"The surgeon was Michael Knight, wasn't it?" she continued. "Why does he keep pushing you?"

"No idea," Mac said.

"Because he's a jerk, that's why." She put an arm around him. "But the operating room has telephones. You could have called to say you were going to be late."

"I got distracted."

He gave her a hug. "How was the symphony?"

"Great. Mahler is a kind of specialty of the orchestra now. I kept looking at the empty seat beside me." She lay her head on his shoulder.

They sat without speaking for a few moments. Lights around the rink created magical shadows and some music played. Mac was only aware of the lovely woman beside him.

Peter interrupted them with the shushing of skates on ice. "Can I get hot chocolate?"

"No problem. I'll go with you," Mac said.

"Do you have to?"

"You know our rule. A new place, I come with you."

"It's been years since I had an allergic reaction. I'm seven now. I can take care of myself."

"You can't read all the ingredient information on labels yet, and you might not know what counts as a tree nut."

"OK, OK, let's just go. Can I get a chocolate bar too?"

There wasn't much of a line at the concession stand. Seeing the prices, Mac understood why. "Hot chocolate," he ordered as they got to the window. "And a plain chocolate bar if you have one. No nuts."

"No chocolate bars of any kind left," the parka-clad teenager with nose and eyebrow rings replied. "Whipped cream on the hot chocolate?"

"Yes, please," Peter said. He swallowed the entire topping in three gulps, then began to sip at the chocolate.

Half-way back to the bench, he put a hand on Mac's arm. "Dad, I don't feel right. My mouth's itchy and the back of my throat feels weird."

Mac's heart raced. He knew these were the early signs of an allergic reaction, though he had no idea why Peter would be having one. He felt cold sweat on his brow despite the freezing temperature. Where was the epipen he vowed always to carry? Had he left it in a lab coat or suit jacket at the office? Picking it up had become so automatic, he didn't remember exactly what he had done.

"Call 911," he called to Lauren. "Peter's having a reaction."

She stood up and began to shuffle over to them on her skates.

"Don't come over. Just call," Mac yelled.

Lauren found her cell phone and punched in the numbers.

Mac tore off his gloves and reached into his ski jacket, hunting for the epinephrine that would save his son. Not in the glove pockets. He turned them inside out to be sure. In his pants? He rifled through them. During surgery his hands never trembled but they now shook uncontrollably. He knew that a few seconds could make the difference between death and life.

He looked over at Peter, now sitting at the edge of the pathway. "You OK?" he asked, but he knew the answer.

Peter stared, unable to speak. His breath came in short gasps and ribcage retracted with each attempted intake of air. When his mother appeared behind him, he lay back against her, closing his eyes as he fought for breath.

Mac explored his shirt pockets, then patted his chest and everywhere else in a panicked search for the epipen. The back of his hand grazed against a tubular shape in the inner pocket of the parka. He gave a cry of relief as he drew out the yellow container, uncapped it, and slapped the pen hard against his son's pants at the thigh.

He watched Peter continue to struggle. In his mind he visualized the landmarks for a crico-thyroidotomy, the procedure he might have to do to open an airway.

A press of onlookers had gathered, pushing in toward him. "Does anyone have a knife?" Mac called out. "I'm a doctor."

The teenager who had sprayed him with ice emerged from the crowd. "Would this be OK?" he asked, eyes wide as he flipped open a large Swiss Army knife.

"Thanks. I just hope I don't have to use it," Mac said. He could hear the sirens of the ambulance come closer, then stop.

"Slow and easy, son," Mac said. "Don't try to take a big breath. The air will come if you give it a chance." He took Peter's hand and squeezed it. Peter looked out of the corner of his eyes, then shut them and squeezed back.

Mac felt the pulse. Rapid—one hundred forty. The epinephrine was doing its job, speeding the heart, increasing the blood pressure, and opening the airways.

"What've we got?" the medics asked as they arrived with stretcher.

"Anaphylactic reaction," Mac replied. "Tree nut allergy. My son Peter. Seven. No idea what set it off. I gave him intramuscular epi four minutes ago." He looked at his watch to confirm the timing. It seemed centuries ago.

"I'm Dr. Duncan MacGregor," Mac added, flashing his hospital ID card. "Neurosurgeon at Harbor Hospital."

The medics put an oxygen mask on Peter as they moved him to a stretcher, then loaded him onto the ambulance. One slid behind the steering wheel. Mac stopped the other. "I want to ride with my son."

"But—"

"The bronchospasm can return once the epi wears off. If Peter needs a tracheostomy on the way to the hospital, you'll want help."

The medic shrugged. "Sure, you can ride with us. The rest of the family will have to follow in their car."

The pediatrician on call stood in the triage area waiting for them. The entire family crowded into the cubicle in the treatment area where she did a quick evaluation and arranged to have Peter admitted. An hour after the crisis at the skating rink, Peter was comfortably in a hospital bed.

"I'll stay tonight," Mac said.

"Thank you," Lauren said. "But there's one thing I want

before I leave. Can you go over the epipen mechanism? It's been a while since I've reviewed how to use it."

Mac held up the yellow cylinder. "The needle is thin, long, and spring-loaded. It punches out, then pops back into the handle so it won't stick you. All you do is press it hard against the skin. The spring mechanism does the rest."

"How much drug goes in?"

"A whomp of epinephrine. Enough to push the blood pressure sky high and cause a brain hemorrhage if you hit a big blood vessel. That's why we give it into muscle."

"How long should it take to act?"

"Less than a minute."

"OK," Lauren said. "Thanks. I'll take Maggie home. I hope we can all rest."

"I expect Peter'll be discharged in the morning, but no school for him," Mac said.

He looked over at his son, already snuffling in his sleep. His heart skipped several beats as he thought about what might have happened.

CHAPTER SIX

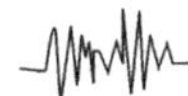

BOSTON AND BROOKLINE

FEBRUARY 16

Lauren arrived at the hospital room at eight the next morning. "How's Peter?" she asked as she came through the door and hugged Mac.

"Slept like a baby," he said. "Even in hospital pajamas in a strange environment. I think he's going to be a surgeon—he can sleep anywhere under any circumstances."

"I made some coffee for us," she said, handing Mac a travel mug. "Dark roast. Thought you could use it after last night."

Lauren took a long swig from her own mug. "We have so many things to be grateful for, Mac. Last night the ambulance guys and hospital staff were great, and you were unbelievable. I called Mom to tell her what happened, and she offered right away to take Maggie to the school bus or do anything else helpful. Says she cleared her schedule, so we should use her."

"And we can go home now. The pediatrician has already signed us out."

Lauren went over to Peter, snuggled beside him in the bed, and whispered something in his ear. He frowned, wriggled, and opened his eyes. Without a word, he hugged her as she put her arms around him.

"I'm scheduled to have clinic today," Mac said. "Thirty patients from all over the place. Should I cancel?"

Lauren looked up from the tear-soaked embrace of her son and said, only half smiling, "If you don't, I'll break your neck so you'll have a good reason to cancel."

Mac shrank back with a quizzical look.

"Really, Mac, I need you to be around just in case. And I have a couple of things I must do at work."

Mac moved to a place behind her and massaged her neck.

"OK," he said. "I wouldn't do justice to my patients anyway—my mind would be at home. I do want to visit the Frog Pond this morning if you can watch him for an hour. I need to find out exactly what caused his attack. It must have been something in the hot chocolate, and it would be good to track it down while everything is fresh."

"Let's take him home together," Lauren said, "and you go off to the Frog Pond to find out what you can. At noon I have an important school meeting with the Board, so please get back before then. We can work out the rest of the day after I return."

Mac nodded, picked up his cell phone, and called his clinic administrator to notify him that he would not be coming in. He listened to the response for a moment, then said, "I know it's a problem, but my son was very sick last night and I have to watch him."

He held the phone away from his ear so he wouldn't have to listen to the comments that followed. Lauren stood beside Peter as he brushed his teeth. "Just reschedule my patients," Mac instructed, cutting the connection and switching the phone to emergency only. He joined Lauren in the preparations for discharge.

A few seconds later the telephone in the room jangled with an unpleasant tone. Lauren answered, listened a moment, then passed the phone to Mac with her hand covering the mouthpiece. "It's Tony Whitemore. I know he's sort of your boss, but right now he sounds like a jerk."

Mac put the receiver to his ear. "I heard you canceled your clinic session today," Whitemore said without preliminaries.

"Our son had a bad allergic reaction and is still in the hospital."

"I know that. Why do you think I called you in his room? And I checked the records. He's fine today and able to go home. That means you can come the clinic."

"He still needs close observation," Mac said, furious that, even though he was chief medical officer, Whitemore had violated HIPAA regulations by getting information on a patient he had no business knowing about.

"That's what mothers are for, isn't it? They're the ones who are supposed to stay home with the children when they are sick. You have a job to do."

"So does my wife. We share duties."

"Do you realize how disruptive canceling a clinic is? It means our patient care assistants will sit around being paid for nothing."

"I have to stay home today," Mac said. "I'll make up the clinic next week." He thought about reasons he himself might give against canceling a clinic—patient inconvenience, delay in care, extra work for the scheduling staff. Having to pay idle clinical assistants was nowhere on that list. "I can run the clinic after hours without staff if you want. Maybe you could give the assistants a morning of free time while my clinic would have been active. I'm sure they would be very grateful."

"You know we can't allow that. They might come to expect it whenever a doctor cancels. As chief medical officer, I'm obligated to draft an email to document your action. While I have your attention, I should also mention that I'm also disturbed by your interference with the recent surgical case you barged in on. I've made an appointment at the end of the week about that."

"What do you see as the problem?" Mac asked.

"That can wait until our meeting, since you're so busy babysitting your son," Whitemore said as the call disconnected.

"Nice to have an understanding boss," Lauren said, shaking her head. "And I thought my department head was a problem."

They traded Peter's hospital sleepwear for his rocket pajamas from home and headed out the door. Peter climbed into the child seat in the back of the car and was asleep before the SUV had left the parking lot. Mac covered him with a blanket.

When they arrived home, Mac gently deposited Peter

and blanket together in bed. He listened to his son's chest. No wheezes.

"Just let him sleep," he said. "I'll be back at 11:30."

Mac arrived at the Frog Pond concession just as it opened for business, although no skaters had yet appeared. A Zamboni scraped back and forth on the pond itself, leaving a layer of freezing water as it passed. The tree lights were off but the snow reflecting the morning sun created a bright and cheerful scene.

The same teenager who served them last night was lifting the wooden shutters off the concession window.

"Aren't you the guy whose kid got sick last night?" he asked as Mac approached.

"Yes. Doctor Duncan MacGregor." Mac extended his right hand.

"Sorry, I don't shake hands, even with gloves. Germs, you know," the teen said.

"Right. I need to ask some questions about your food preparation."

The boy stopped. "Are you trying to pin the allergic reaction on me?"

"Not at all. Just wondering what's lying around on the surfaces back there. Can I take a look?"

"I'd have to ask the owner. We don't want trouble."

"No trouble. I'm trying to track down the allergen that almost killed my son. Any nuts or nut products in the shop?"

"Peanuts for the sundaes and some nut chocolates, but they're not lying around."

"Anything with tree nuts?" Mac asked.

"What are those?"

"Walnuts, almonds, cashews, pistachio, hazelnuts."

The boy paused, then slapped his thigh. "Whipped cream."

"Whipped cream?"

"Yeah, the whipped cream contains hazelnuts. Gives it a distinctive taste, you know. Made with real hazelnuts. Our own special—"

Mac realized his face must have changed, because the teenager stopped. "That was it, wasn't it? The hazelnuts. Jesus, I'm sorry. I was responsible. Never thought..."

"It's a rare allergy, but at least we know. It may be best in the future to tell customers exactly what they're getting."

"I will, Mr. MacGregor. I will. I had no idea."

"Enjoy the day," Mac said as he turned back toward the car. What kind of unsafe world was his son entering when a swallow of whipped cream could almost kill him?

Mac called for Peter as soon as he arrived home. There was no answer. He heard the intermittent noise of television from the family room. Walking toward it, he could make out Peter's voice.

He passed through the kitchen into the comfortable family room outfitted with a huge TV, rug, couch, lounge chairs, fireplace and windows looking into the back yard. Peter lay on the couch transfixed by a movie flashing on the television. Lauren was sprawled under a blanket beside him.

"You're home early," Lauren said as he came through the door. "Nice work."

"Whipped cream," Mac said.

"Whipped cream?"

"It was the whipped cream. It had hazelnuts as a special secret ingredient."

"How are we supposed to anticipate something like that?"

"I don't know, but I kick myself for not checking more carefully last night. Most important, I've made myself a promise always to know where the epipen is."

Lauren threw the blanket aside and stood. "He's been having a great morning. No wheezing. Everything back to normal."

"What's on the TV that's so fascinating?"

"A Supergirl episode about an atomic bomb. Peter'll explain. Wish me luck in the meeting."

"Luck in the meeting. Really." Mac gave Lauren a quick kiss on the cheek, then turned to Peter. "So what're you watching?"

"Shhh," Peter said and put his finger to his lips. The movie mounted to its apparent climax, where the heroine had to cut either the red wire or the blue wire leading to the timer of an atomic bomb. She stood trying to decide which to do.

"That's so bogus," Peter shouted. "In a real bomb, you couldn't even get through the shell to find the wires, and besides, they have failsafe devices that cause the explosion if you mess with the wires."

"So how would *you* prevent the bomb from going nuclear, Mr. Expert?" Mac asked.

"Stop the chemical explosion that starts the whole sequence. At least, that's what they do in the best comics."

"What?"

Peter turned as if he were talking to a two-year-old. He jumped off the couch, ran to the corner where a pile of graphic novels lay in a heap, and pulled out one of them. He read, slowly and with several errors, "The nuclear sequence is begun by a chemical explosion that directs neutrons into the fission device. Preventing that will abort the detonation.' What's 'abort'?"

"Stopping something."

"Anyway, this shows you how," Peter said, pointing at one picture.

"Are the explosive chemicals really removable?"

"Yes," Peter said. "They're in packets arranged to focus their energy."

"How did you get to be such an authority on atomic bombs?" Mac asked, ruffling Peter's tousled hair.

"It's all in the comics, Dad." On the screen, the heroine picked the right wire and saved the world. "No surprise," Peter said. "Otherwise they couldn't make the next movie."

Mac decided his son had recovered without serious side effects. "Let's get lunch," he said.

After lunch, Mac suggested they read a book. Peter wanted to watch another TV episode. Mac again suggested a book. Peter insisted that if it were going to be a book it had to be one of Maggie's. They rifled through the stack on her desk and found one with a helmeted GI on the cover.

"That one," Peter said, "And I'm not going to sleep."

"Of course not," Mac said, "Just quiet time. But if you feel like closing your eyes, I'll stop reading and let you rest."

"Are you going to stay at home all day?"

"Yes, of course."

Mac sat on the bed with his arm draped over Peter's shoulder. He got through two pages of the volume describing the Korean war when Peter interrupted.

"Dad, is Korea as far away as China?"

"Yes."

"Could we go there some day? Or to Disneyworld?"

"Maybe," Mac said, "but for now, let's just be glad we're here in Brookline." He began to read again, but after one more page Peter was asleep.

At three thirty, Lauren's mother appeared at the door carrying what she described as "a tiny chicken casserole." She was a silver-haired woman, fifty-eight years old and still young in mind, who worked full-time as an editor. "Nothing much was going on today, so I decided to take the day off and do what I really like, which is to cook. And if I'm lucky, maybe I can watch over Peter for an hour while you take a break."

"Wonderful," Mac said, grateful for his mother-in-law's generosity.

With a free hour, Mac headed for the music room. He yearned for his piano's calming effect after the trauma of the last two days. The quiet simplicity of Debussy's Reverie floated from his fingertips, followed by the opening Aria of the Goldberg Variations.

Soothed, he moved to the living room where he fell asleep on the couch.

CHAPTER SEVEN

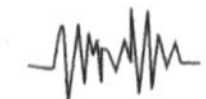

BOSTON

FEBRUARY 17

Dr. Julia Pedroza was as attentive as possible to Mrs. Clark in the days after the surgery. Following hospital protocol, she had told the patient about the intraoperative cardiac arrest. No problems had appeared by the third postoperative day and Mrs. Clark seemed to be quite pleased by her recovery.

When Mrs. Clark's executive assistant asked for a private meeting, Julia felt a twinge of apprehension. Was this the start of a malpractice claim?

They met in a consultation room outside the intensive care unit. The assistant was a woman in her thirties with hair pulled into a bun, blue-rimmed designer eyeglasses, and a dark blue Chanel suit. "I want to thank you and your team for all you've done," she said. "Mrs. Clark has made remarkable progress since her surgery, but—"

Julia felt her stomach tighten.

The assistant continued. "But something strange has happened. I've worked with her for three years and pride myself on being one of the longest survivors in my position. She's difficult, I mean *very* difficult, to work for. I assumed she needed to be that way to succeed in a male world."

"Probably did," Julia said.

"Anyway, something seems to have changed. Before the surgery, she ordered me to stay in the waiting room throughout the case. I was to see her immediately afterward and notify the corporate world that she was not fazed by the procedure, was still invincible."

"And?"

"And when I did approach her after the surgery, she reached out and touched my hand. She apologized for making me wait and told me I should take the rest of the day off. She didn't even mention spreading the news that she had survived.

"I asked her if she was OK, really meaning it. She smiled and said, 'Never better, and I'm so grateful you are here."

"I thought maybe it was the drugs talking. Over the last few days, I got the impression that it's something more permanent. At the office, she rarely said good morning and never said thank you. Now she wants to be friends with everyone. Did you guys implant some niceness module in her?" The assistant looked directly at Julia.

"Wouldn't it be wonderful if we had such a thing?" Julia said. "I know a few people I'd use it on."

"Well anyway, I'll give you another example. She had been estranged from her younger sister for five years, believing that sister had disrespected her. Two days after her surgery, she asked me to arrange a visit. When her sister entered the room, Mrs. Clark apologized for being so resentful and started to cry. Even the nurses were teary as they watched the reunion, both sisters hugging and saying how much they really loved each other."

The woman dabbed at the corner of her eye. "This probably sounds wonderful to you—a hard-boiled CEO comes to Jesus. But it's not really who she is. If she doesn't revert to her former self, I'm worried about what's going to happen when she gets back into the corporate world. She deals with some tough people, and if she stays this way, it could be a disaster."

"This was major surgery," Julia said. "Sometimes there are temporary effects that go away with time. I'd wait a little longer."

She didn't feel as confident internally as she sounded on the outside. She would have to talk about this at her meeting with Mac in the morning.

CHAPTER EIGHT

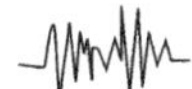

BOSTON

FEBRUARY 18

At six-fifty the next morning, Julia and Mac met in the hospital cafeteria.

"Mrs. Clark is doing great, ready for discharge in a couple of days." Julia reported. "Her heart is fine, but she seems to have had a personality change. Her executive assistant says she's become much more pleasant and reasonable. She initiated a reunion with her estranged sister and is being nice to everyone around her."

"That doesn't sound like a bad outcome."

"Her family's happy, but her stockholders might not like a kinder, gentler CEO."

"Sounds like it's important to see whether her brain has been visibly affected to cause the change," Mac said. "Can we get a high field MR with diffusion tensor imaging?"

Julia smiled.

"Does that mean you've already scheduled it?" Mac asked.

"Yes, for tomorrow morning. We can look the images as soon as I've done the post-processing to show the brain tracts and nuclei. But there is a potential complication."

"What's that?" Mac asked.

"If she thinks there's any chance you can be her doctor, she's going to switch from Knight. I don't envy you dealing with that."

"A day at a time."

Julia laughed and left. Mac continued to enjoy the spectacular view of clouds, airplanes, and boats that Boston Harbor displayed on a sunny February morning. A blessing to work in a hospital with such vistas around it. After a second cup of coffee, he reluctantly headed for Whitemore's office.

The slick-haired male assistant told him to sit until called. Ten minutes past the appointed time for his meeting, Mac returned to the desk. "Should I reschedule?"

"He wanted to see you today." The assistant picked up the phone and buzzed into the inner office.

"Five minutes," he said in a tone that ordered Mac to wait.

Mac returned to his seat. In his own work he tried to keep on schedule despite the many interruptions in his day, considering it an insult to keep a patient or colleague waiting. The thought occurred to him that the chief medical officer might have just such an insult in mind.

Whitemore appeared fifteen minutes later. He was a heavyset man with thinning hair and horn-rimmed glasses covering eyes that blinked too often. His hands were as meaty as his jowls, always moist with sweat.

"We need to talk," he said as he slid his hand out of Mac's.

The office occupied a choice space. Located on the top floor of the hospital, it looked out over the Harbor with an all-window wall. Whitemore had placed his desk in front of the window, turning his back on one of the most spectacular views in the city. It did mean that the visitor saw the chief medical officer outlined against Boston Harbor and Logan airport. Power was more important than aesthetics on this floor.

"To start, I'm very disappointed that you canceled your clinic earlier this week," Whitemore said. "I've received several client complaints that have been added to your dossier."

"I couldn't have given the patients my full attention. My son had a severe allergic reaction. I did a makeup clinic yesterday."

"Whatever. That isn't the main reason for the meeting today. There is a serious issue arising from your operating room antics last week. I've talked at length with Dr. Knight."

"No doubt," Mac muttered under his breath. Whitemore continued without acknowledging the comment. "We're concerned that this action constitutes assault and battery—that since Mrs. Clark didn't consent to your coming into the procedure, your participation was effectively a physical attack on her."

Mac felt the blood rush to his face. He restrained himself from waving his fist and shouting.

"What do our lawyers say?" he asked with as much self-control as he could muster.

"They're working on it. Of course, this is all internal—we don't want any publicity."

"And the fact that this action saved her life?"

"Dr. Knight thinks the cardiac problem would have corrected itself."

Mac felt his blood pressure rising even further. "I don't think the code team leader agrees."

"I have to support Dr. Knight as the surgeon."

Mac stood. "Anthony, let's put our cards on the table. Knight thinks he can do any procedure as well as any person on staff, even though he's not yet technically finished his residency. I don't even see how you can let him operate alone."

"No use in bringing that up. It's hospital policy."

"It's a bad policy. You know I've tried to get it changed. I also know you want to hire him when he finishes. I expect you think he will increase our volume because he will operate on anything."

"What's wrong with that?"

"Everything. Look at the potential disaster in the case we're talking about. Removing a hypothalamic hamartoma requires experience."

"Can you be more specific?" Whitemore seemed taken aback by MacGregor's aggressiveness, but cool, as if he were collecting data for later use.

"Knight completely missed the blood clot. I've operated on more than a hundred people with this tumor. This was the first of these cases he had ever attempted."

"How are people going to learn if they can't try?"

"By working with a senior surgeon to learn, not just going ahead blindly alone." Mac almost shouted, pounding his fist into his hand.

"Knight says you would have just done the whole case by yourself if he let you help at all."

"Wrong, but it doesn't matter. A patient should not be put in harm's way to stoke a surgeon's ego. If there is a more experienced person in the hospital, take advantage of that fact to learn."

"Well, we'll get this all sorted out at the Morbidity and Mortality conference," Whitemore said with a flick of his hand, shooing Mac out. "I'll be setting that up for mid-March. Now if you'll excuse me, I have another meeting."

CHAPTER NINE

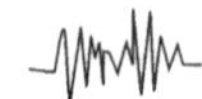

BOSTON

FEBRUARY 20

Julia called Mac in two days as promised. “Great news,” she said. “The new MRI scans on Mrs. Clark are done. You’ll be impressed when you see them.”

“Is the hamartoma gone?”

“Yes.”

“And the area of the clot?”

“I’m working on that now. The diffusion tensor imaging should be done by tomorrow morning.”

“Does Mrs. Clark know I’ll be reviewing them?”

“Absolutely. She said she would just as soon have you be the only person to analyze them, since you know so much about this condition. I guess she’s been doing some research on her own.”

“Any new postop developments?”

“Nope; she’s still a gentler, kinder person, except when it comes to Dr. Knight. Says he bamboozled her into thinking he was an expert in this problem.”

“I wish I could meet her face to face without antagonizing Knight.”

"You can meet her MRI scans tomorrow morning. Is that a reasonable substitute?"

"No. I treat patients, not scans."

"Six-thirty tomorrow in the neuro-imaging laboratory?"

"Deal."

The laboratory, a large basement room with forty computer workstations, was empty when they arrived the next morning.

"Can you talk about this as if you were lecturing at a conference?" Mac said. "You should practice your presentation."

"But I'm not very good at public speaking. My English sometimes fails me, and my accent—"

"You're as good as anyone. I've never had a problem understanding you. Stand here."

He wrestled a lectern from a corner of the room.

"Our next speaker will be Dr. Julia Pedroza," he announced as if he were talking to a large audience. He placed a chair ten feet in front of her and sat.

Julia stood behind the podium and began to speak in a voice so soft Mac could barely hear. "I am pleased to have the opportunity to present my work analyzing brain tracts and nuclei of the hypothalamus. I used a volunteer to create a hologram of the normal human brain."

She looked at Mac, continuing with a conversational tone. "It's my brain. The scans took hours to acquire. I was the volunteer."

"Louder, and no editorial comments," Mac said.

Julia started again in a more robust voice. "Ladies and

Gentlemen. Today I want to demonstrate how powerfully MRI can demonstrate brain function in both health and disease."

She waved her hand and a three-dimensional image of a brain spun before them. "This is a hologram from a volunteer's MRI."

Julia moved both hands. The hologram enlarged. A network of neural fibers flashed by them as they seemed to fly into a chamber filled with clear fluid.

Mac sat straight up. "We're in the third ventricle."

Julia nodded, bringing into focus one small area. "This is the part of the hypothalamus that houses a hypothalamic hamartoma, the tumor we are going to discuss. Here's a reconstruction of nuclei and fiber tracts in this neighborhood. The tracts are colored by their paths and neurotransmitter type."

The fibers, which had been white, now became multicolored—blue, red, green, yellow, creating a brilliant display. She spoke louder. "The blue fibers carry oxytocin, the love transmitter."

"Your voice volume is much better."

"Thanks. Watch this!" Julia lifted both arms like a sorceress casting her spell.

The images came to life. Arteries expanded and contracted sixty times a minute with the heartbeat. The fluid ebbed and flowed with the pulse. The fibers dazzled with psychedelic explosions of sound and colors. Mac leaned back in wonder at the pyrotechnical model of neurons in action.

"This is the way the brain might look if you could display

its connections and electrical activity," Julia said, almost shouting to be heard over the buzzing and snapping around her. "Neat, huh?"

"Awesome." Mac felt like a kid with a new video game.

"So that's a normal brain," Julia said as she lowered her hands and the holographic display faded. "Now look at Mrs. Clark's brain before surgery." She displayed a glistening white surface with a large hillock. "Here's the hypothalamus with a hamartoma bulging out from it."

"Looks just like what we see in surgery," Mac said.

"It does, but we can identify something you can't." She pointed to electrically inactive blue fibers compressed by the hamartoma.

"The fibers you called the 'love' fibers are silent," Mac said. "The peace-making pathways are blocked."

"Exactly. And the fibers that carry aggressive impulses are still firing like crazy." She pointed to red fibers sparkling with activity. "This was Mrs. Clark before surgery—bristling, aggressive. A CEO to be feared."

"And after surgery?"

The blue fibers flashed. "The whole scenario is reversed. The peacemaking fibers are working again." She pointed to a dark spot behind the tumor removal site. "And the blood clot destroyed the center for aggression, so no more flashing red fibers. The peacemaking neurons now run the show."

Mac began to pace.

After a few seconds, he said. "So a person with a hypothalamic hamartoma will be aggressive and impulsive because the peacemaking fibers are blocked. Taking out the hamartoma will change that, especially if the aggression area behind the hamartoma is damaged."

"Right," Julia said.

He shook his head. "That's too simple. All the learning and psychological adaptation we do to be civilized. It's all gone in some people because of a simple brain lump?"

"Yep."

"And the brain tumor makes it impossible for the mind to overcome the problem."

Julia nodded. "Maybe we need a specialty called 'brainiatry' to replace psychiatry."

"Sure we do," Mac said.

"Could be really important in surgery," Julia said. "My message is simple. A person suffering from a hypothalamic hamartoma is normally impulsive and violent. If you remove the tumor, including a little bit of brain behind it, that person becomes a peacemaker."

CHAPTER TEN

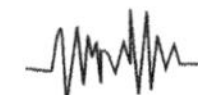

BOSTON

MARCH 14

Whitemore scheduled the Morbidity and Mortality Conference for March 15, claiming that was the day most convenient for his schedule. As that date approached, Mac became more and more irritable.

At seven a.m. the day before the meeting, he met Julia in the hospital cafeteria. A sprinkling of other customers dotted the large space. The sun was just starting its daily ascent over Logan Airport with a luminous dappling of clouds. The harbor was already active with boats and planes.

"I think the conference tomorrow is going to be a mess," Mac said as they took their usual seats beside the window.

"Because?" she asked.

"Knight has been meeting with Tony Whitemore all month. From what I've heard, he keeps emphasizing the idea of a surgeon being the captain of his own ship and the legal danger of unconsented surgery."

"Can Whitemore really hurt you? You have a big tumor practice and a lot of respect here."

"He's chief medical officer. I don't think he likes strong-willed staff surgeons like me. There are lots of ways he could hurt me. He could try to kick me off the staff because I barged in on Knight's case, or open an investigation of all my cases, or suspend me until some committee meets."

"Would he?"

"Absolutely, but more likely he will do something sneaky and subtle."

Julia swirled the remaining coffee in her cup. "You think he's that bad?"

"You don't have to work with him regularly."

"Thank God. I do think another person is out to get you too. Knight wants to be hired onto the permanent staff when he finishes this year. He has his eye on your job."

"I'll have to face that when the time comes. Right now, I just want to get through tomorrow's meeting."

"Can they attack you even if you saved her life?"

"Knight will claim Mrs. Clark would have recovered on her own if we left her alone."

Julia shook her head. "You know that's wrong. And the clot did other damage, as we saw on the MRI. She's still not her old self."

Mac's eyebrows furrowed. "Still too kind?"

"I met with her executive assistant again yesterday. Mrs. Clark is back at work and her co-workers are amazed at her quick recovery. However, she has made some business decisions that are unusual."

"For instance?"

"One of the company's warehouses burned down and she said she would continue to pay the employees' full salary until a new one was built. The old Mrs. Clark would simply have furloughed them."

"I like the new Mrs. Clark better."

"You're not on her Board of Directors."

"Other changes?"

"She's talking about collaborating with a competitor. It's stirred up a lot of controversy."

"Again, seems sensible to me. Industry leaders could use a little more trust."

"It all depends on your point of view." Julia said. "But to get back to the complications conference tomorrow. I have no question you saved Mrs. Clark's life. I also believe that my analysis of the fiber tracts and her behavior is correct."

She started to get up from the table. "I'll be presenting the background of the case. I have to check on some details and get slides ready. I should let you know I have a little trick up my sleeve. My business-savvy husband gave me a great idea about how to deal with the hospital. You might be pleasantly surprised."

Mac stood, then moved to the window as Julia left the cafeteria. He stood watching the early traffic on Boston Harbor: ferries and commuter boats emptying their passengers, water taxis zipping in and out, airplanes rising and descending at Logan. He never tired of the vista and the idea that Boston had reclaimed its waterfront as an integral part of its life.

"You're going to get blasted tomorrow," a voice behind him said. Mac knew that voice and did not want to give its owner the pleasure of turning around.

"How so, Michael?" he asked, still looking out at the harbor traffic.

Knight moved up beside him. "I've been talking a lot with Tony Whitemore. He's concerned about your arrogance. He thinks, and our lawyers now agree, that in technical terms you may have assaulted my patient. She did not sign a consent to have you operate on her."

"Really? And the code team that came and pumped her chest? Did they assault her too?"

"They were just doing their job. Badly, I would say. Whitemore is also against your trying to create a center of excellence to understand and treat brain tumors. He thinks it's just a marketing ploy to keep other surgeons from building their practices."

"Sounds like you have him eating out of your hand."

"I know I'm not yet on regular staff, but I do have some good ideas. Anyway, see you in the boxing ring tomorrow." He punched Mac's arm with a not-so-gentle fist as he left.

That evening, Mac and Lauren had tickets to the Boston Symphony Orchestra. They had not been to a concert since the Valentine's Day fiasco. March had delivered a relatively warm day and they made fast connections to the Symphony stop on the Green Line, arriving twenty minutes earlier than they planned.

They sat at a cement table on a plaza at Massachusetts Avenue and Huntington, sipping hot bubble tea and watching early concertgoers assemble.

Snow lay in the shadows of the plaza, but the air temperature was in the low forties. Streetlamps glared orange in the early stages of darkness. Although the honking of rush hour traffic had diminished, Mass Ave was still a line of car snails.

Lauren's auburn hair and lively expression captivated Mac as much as it had on their first date. Her intelligent eyes cast a spell he had never escaped. He was, he thought, the luckiest man in the world to have such a wife. Her red puffer coat, pompom hat, and leather backpack made her look like a student again.

"Tell me everything about your day," Mac said.

"It was terrible," she said. "We're in the middle of mid-terms and I have a lot of papers to grade. I'm trying to get a new course on movie heroes and their Greek predecessors organized. It's fun, but a lot of work."

She sloshed her tea, looking at the dark bubbles in it. "How about you? What's in your week?"

"The Morbidity and Mortality conference I've been dreading is tomorrow. Michael Knight says I should not have scrubbed in."

"You saved the patient's life."

"Right. Most surgeons would have been grateful. Knight thinks he can do anything alone."

"Did you ever believe that?" She looked at him with a steady glance.

"Never." Mac looked at his hands as if the memories were encoded physically in them. "I asked for a lot of help. Even today I have limited surgical ambitions. I just want to remove brain tumors safely, especially tumors in places no one else can touch."

"And Knight?"

"He wants to be macho man. He decided to operate on a hypothalamic hamartoma without asking for assistance.

He got into trouble. I helped him. Now he has to protect his ego by saying I operated without consent."

He drained the last of his tea. "There's also another thing bothering me. The World Federation Program Committee just rejected the paper on surgical results for hypothalamic hamartomas I wanted to present at the World Congress in Seoul this summer. There's no point in developing a safe surgical technique if you can't teach it to others."

"Saves you a trip to Korea."

"Yeah, but I'm getting discouraged about being able to get my message out. The techniques for hypothalamic hamartomas I've developed *do* allow safe surgery. Most people feel operating is too dangerous. And they're right. As Knight showed, in the hands of an amateur, it too dangerous. You need a pro. I really want to let other neurosurgeons know this."

"Time to go," Lauren said, looking at her watch and the streaming crowd. "We don't want to keep Mr. Mahler waiting. And Mac," she added as they entered Symphony Hall, "I'm sorry you're feeling so stressed."

"It's helpful to talk about this situation. Now I just want it to go away."

CHAPTER ELEVEN

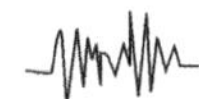

BOSTON

MARCH 15

"Wish me luck," Mac said to Lauren as he climbed into his car. "The complications conference is first thing."

"Luck. You should be proclaimed a hero when it's done."

"Thanks," he said with a trace of a smile. "Somehow I don't think the hospital will agree."

"Screw the hospital. And it is the Ides of March. Julius Caesar had his comeuppance on this date. Maybe the chief medical officer will be assassinated."

"I'll hope for the best."

"Me too. I love you." She blew him a kiss as the car backed out of the driveway.

Mac disliked the monthly Morbidity and Mortality conference the hospital required as part of quality assurance.

The concept seemed sound. Surgeons were supposed to analyze problem cases so future care would be improved.

Instead, some surgeons used the conferences as an exercise in blame and shame. They blamed trainees for any bad outcomes and then shamed them in public.

When Mac arrived at the conference room, he found the same configuration as usual. Residents and students sat scattered toward the back of the room, hoping to avoid questions. Surgical staff sat at the front.

Mac joined the surgical staff, nodding to colleagues and collecting a large cup of dark roast coffee as he sat. He missed the doughnuts that used to be served. Budget cuts and conflict of interest rules had eliminated them.

The chief of surgery called the conference to order. Mac saw him as a decent person who tried to stay out of intra-departmental politics. He could not be counted on for support, however.

The Chief added to his usual introductory remarks: "We welcome two special guests today: Dr. Whitemore, the chief medical officer of the hospital, and Ms. Lynette Murphy, from the Massachusetts Department of Public Health."

Knight, sitting behind Mac, raised his hand. "I understand why Dr. Whitemore's here. I invited him. However, I don't know why we have a public health official. I suggest that Mrs. Murphy's time could be spent more profitably elsewhere. We could send a transcript of the proceedings if she needs to know what happened."

The chief scowled at Knight. "Dr. Knight, as someone still finishing his residency, you're rather outspoken. Your suggestion is overruled. Ms. Murphy's presence is not optional. She can close down our hospital. If she asks to sit in on one of our complication meetings, we comply."

Mac felt some sympathy for Knight's position. This conference was meant to be an internal event for the department, not one that included anyone from outside. He got ready to comment, but looked first across the aisle at Julia Pedroza with the unspoken question "*Is this part of your plan?*" Julia nodded. He remained silent.

The chief continued. "This is a special meeting of the department convened at the request of Dr. Whitemore. There is only one case. As the assistant in the procedure, Dr. Pedroza will present the history."

Julia moved to the podium. "Mrs. C. is a fifty-year-old successful businesswoman who started to have gelastic seizures two years ago." She looked at Murphy. "Gelastic seizures are inappropriate laughing spells."

She continued. "As expected, an MRI showed a hypothalamic hamartoma and she was prescribed anticonvulsant medication." Again directed at Murphy, "the hypothalamus is at the base of the brain and controls many vital functions for body stability, including heartbeat, aggressive behavior, eating, and reproductive function. Some people say it controls the four f's—fighting, fleeing, feeding, and sexual behavior."

Isolated smiles and snickers erupted from the students.

"On February 12 of this year, our patient had a generalized seizure and was rushed to our emergency room. Dr. Knight, the neurosurgeon covering the emergency room, admitted her to his service. She consented to have the tumor removed. On February 14, he took her to the operating room."

Pedroza showed a slide of blood pressure, heart rate, and respiration during the early phases of surgery. "Mrs. C's initial course was unremarkable. We could identify the tumor because it was firmer than the brain tissue that surrounded it. As we were dissecting behind it, the anesthetist informed us her heart had slowed, then stopped."

The slide showed the tracings for heartbeat and blood pressure flattening two hours into the procedure.

"We stat paged the code team, who arrived within two minutes and carried out the usual resuscitative procedures. The heart remained flatlined."

Julia looked over at Mac, then at Knight. "I knew that Dr. MacGregor was next door. He has extensive experience with this surgery, so I asked him to look in. He identified a blood clot behind the tumor and removed it. The patient recovered and is doing well back at work. She has had no cardiac or other complications."

"Any comment from the anesthesiologists?" the chief asked.

"Only that this happened suddenly," the anesthesiologist from the case said. "We couldn't identify anything that had changed in our anesthesia. And the problem reversed immediately after Dr. MacGregor took out the clot."

"Dr. Murtha, you were the leader of the code team. Anything to add?"

"We tried everything to get the heart started, including intracardiac epinephrine. Nothing worked until the clot was removed. The heart recovered spontaneously then."

"Dr. Knight?"

"As the attending surgeon, I did not invite Dr. MacGregor into my operating room. The patient did not consent to have Dr. MacGregor operate on her. Legally I believe that this is assault and battery." He looked over to Whitemore, who nodded and smiled.

"More than that, however, I would like to ask the surgeons on staff whether they would accept the uninvited intrusion of another staff member on one of their cases. We don't even know whether this could have been spontaneously reversible. MacGregor's interference was unjustified."

"Dr. MacGregor, do you have any comments on this?"

Mac took a deep breath. "I agree with Dr. Knight that surgeons are responsible for their patients and no one else should interfere with that relationship. In this case, I felt it might be possible to help Dr. Knight. I'm sorry he feels differently, and I apologize to him."

"Dr. Pedroza, you called Dr. MacGregor to look. What are your thoughts?"

"Dr. MacGregor is an expert in surgery for hypothalamic hamartomas. Everyone here knows that, as do neurosurgeons around the globe. He has done more than one hundred of these operations. Our patient was about to die, and Mac had finished his own surgery just down the hall. I felt it was appropriate to call him in to help."

Knight stood up. "I want the record to note that Dr. Pedroza just admitted she asked for another surgeon to interfere in my surgery. I will insist she be put on probation by the residency committee."

Murmurs circulated around the room. The situation seemed to be escalating. "Let's have a little more order," the chief said. "Dr. Whitemore, do you have any comments?"

Whitemore stood and moved to a position at the head of the table. "As the chief medical officer of the hospital, I am responsible for the behavior of staff members. I believe Dr. MacGregor overstepped his bounds and in effect assaulted this patient. We have some legal opinions that agree with me. I am proposing that he be suspended until the hospital ethics committee can evaluate his actions."

The staff members gasped and looked at each other. Mac's heart pounded as he grasped the chair arms, about to stand and protest. He looked over at Julia, who put up her hand to suggest restraint.

"I would like to say something," Ms. Murphy, the DPH representative, said as she strode to the podium and signaled for Whitemore to sit down. She waited for complete silence. "As you know, the Department of Public Health is charged with protecting the well-being of Massachusetts citizens. The Commonwealth of Massachusetts mandates us to do this."

She leaned on the podium. "I have reviewed the records of this case extensively. The position of the DPH is simple. Dr. Knight should not have attempted this surgery without help. You have Dr. Duncan MacGregor, the world expert, on the hospital staff. A patient almost died as a result of Dr. Knight's misplaced self-confidence."

Murphy looked around at the hushed audience. "I am ruling that at Harbor Hospital any further hypothalamic hamartoma procedures or other operations in this part of the brain can only be done through a program directed by Dr. MacGregor. I will be informing the hospital president and Board of Trustees of my decision later today. Do you have any questions?"

Mac looked around a room of stunned and confused faces. Ms. Murphy turned and said to Whitemore, "Dr.

Whitemore, as you know, my report becomes public record. It will be very critical of your behavior at this meeting and your ability to keep this hospital safe. As for your suggestion that we put Dr. MacGregor's name before the ethics committee, I am going to recommend that he be given a letter of commendation for his courage in doing what he did. And my report will also commend Dr. Pedroza for her judgment and courage, with a copy to the American Board of Neurological Surgery. We'll see whose voice has more power."

She gathered her papers and asked, "Once again, are there any questions?" Observing only silence in the room, she walked out.

The surgical chief closed the meeting, looking as bewildered and stunned as all the other participants.

CHAPTER TWELVE

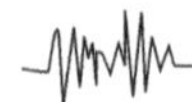

PYONGYANG

MARCH 21

Five weeks after he had begun to prescribe anticonvulsants for the Supreme Leader, Dr. Ahn continued to attend all official meetings. He lived in a state of terror that this day would be the day for a generalized seizure. He had no way of knowing whether his patient even took the prescribed medication, since he could not obtain blood levels.

His patient. What a joke. The Supreme Leader had no interest in following a doctor's advice. Why would a man whose word could kill hundreds, who believed he had divine blood, pay any attention to a lowly physician?

This morning, as every morning, Ahn crawled into an oversized chair in the corner of the War Room below Ryongsung Palace, trying to make himself as inconspicuous as possible. Around a massive table in front of him, the Supreme Leader and his Military Chiefs of Staff discussed the next step in an escalating war of words and missiles.

"I am worried about the possibility of a joint United Nations response to our latest missile flights over Japan," a senior staff member began.

"They will never get their act together enough to oppose

us," General Kung replied. Even in this group of seasoned military officers, his voice carried depth and authority that brooked no opposition.

"But are we prepared if they should by some miracle create unified opposition? We are only twenty-six million people against the world."

The Supreme Leader appeared to be more and more agitated during the discussion. Finally, with his face reddened and temporal artery throbbing, he stood and pounded the table with his fist. "We will never yield to the capitalist warmongers. We will do whatever is necessary to strengthen the Democratic People's Republic of Korea's nuclear capability. We know we would win any nuclear war by retreating to our tunnels. Meeting dismissed."

He remained standing at the podium as the chiefs exited. When only Kung and Ahn remained, he pounded his fist again for emphasis. "No need for discussion in this kind of meeting. I will not let our country become tools of the capitalist enemy. If necessary, we will—" His right lip began to twitch. His mouth moved silently as he stared with a puzzled expression that became one of fear. His face twisted and the right arm began to jerk rhythmically. In a few seconds the jerking spread to his entire body, his eyes rolled up, and he hit the floor as Ahn and Kung ran toward him.

Ahn pulled out a preloaded syringe, wrapped a rubber tourniquet around the Supreme Leader's arm, palpated the antecubital vein, and injected Ativan.

Ahn saw fear appear in Kung's eyes, a look Ahn never imagined he would witness.

"What should we do?" Kung shouted.

"It will stop in a minute," Ahn replied. "We just have to make sure he doesn't hurt himself." He tried to drag the seizing Supreme Leader away from chairs and table legs but had to wait for Kung to help move the mountain of twitching flesh.

As soon as the body was moved, Ahn pulled out his phone and went to video mode. "What the hell do you think you're doing?" Kung screamed.

"We have to convince our Supreme Leader that he has a serious medical problem. When he wakes up he will not remember anything. But he must understand how ill he is, so we can help him."

"If that video gets into any hands but yours, you and your family are dead. Painfully dead."

"I know that, but how else can we convince him to get the tests we need?"

Two minutes later the Supreme Leader of the Democratic People's Republic of Korea lay silent on the floor, eyes closed, foam on his lips, pants soiled with urine. He began to grunt and shake his head.

Kung looked up at Ahn from his kneeling position. He said with words that cut Ahn like knives, "It's your job to convince him to have the MRI done and to find a suitable scanner. Meet me here after you have convinced him, in no case later than ten tomorrow morning."

Ahn arrived at the Great Leader's office six hours after the incident. He drew in his breath as he always did crossing the threshold. Kung had refused to come to the meeting, saying something about leaving medical issues to doctors. Ahn thought he was just protecting himself. Ahn realized that one reason Kung remained chief of staff was his masterful avoidance of anger from above.

Ahn had entered the office many times, but each filled him with apprehension. He never knew what the Supreme Leader would do. He worried that his suggestion might meet with a violent response. How could he convince the most powerful and erratic man he knew to have an MRI?

He took a deep breath and entered the huge office space.

A large conference table filled the far corner of the room. One wall had a bookcase without any books. Another had maps of the Korean peninsula, Japan, and China. On the third, a screen and chalkboard sat ready adjacent to the conference table. The fourth wall contained two large windows with official photographs of the Supreme Leader and his father, the Great Leader, hanging between them.

The Supreme Leader himself sat behind a large desk with a Macbook Pro in front of him. He seemed to have recovered completely from his seizure, put down the videogame controller he had been holding, and looked at Ahn with a frown.

"What happened to me today?" he asked.

"You may have had a blackout, Supreme Leader. Probably too much work and stress with the magnificent job you are doing to develop our military and nuclear capability."

"I have never had such a thing before, and my father never suffered such an event."

"Your father did not have to put up with such warmongering from the United States."

"Listen, my muscles feel strained and I wet my pants. That's more than stress. I just don't remember what happened."

"Would you allow me to show you?"

"You have a video?"

"Only for part of the episode. After I medicated you."

He started the video showing the seizure, with shaking and mouth frothing. The Supreme Leader stood for a moment with wide eyes and clenched fists.

"Give me that," he shouted as he grabbed the phone from Ahn and smashed it to the floor. "This is just propaganda. Who are you working for? Who else has seen this? You are a dead man."

Ahn stepped back with a hammering heart and rapid breathing. He could feel the vasoconstriction in his skin and felt he would faint. "N-no one; absolutely no one, has seen it," he stammered.

"Not even Kung?"

"Not even him.

"Did you make a copy?"

"No."

"Did anyone else see this happen?"

"No, everyone had left the room."

The Supreme Leader paced. "How do you explain this? Someone must have bribed you to fake this video."

He poked his finger at Ahn, who stood twisting his hands, shoulders in, head down. "Supreme Leader, you yourself said you wet your pants. How could we fake that?" He winced as he said the words.

The Supreme Leader screamed several obscenities, shook his head, moved toward Ahn as if he were going to throttle him, then turned back and paced more.

Ahn would rather be with a caged lion. He could feel

the leader's fear and anger and effort to integrate what had happened.

After what seemed like a long time, he said to Ahn, "Is it possible I could have another episode like this?"

"Yes. Have you taken the medicine I gave you?"

"Some of the time." He paused. "Wait. That's it. Your medicine must be doing this to me."

"That medicine is the only anticonvulsant known to be effective in the condition you have."

"The condition I have?" He stopped pacing. "You know what might be causing this?"

"I believe we could find out if you wish, Your Excellency," Ahn began, trying to capture the right tone between deference and authority. "There is one test that would help. It would also demonstrate your superiority in intellectual and political matters by emphasizing the size and structure of your brain."

"What test is that?" the Supreme Leader asked, frowning.

"A high-field MRI scan. It's like a secret portrait."

"What does it involve?"

"Just lying still for about an hour. We can give you some sedation to make sure you're comfortable with it."

Ahn recognized his boss was now listening to him. "Look at the portraits the world sees of all the leaders who oppose you. You would have something none of them have—a very detailed image of your own superior brain. No one but you would have access to it, but you would know no other world leader can see his own brain. Even the premier of China has no such brain image."

The Supreme Leader paused, looked at Ahn with narrowed eyelids. Ahn shifted in position, wondered whether he was now going to be terminated.

"You mean this would be a unique portrait, one no other world leader has?"

"Yes."

"It would have to be done here. And not with any of our equipment or technicians. I don't trust any of them."

"I will arrange it," Ahn replied. He had no idea how.

The Supreme Leader paused and drummed his fingers on the desk, looking at the far wall. "Do you remember the men who were found to be dealing pornography a couple of years ago?"

"The ones tied to the muzzle of an antiaircraft gun and publicly executed by firing?"

"Those very men."

"Yes, Your Excellency. Everyone watched it. By decree."

"You should know that their parents, grandparents, children, cousins, brothers, business associates, and pet dogs all had similar deaths. Burned alive, waterboarded, devoured by rats, amputated limb by limb. The lucky ones were just decapitated or shot. My staff has a long list of techniques to kill criminals."

"Yes, Your Excellency." Ahn felt like throwing up as the memory of the blasted bodies of the antiaircraft victims filled his memory.

"If you tell anyone about this conversation or about my condition, you and your family will die. Horrible deaths. Do you understand me?"

"Yes, Your Excellency," Ahn shuddered. Even though he only had parents, no wife and no children, the thought of them arrested and shamefully executed filled him with horror. The person talking to him a few moments ago had seemed a receptive patient eager to understand. The person who glared at him now was a despot who destroyed all opposition.

Ahn backed out of the room as fast as he could, both to show respect and to make sure his back was not left exposed.

CHAPTER THIRTEEN

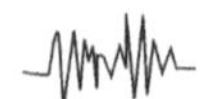

PYONGYANG

MARCH 22

"My niece, Rhee Sung," General Kung said as Ahn entered the office at eight a.m. the next morning. Kung nodded toward a beautiful Korean woman in her twenties sitting across from him. She had the same onyx-hard eyes as Kung, making the family resemblance unmistakable.

Kung turned back to his computer. "Sung will get you what you want. I know about your conversation with the Supreme Leader and what you need."

Ahn wondered how Kung acquired his knowledge so fast. He knew the Supreme Leader had not communicated that information. He never rose this early. Was the Supreme Leader's office bugged by the general? What did all this mean?

"Follow," Sung said, already crossing to the far wall. She put her handprint on a panel, which slid open.

They stepped into a room and a world that Ahn never dreamed existed.

Rows of monitors lined the walls and a dozen high-speed computers sat at individual workstations. No one manned any of them. Twenty television channels played at once, in twenty different languages, all muted, but giving a snapshot of the entire world. Just as many feeds seemed to show rooms and vistas he knew in Pyongyang: the Palace Grounds, Kim-Il Sung Square, many others, in apparent real time.

He gasped when he recognized the Supreme Leader's office among the feeds.

"What is this place?" he asked Sung.

"Do you think the leadership of our country is stupid?" Sung said. "In this office I monitor everything happening in the DPRK and around the globe. When the American president makes a fool of himself, which is often, we know. When an African dictator is forced out, we know. When someone in the Palace does something against the Party, we know."

But this is not the office of the Supreme Leader or military personnel, Ahn thought. *It is General Kung's office. If knowledge is power, who is running the country*?

"Does the Supreme Leader have an office like this somewhere?"

She gave him a look full of pity. "He relies completely on my uncle. No more stupid questions. You want access to a 3 Tesla MRI? There are none in the DPRK, even at the Pongwha Clinic. We must search out of the country."

She tapped into a computer that responded more quickly than any Ahn had ever seen. "There are many 3 Tesla scanners in South Korea, but getting them across the border is out of the question. China is possible, but in the northern sector there are no cities with high-field scanners. It's almost as backward as we are."

Ahn, still struck dumb by the sophistication of the room, continued to stare.

"That leaves Japan or Russia. We could ship an MRI across the Sea of Japan from Tokyo and Honshu Island, but that poses problems."

"You mean finding the ships?"

"No. We have access to any ship or airplane network we want. It's the political immunity and discretion we need. A Westernized country is not sympathetic to us and smuggling an MRI takes a longer unguarded border than Japan has.

"No," she shook her head. "It has to be Vladivostok."

She called up a satellite map of the Japan Sea and shrank the view to target the eastern Russian city.

"Do we have satellites to take pictures like that?" Ahn asked, his eyes wide.

"Google maps does it, idiot," Sung said.

"Google maps? What's that?"

She ignored him, muttering in a voice so low he thought she was talking to herself. "A railway comes to our border, then direct to Pyongyang. Yes, that's the city we want."

She raised her voice, including him in the conversation now. "The Vladivostok Clinical Hospital Number One looks like our best choice. It says it has full imaging equipment and an MRI scanner that provides care for the territory around the city. Must be a scanner that loads onto a train, since the roads seem difficult to travel."

She turned to him and faced him directly. "Dr. Ahn, you are about to change your perception of everything you know. I want you to remember three things my uncle taught me."

She held up one finger: "Our country must be preserved at all costs. Our honorable history must be defended against the west, especially America."

Finger two went up: "There are worse things than death. Dishonor, for one, and especially dishonor for your family. You come from a loyal heritage, which is why we chose you to be the personal physician to the present leader. If you make a misstep, all of that will change."

"And three?" Ahn asked.

"Look around you," she said. "Our surveillance capabilities reach everywhere in the world. We have hacked into the monitoring system of every government. Wherever you go, we can see you."

"Why are you saying that?"

"Tomorrow you will leave for Vladivostok. We will make all arrangements. You will experience things you have never seen. Normally I would travel with you, but I have another assignment. My uncle will tell you the rest."

She paused, then reached into her purse. "You'll need this." She handed him a sealed thick envelope. "It may smooth negotiations. Do not take even one bill from this envelope for your own use." She nodded at the monitors around her. "Remember, we are watching."

"These rubles are for your own personal expenses, but you shouldn't require even this much," she said as she handed him a much thinner envelope. "We'll need a precise accounting of everything you spend."

They exited the room to find Kung still sitting at his desk.

"No need to talk. I heard everything," he said. "You leave for Vladivostok tomorrow at six a.m. You have five days after that to be back with the scanner."

CHAPTER FOURTEEN

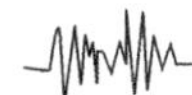

VLADIVOSTOK

MARCH 23

Ahn vaulted back onto the curb as a car sprayed him with icy water. The Russian cold penetrated through his thin wool coat. Slush soaked through his shoes. Honking horns and screeching brakes confused him.

His hour and a half flight to Vladivostok had been smooth, perhaps because Sung gave him a pill to take before he got on the plane. She also arranged companions to help with the airport departure, accompany him on the nonstop Koryo flight itself, and steer him through the Russian arrivals process. Ahn passed from one to the other like a diplomatic pouch.

Now he had to find the Clinical Number One Hospital Vladivostok and persuade the director of MRI to take a scanner to Pyongyang. For this, he was on his own.

He had a letter of introduction. But where was the hospital? His official chauffeur abandoned him at a corner after pointing to the one-way arrow and shouting something unintelligible in Russian.

He already longed for the empty streets and quiet pace of his home city. Only during military ceremonies did traffic like this crowd the boulevards in Pyongyang. Vladivostok teemed with cars twisting and turning and making crossing impossible despite the traffic lights.

Ahn searched for the large institutional architecture and Emergency signs that marked hospitals in his country. He shouldered his way through the crowds, repeating the word hospital in Russian to those who would listen. Most kept on moving.

One older woman finally stopped and pointed to an entrance just behind him that led up to what seemed an elegant embassy. Only as he ascended the stairs did he see the modest sign that he sounded out as the Vladivostok Clinical Hospital Number One.

A young Korean male met him at the door. Ahn's heart jumped a beat when he heard the sounds of his native language. He learned that this was a doctor doing extra training in Vladivostok. After the usual pleasantries, Ahn followed his guide with open mouth and wide eyes through spotless corridors. Crisp nurses and proud physicians passed him without comments. On the wards, most rooms had only two patients and there were no families eating breakfast on the floor.

His guide took him downstairs to the radiology suite, then to the director's office. It was a windowless box with fluorescent lights and bare walls.

"This is Dr. Pavel Ostrowsky, our director of radiology," the young Korean guide said, remaining to translate.

Pavel had a nose made crooked by several old fractures, a thick face with perpetual scowl, and an attitude that suggested only unpleasantness.

"Let me get this straight," he said as he took a bottle of vodka from his top drawer and filled two glasses. "You want to take a three-tesla scanner to the Democratic People's Republic of Korea?"

"Exactly," Ahn replied. "Do you have such a machine?" He handed over a sheaf of paper written in Russian that the Presidential Palace had provided as a formal request.

"Of course," the director replied, emptying one glass and pushing the other to Ahn. "We supply scanners for all cities within five hundred kilometers of Vladivostok. But I can't see how we could provide a three-tesla scanner for Pyongyang on short notice."

Ahn picked the glass up, wrinkled his nose after smelling it, and pushed it back toward Pavel. "How do you transport the scanners to other cities?"

"We have flatbed railway cars that carry truck, scanner, and radiologist. There is a regular schedule. But why do you want to borrow a scanner?"

"To assess whether we need your technology."

"Understood," said the director, drinking Ahn's vodka and filling both tumblers again. "But it might take a long time to arrange."

He waited, expression expectant. Ahn's brows furrowed. He sat wondering what he was supposed to do next. The director's face assumed an inviting smile.

Ahn fidgeted with the good-luck charm in his coat pocket. His arm brushed against his jacket and he remembered the thick envelope Rhee Sung had given him. He took it from the inner pocket of his coat, now remembering the comment *It may smooth negotiations.*

Ahn pushed the envelope toward Pavel. "We hope this will help any inconvenience and compensate the person accompanying the train."

The director looked at the envelope for a moment, then ripped it open, making no attempt to hide its contents. American hundred-dollar bills poked out at him, the first Ahn had ever seen. The man flipped through them and looked up with a gap-toothed smile.

"Yes, I think we can do something to help our Korean colleagues. For the Communist cause."

"Of course," Ahn said. "We will also need technical help. And someone to read the images. The man who gave me these said he will provide twice as many more to the person who comes to Pyongyang with the scanner."

"For our comrades in the People's Republic, I, Pavel Ostrowsky, will provide assistance myself," the Russian said as he pocketed the envelope and finished the rest of the vodka. "We leave tomorrow morning."

He turned to the Korean doctor, who Ahn now realized was in Kung's service.

"And, of course, you must join us to translate."

CHAPTER FIFTEEN

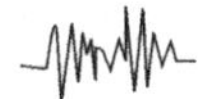

EN ROUTE FROM VLADIVOSTOK

MARCH 24

The next morning Ahn emerged from the waiting room of the train station, hugging himself to stay warm. Halogen lights punctuated the darkness with a dazzling glare. The stench of diesel oil filled his nostrils. Slippery deposits of grease made the path treacherous as he picked his way to the passenger carriage.

He had thought this would be a simple trip. Rhee had selected Vladivostok to borrow an MRI scanner because of its proximity to the DPRK. He thought he and Pavel would drive a truck with a mobile MRI unit from that city to Pyongyang. They would persuade the Supreme Leader to have his scan and Pavel would take the rig back to Vladivostok. All the complexity would rest in persuasion and subsequent decision-making.

Instead, the logistics had become a nightmare. The only ground passage between the two countries was a railway bridge. The journey, at the mercy of train schedules, freight yards, and border guards, might take a week or more and provide no flexibility in schedule. General Kung had given him five days.

The revving of a truck engine blasted through his self-absorption. Twenty meters from him, a fourteen-wheel tractor-trailer spewed exhaust as the driver gunned the idling engine, straining like a sprinter ready to race. Ahn startled to see Pavel, the director of radiology, waving from the cab.

Ahn identified the passenger carriage waiting for him halfway across the railway yard and scurried toward it, noting that the young Korean translator was already in the car at the window. As he boarded the train, he saw Pavel begin to inch the truck toward a single flatbed car sitting isolated across from him. Pavel shouted something the translator bounced back to Ahn as "Watch this!"

Ahn held his breath. He had never seen a civilian vehicle this big. With his mouth open and eyes wide, he watched Pavel inch the vehicle up a metal ramp onto the railway flatcar, squeal to a halt, jump down from the cab, place blocks under the wheels, and lash it with chains in conjunction with a crew of railway attendants.

Pavel joined them a few minutes later. Ahn envied the thick greatcoat that wrapped around his large body, dripping snow but keeping its wearer safe from cold and wet.

"Not bad, eh?" Pavel grinned. "It took me forever to get funding for that rig. The Primorsky Krai regional health authority busted my balls for three years before they saw how important it was. I've wheeled it to all the small towns around Vladivostok to get MRI scans. Maybe I should have been a truck driver."

Pavel sat in the compartment but did not remove his coat. A prolonged whistle pierced the air; the car lurched forward, stopped, jerked backward, and shook with a loud crash.

Ahn's head whipped back and forth and he almost flew off the seat. He grabbed the window handle to stabilize himself.

"Be careful," Pavel said. "That handle could come off in your hand. Not very sturdy."

"What happened? Did we hit something?" Ahn asked.

"No, the engine is just coupling to our railway car. Next, it'll link with the flatbed car containing my MRI truck. We'll move out after that."

Five minutes later the train screeched and lurched out of the station, billowing the gray haze and acrid odor of diesel exhaust.

"Next stop, Ussuriysk. We change track gauge there," Pavel said as he uncorked a bottle of vodka and tore into a sandwich of sausage, onions, and peppers on thick slices of peasant bread. Ahn turned away, trying to decide which of the items provided the worst olfactory experience. He decided it was the onions, which blasted across the coach on a stream of alcohol vapor.

For the rest of the trip, the young Korean translator sat curled asleep in the corner, giving up any pretense of amicable conversation. Ahn turned to a book that claimed to reveal the secrets of the Russian language in two hundred pages. The radiologist continued his breakfast feast.

Thirty kilometers of thick forest later, the train squealed, thumped, and halted at a station that Ahn spelled out as Ussuriysk. The clunk of the uncoupling melted into receding engine noises, then silence.

"What now?" Ahn asked.

Pavel gave him a smile and thumbs up as he disappeared through the compartment doorway. The translator pointed to the railyard. Lifting the window, Ahn craned and stuck his neck out to confirm that their car had been uncoupled along with the flatbed holding the MRI scanner. Another flatbed and passenger car sat on separate tracks a few meters away.

Ahn heard the truck engine roar, felt the bumps of the truck driving off the flatcar, then saw it lumber toward another flatbed several meters away and jerk forward up its ramp.

Pavel reappeared with a satisfied smile on his face and his coat again covered with snow. "We had to switch railway cars from the wide gauge tracks used in Russia to the standard gauge of the DPRK. Now we will move to a new car ourselves. Then we wait."

They transferred to the new car and left Ussuriysk four hours later. The chugging of the engines, lurching of the car as it rounded all-too-frequent bends in the railbed, and clacking of the wheels made reading impossible. After six hours of travel, the train stopped with a screeching shudder.

"K-H-A-S-A-N," Ahn spelled. "What happens here?"

"We're at the border with the DPRK," Pavel said, and went back to his vodka bottle.

Ahn slid to the window. A pair of army vans loomed a few meters away. From them, four soldiers in Russian uniforms headed for their car with rifles slung over their shoulders.

CHAPTER SIXTEEN

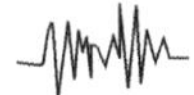

KHASAN, RUSSIA

MARCH 25

Ahn's hands trembled. He tried to squeeze them together in his lap. That failed, so he sat on them. In Pyongyang, soldiers approaching a train with guns meant trouble. In Russia, he did not know what they had in mind, but he expected the worst.

"What's going to happen?" he asked his vodka-sodden companion.

The radiologist shrugged. "Who knows. Give me your papers. Let me deal with the officials."

Ahn handed over his letter and identity papers and looked out the window again. He saw a Korean civilian surrounded by several soldiers. Before he could ask about that man, he heard voices from the rear of the car and felt a blast of cold air as footsteps approached. Moments later, he heard a loud knock on the door.

The radiologist jerked the door open. Two soldiers in their twenties, wearing Russian uniforms, stood with assault rifles at the ready. When the radiologist confronted them, they pulled back. Even from behind Ahn could smell the onion and vodka on Pavel's breath.

He could only follow the gestures of the discussion that followed. He dared not ask for translation, and even if he did, the translator was huddling in the corner about to collapse from fright. After several minutes, the soldiers pushed Pavel aside and snatched the bags from the baggage compartment, opening them on the seat beside Ahn and scattering their contents everywhere. They pulled the top off the back of the seat and inspected the space behind it. Finally, they looked at Pavel with narrowed eyes.

Pavel shrugged and with a smile opened the greatcoat that enveloped him. In its inner lining were pockets containing four bottles of vodka claiming to be the Czar's finest. The soldiers removed them one by one, twisted the cap off each, took a sniff, and left.

"They deduced that I might have some extra vodka and wanted to find it," Pavel said with a grin after the compartment door closed. "These poor boys get paid very little and have to spend their days in this godless place. I'm more than happy to provide them with something to lessen their stress."

"What's the story with that man?" Ahn asked, pointing to the Korean civilian standing apart from the group, now manacled.

"Poor bugger," Pavel said. He pointed to the bridge that lay before them. "The Friendship Bridge is the only land connection between my country and yours. That man is one of your countrymen who thought he could sneak across last night. Not long for the world."

As they watched, one of the soldiers marched the man to the precipice, shot him, and rolled his body into the Tumen river.

"Your country does not like defectors," Pavel said, not smiling now.

Later that night, Ahn counted the reasons he should be able to sleep as he lay in the lower bunk of the train compartment. The train car rested quietly in the station without jerking. The day's experiences had exhausted him, so he should have just drift off. The berth had the same firmness as his floor at home. His medical training had taught him to snatch sleep whenever possible.

None of those helped. He could not get the picture of the dead man or the soldiers out of his mind. He stared at the mattress above him hour after hour, trying to block out the snoring that pummeled his ear drums. Twice he kicked the mattress when the raspy exhalations from his radiology colleague in the upper bunk overpowered him. His drunken comrade merely rolled over. He considered that inebriation might be a useful travel state after all.

A familiar shuddering of the car and loud crash disrupted his musings. By now, he recognized the sound—coupling with a new locomotive. A few minutes later, the train crawled out of the yard. Enveloped in darkness, it rumbled onto the Friendship Bridge that spanned the Tumen River and separated Russia from the DPRK. Ahn noted the time. Eight a.m.

The bridge was fifty years old. Clearly it had not been upgraded. It swayed and creaked with each turn of the locomotive wheels. The six-car train crept across as if it feared to awaken some destructive demon. The stench of the polluted river filtered through closed windows. Ahn could only imagine how much it must stink in the summer months.

None of that mattered when he got to the other side of the bridge. He was in his own country at last. As the train rolled onto solid land, Ahn smiled with relief at the recognition that he could read the signs. The stress of Russia, whose Cyrillic linguistic building blocks were unfamiliar, had bothered him more than he had admitted.

His radiology partner remained asleep until the train groaned into the Tumangang station. When the convoy came to a full stop, Ahn sprinted for the door and jumped onto the frozen earth. He did not kiss it—there was too much animal excrement for that—but he did raise his arms in a small victory dance.

A train attendant in neat brown uniform approached him with a scowl.

"Just glad to be back home," Ahn said to the unasked question. "Are we on schedule for Pyongyang?"

"We get in at eight o'clock tomorrow evening," the man replied. "Now I must ask you to return to the car. No one is allowed off the train in this rail yard."

Ahn passed the rest of the agonizingly slow trip meditating on how he would deal with the results of the MRI once he got it.

"Can your machine identify a three-millimeter lesion?" Ahn asked Pavel when the radiologist had finished his liquid breakfast.

"Even one millimeter," the radiologist replied.

"And can you know for sure whether it is a mass and not just some normal outgrowth?"

"You already asked these questions in Vladivostok," Pavel said. "Let me be clear. We can diagnose an abnormal mass in the hypothalamus with thin section MRI. We can identify whether it is a tumor by MR spectroscopy. We can establish how it affects the fibers around it with diffusion tensor imaging. We can give you a complete picture of the problem."

"How long will it take?"

"About an hour, but your patient can wear headphones and listen to whatever he wants. Most patients just go to sleep."

"But can you be absolutely sure?"

Pavel turned back to his book. Ahn realized he had used up his companion's patience. He stared at the barren countryside for hours at a time, stoking his anxiety. Occasionally he drifted into uneasy sleep, tortured by the path that led ahead.

What if the MRI showed no mass in the hypothalamus? Would he be killed for his error in diagnosis? What if the Supreme Leader had side effects from the medication?

And the biggest problem of all—what if the mass needed surgery? He knew there was no one in the DPRK who would carry out such an operation. Would he have to try to persuade a foreign neurosurgeon to come and operate in the DPRK?

And Ahn's own family. Would they be safe if he failed to resolve the problem? He knew only too well stories of citizens who had disappeared when they had displeased the government.

He wished he had never gone to medical school. And for the first time in his life he wondered whether life would be different if he lived on the other side of the border that separated the two Koreas.

CHAPTER SEVENTEEN

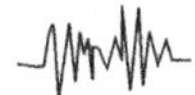

PYONGYANG

MARCH 26

The train pulled into the Pyongyang train station under the People's Palace at eight-thirty that evening. Ahn wondered how the administration had dispersed the crowds of workers normally leaving the palace grounds at that time. No concern of his. He was home, and he smiled as he stepped onto the platform with his associates in tow.

The smile dissolved when General Kung approached. No handshake; no congratulatory comment. "Where is the radiologist?" Kung asked as he looked past Pavel into the train compartment.

"I'm the radiologist," Pavel said. "Radiologist and MRI operator and truck driver reporting for duty. Where do I move my rig?"

"You don't move anything," Kung replied in what appeared to be good Russian. "You have only one patient, and the scan will start in an hour." He beckoned them all to follow him. The translator disappeared.

"But don't I get a chance to—" Pavel's face froze as Kung impaled him with his eyes. "All right then. I'll fire up the machine." He disappeared in the direction of the MRI scanner.

Ten minutes later, the Supreme Leader appeared, flanked by two guardsmen. He mounted the train, came up to the place where Ahn and Kung waited in the antechamber of the scanner. He looked at the narrow tube for his head. "I have to put my head in that?" he asked

"Yes, but you only have to keep still for about half an hour," Ahn said.

"I'm not going to do it," the Supreme Leader turned away.

"It's the only way you can get your unique brain image and we can find out what's going on," Ahn said.

The Supreme Leader looked like a child just told he had to have an injection. "I don't want—Kung, you have one first, just to prove it is safe."

Ahn turned to General Kung. "What about that?"

Kung shrugged. "Of course. No problem for me." He moved onto the gantry and lay back. His head barely fit in the magnet's bore. The scan took forty minutes, a time in which the Supreme Leader sipped beer, smoked a cigar, and looked at his smart phone.

Kung emerged looking rested and comfortable. "It was easy," he said to his commander. "Just a little banging. Wear the headphones and listen to some music you like." He put his arm out toward the door to the scanner as an invitation.

"I-I am still going to have to think about it," the Supreme Leader said. "Give me a few minutes."

"Dear Respected, we really need this. It's not painful at all," Ahn said.

"I'm going back to the waiting area to think it over," the Supreme Leader said and walked away.

Kung grabbed Ahn's arm and pulled him aside. "Do something to convince him."

"I've done my best."

"Some sedative, then." Kung looked angry. "Don't you have tablets in your office?"

"I'm not sure they're safe with his anti-seizure medications."

"Get them. Now." Kung pushed Ahn toward the exit. Ahn stumbled with the force of the push but recovered and kept running toward his office. He found a bottle filled with five milligram Valium pills. He shook his head. He had been saving these for his own use in case life got too difficult. Shrugging his shoulders, he returned to the railway station.

He found Kung waiting where he had left him, looking at his watch. "Give them to him."

"How many?" Ahn held out his hand with three pills in it.

"You're the doctor. Enough to get the scan," Kung said, nodding toward the next room. "He's still in there."

Past the guards outside the door, Ahn could see the Supreme Leader lounging in front of the television with a glass of whiskey in his hand. Ahn tried to keep his voice calm. "It's too dangerous," he said. "I have no idea how much alcohol he's had tonight. Each of these pills might keep a normal man asleep for hours. The instructions warn against mixing them with alcohol. If we give them to him now, he could stop breathing."

"You claim we need this scan," Kung said, "and I guarantee your patient won't hold still unless he is sedated. He's out of the city tomorrow. We have one chance."

"If he gets into trouble it's my head on the line."

Kung withered Ahn with a flaming glance. "You have one job—to do what I say to keep your leader and country free from shame. Your head—and ass—is mine whenever I want it. Give him the damn pills."

Ahn hesitated. Kung grabbed the tablets and marched into the president's room, leaving the door open so Ahn could hear everything.

"Your doctor says you must take these to relax."

"Tell my doctor to go fuck himself," Ahn heard through the open door. "I take what I want."

"But they might give you a new sensation, a special relaxation. I'll guarantee you'll love the feeling."

The Supreme Leader dumped the pills into his whiskey glass and emptied it with one swallow.

Nothing happened for half an hour. When he went to relieve himself, however, the Supreme Leader showed an unsteadiness that worsened on his return to the couch. Kung intercepted his trajectory and guided him to the door, saying, "The opportunity to show your superiority is here at last. You are ready for your scan."

The Supreme Leader mumbled something and continued his uncertain route. Ahn intercepted him. "Do you have anything metallic in your pockets? Pens, change, anything? The MRI has the power of one thousand magnets."

The Supreme Leader shook his head. Kung and two guards continued to maneuver him up the stairs into the MRI car. "You are dead men if you let him fall," Kung said through clenched teeth as he staggered back in response to an unexpected lurch. Pavel, clean shaven and with combed hair, waited at the entrance to the MRI.

"Leave anything metallic outside the room," Pavel shouted as the guards began to enter. One guard shoved his way through despite this admonition. Ahn watched as the man's jacket tore open and a Sig Sauer P320 flew into the magnet's bore.

"Thank God our patient wasn't in the magnet. I'd have to quench the magnetic field to get the gun off," Pavel shouted.

"Can you do the scan with a gun on the magnet?" Kung asked.

"Yes, it's just stuck on the surface."

"Then do it," Kung ordered. He turned to the guard cowering in the corner. "And you will pay for your carelessness."

The Supreme Leader crawled onto the gantry and was snoring within five minutes.

Pavel arranged the head coil with no visible sign of recognition of his patient's identity. The scanner began its banging.

CHAPTER EIGHTEEN

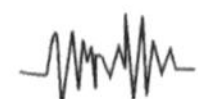

PYONGYANG

MARCH 26

Ahn climbed into the back of the truck and slid into a seat beside Pavel while the scan was being done. Pavel scrolled past General Kung's scan and moved to the patient whose identity was marked only as X on the images. He hunched over the MRI console with a posture of intense focus as slice after slice of image rolled through.

Ahn shuddered to realize he was the first Korean citizen to see an image of his Supreme Leader's brain. He half expected to identify some remarkable feature in the images, something that set them apart from any other man's MRI.

He looked away from the screen for a moment. Kung stood silhouetted against the closing doorway, then rolled a chair behind Ahn and deposited himself without a word.

"There," Pavel shouted as Ahn was returning his attention to the monitor. He spoke in English, as that was the only language all three of them understood.

"Did I miss something? I didn't see anything," Ahn said. He looked at Kung. "Did you catch that, General?"

Kung remained silent and grim.

"I'll replay the scans in a minute," Pavel said. A tone of authority had replaced his casual banter and he seemed to work with precision and purpose. "I'm going to adjust the sequences to pick it up better."

He turned to his companions. "I'm sure you know that MRI scans vary with the settings of the imaging. What you see depends in part on the acquisition parameters selected by the radiologist." He turned to Ahn as if he expected confirmation. Ahn stared at him with a blank expression and noted that Kung had the same uncomprehending stare.

"It's like tuning a radio," Pavel said. "I have to define the MRI sequences to get the best pictures. I believe we have an abnormality here, but I want to visualize it better." For the next ten minutes he worked like a boxer closing in on his opponent, bobbing and weaving as he dialed up scans and adjusted parameters of scanning. His fist clenched and unclenched while the images formed.

"We're done," Pavel said. "And we have what we need. I'll show you." He twisted knobs and punched buttons until the image of a dark cleft making a V between two smooth surfaces appeared.

"Observe the hypothalamus," he said. "A valley between two slopes. Pretend you're a helicopter pilot flying through it. These coronal scans show you what you would see when the landscape passes around you."

As the sequences progressed from the front of the hypothalamus to the back, Ahn noted a large hillock protruding from one side of the valley, distorting but not destroying the smooth margin of brain tissue. At its maximum, the hillock filled the entire V and pressed into the surface of the opposite side.

"Is that a hypothalamic hamartoma?" Ahn said. He could not keep the excitement from his voice, although he tried to sound calm. He noted that Kung remained completely still.

"Yep. Sizable, too. You can see here how it bulges down toward the optic nerve."

Kung stood. "Prepare to leave in an hour. Our palace guards will escort you to the edge of the city. Ahn, come with me."

"But I haven't had the opportunity to see your beautiful city," Pavel said. "And don't you need copies? I've made these for your records." He handed a CD to Kung with a silent appeal in his eyes.

Ahn wanted to show off the city he loved, but Kung's body language vetoed that idea. He would have to show his colleague around another time.

Kung exited from the truck, and Ahn followed him like an obedient puppy.

The two men faced each other across the large bare desk in the general's office ten minutes later.

"You got lucky with predicting what would be on the scan," Kung said. "But now you have a problem—the biggest problem of your short career. That career will end if you don't solve the problem perfectly."

He turned to point to a calendar on the wall. "You're going to have to make this hamartoma go away by October 10, Worker's Celebration Day, the most important holiday in the DPRK. Every citizen will be watching the Supreme Leader then. He must be perfect. Do you understand?'

Ahn nodded. He feared he would vomit if he opened his mouth. His heart was beating so fast he thought he would have a cardiac arrest.

"And in case you don't realize the stakes, let me be clear. If you fail, we will inflict unbelievable pain on you and your family before you die. Your blood line will be disgraced. You will lose the most important thing we Koreans have—honor."

He turned to the computer and added, "Nothing personal, you understand. You're just in a bad place at a bad time. Have a nice day."

CHAPTER NINETEEN

VLADIVOSTOK

MARCH 30

Happy chaos reigned in Mumiy Troll, Pavel's favorite Vladivostok bar. *Nostrovia* echoed back and forth as the customers took advantage of his promise of free drinks. Pavel himself sat at a table for eight at the epicenter of the jollity.

"Another round of vodka for everyone," he shouted to the bartender, "and a round of your special scotch for my table."

As the liquor flowed, the questions from the friends around him flowed even more. "Where have you been, Pavel? We've missed you for the last week."

"Did you shack up with that hot dancer from the night-club?"

"You must have been out of town. The hospital closed down MRI's the last few days."

"Were you on a secret mission? Someone said they saw your train heading for China."

Pavel decided it was time. With the train engineer Dmitri at his side, he began a detailed story of the adventure that had taken them from Vladivostok six days ago and returned them today. It was funny, carefully rehearsed, and false.

General Kung had warned him and Dmitri to keep their excursion secret, with death the penalty for indiscretion. He slipped them one million rubles at the same time to show he could be generous if they complied.

The money burned in Pavel's pocket until he could get home. He would divide it seventy-thirty with Dmitri, but take fifty thousand rubles first to be sure his friends had an enjoyable evening.

Dmitri agreed enthusiastically with this plan. The two travelers sat together so they would also agree on the details of the story as they wove it. They knew Kung would have spies here who would report everything they said.

"A week ago we got a request to take our MRI train to Dalnerechensk," Pavel began, "way up in the most northerly part of Primorski Krai. Has anybody ever been there?"

He looked around, was delighted to see no one raise a hand. That would make the story spinning easier.

"We were obligated to do this because the regional government paid for our MRI machine and the flatbed it rides on. It's part of our civic responsibility to go wherever in the region we're asked."

"The trip was a bitch," Dmitri took up the tale. "There was still snow on the tracks, and when there wasn't snow there were trees and poles and sometimes dead animals. It took us two and a half days to get there."

Pavel resumed. "We had to do minor repairs on the engine several times, and finding fuel was more and more difficult as we got further north. Several times I thought my machine was going to be bounced off the train."

Dmitri chimed in, "When we got there, there was not a f**ing thing to do. I had to hang around bars while Pavel did his imaging stuff just for an afternoon. Then we climbed back in and came home."

"In summary, gentlemen," Pavel finished, "I would not suggest that any of you decide to move there." Laughter and calls of "Don't worry" and "We won't."

"Did they pay you well?" someone shouted.

"Hardly anything at all, but I'm a generous man and glad to be home. I decided to use the pittance they provided to help you celebrate our return."

Pavel avoided further questions by excusing himself, leaving Dmitri behind. The engineer was now so drunk he could barely speak. He would be lucky to stay upright for much longer.

As for the customers who protested his departure, Pavel repeated, "I have to prepare my official report for the government. Don't worry, though; I've left enough with the bartender for at least two more rounds." Most of them gave him a laughing thumbs up and knowing wink.

The cold slammed into him as he left the bar, still numbing his fingers despite the fact it was officially spring. Some day, he vowed, he would have a cottage on the Black Sea to escape the winter.

Snow had piled up in the streets and the walking was treacherous. His flat was only a few blocks from the bar. As soon as he let himself in, he checked that nine hundred fifty thousand rubles were still hidden in the mattress. *I should try to get a better lock for the door. Suppose some kid broke in and found this?*

Or this. He turned on his computer and twisted at his generous forelock of black hair.

Tugging hard, he pulled off a hairpiece and extracted a mini USB drive that was only slightly larger than a hairpin. He had found the hairpiece useful for attracting women, for making him less depressed about his age, and occasionally for hiding important computer files. The Korean authorities had wiped the storage drive of his MRI machine under the pretense of searching for contraband. They had body searched him but had apparently not worried about what looked like hairpins holding a partial toupee.

Pavel had of course expected that the machine's memory would be wiped. As a precaution, he had downloaded the scans he had taken in Pyongyang onto the mini flash drive that he now held in his hand. It was wise to have a backup.

Plugging into the USB port of his computer, he watched as the images appeared slice by slice on the screen. Again, he saw the hamartoma rise out of the hypothalamus. More important, at the end of the sequence he saw the video picture of the patient superimposed on the scan sequences. This was added automatically to the scan only after it was finished to serve as an extra step in patient identification. He smiled as he confirmed that he had just scanned the Supreme Leader of North Korea.

There was another MRI on the flash drive, the one General Kung had volunteered for when he wanted to show the machine was safe. Pavel had not bothered to look at that scan and was about to delete it when the MR angiogram cuts started to come through. He stared at the screen, then reversed the scans and looked again.

My God, Kung has a basilar tip aneurysm. With that weakness in his artery's wall, he could die if his blood pressure suddenly spiked. Should Pavel call Kung to tell him there was a time bomb in his brain, a blood vessel weakness that could explode at any time?

That, of course, would be evidence that Pavel had preserved a copy of the scans, and such proof might be fatal. He decided that he should think it over in the place he always found conducive to his best decision-making—the bar.

He returned to Mumiy Troll. It looked very different than it had with the riotous drinking earlier in the evening. Most patrons had called it a night. A few prostitutes clustered at one end of the counter, hoping that they could still rescue an unprofitable day. Two men Pavel knew vaguely sat at isolated tables nursing vodka shots. The air reeked of alcohol and old cigarettes, reminders of the earlier festivities.

Pavel ordered a single malt scotch and sat alone at his usual table. He swirled the dark liquid in his glass, considered his options concerning Kung's aneurysm, decided to do nothing, and tipped back the contents of the glass in one gulp. He was signaling for another when the door burst open.

"Dmitri's dead!" the man who entered shouted. Pavel recognized him as one of the colleagues who had been drinking at the table.

"What?" Pavel stood and headed toward him.

"Dmitri's dead." The man pointed out into the street. "Not far from here."

"What happened?" Pavel asked as he wove toward the man.

"Run over. I guess he was walking in the street and didn't see the car. Sounds like no one saw it. Come and see."

Pavel followed into the night. As they got to the accident site, police were loading Dmitri's body into an emergency vehicle. There was no question that he was the victim, and there was no question he was dead. His head had been crushed by a tire, which had left its mark across his temple. The bone and scalp had ruptured with the impact. Brain oozed through a large laceration, dropping onto the puddle of blood and spinal fluid that surrounded his head.

Pavel turned away. "God, that's terrible. He must have been very drunk."

"He didn't seem that much worse than he's been many times before, but I guess this was his unlucky day," the man who had brought the news remarked.

Pavel decided there was nothing he could do and began to weave back toward his old hangout. A couple more glasses of Scotch would feel good about now.

He felt unsteady himself and took care to stay on the sidewalk.

Just before he entered the pub, one possible implication of Dmitri's death hit him. Could this have been a deliberate assassination? His heart began to pound and his breath came in short puffs as he changed course to head toward his own house.

He checked the lock. No apparent tampering. He made the sign of the cross to thank his creator for getting himself safely home, threw his coat on the hallway chair, and flicked on the lights.

A knockout Korean woman sat in his living room armchair wearing red leather gloves and holding a very fancy leather handbag on her lap. At first he thought she was one of the prostitutes from the bar, but the Serdyukov pistol she revealed by moving her purse changed his mind.

"You disappoint us, comrade Pavel," she said in perfect Russian.

"How so?" His eyes darted around the room, trying to find some weapon he could surprise her with.

"This USB drive. Not part of the arrangement." She showed him the USB with gloved hands. "And how did you spend fifty thousand rubles so fast?" She fanned the money he had hidden in the mattress.

"How did you discover that cash? And how did you get in?"

"You think this mini-USB is small? Our GPS tracker in the cash is even smaller. We did this the American way. We followed the money."

"We? Who are you working for?" he asked. He didn't care, but her answer would give him time to think and might allow him to negotiate his way out of this. By now, the alcohol's effect had been chased away by fear.

"It doesn't matter. It's enough to tell you that my employer will be very sad to know what you have done."

"Whoever he is, he doesn't have to know. You speak Russian well, and there is always a place for a beautiful woman like you in Vladivostok. I am very discreet. You can count on me."

He took a step toward her, shrugging his shoulders. "Take the money. It should be enough to get away and start a life of your own."

"What makes you think I want a life of my own?" She cocked her head, reached in her purse. She laid her gun on her lap and extracted what looked like lipstick. She did something with it hidden by her bag.

Just like a woman, thinking of lipstick at a time like this. But it may give me the opportunity I need. He lunged toward her, arms outstretched, desperate to grab the gun.

She stood, let the pistol fall from her lap, and put her foot on it as it hit the floor. His momentum carried him toward her, but she had stepped back. He careened past her, barely feeling the touch of her gloved finger on his lips as he smashed into the radiator. His scalp must have split, because he could feel blood coursing down his face. It didn't matter; he could still get the Serdyukov if he turned fast enough. Whipping around, he looked to see what she had done with it.

She hadn't even moved to pick it up. He smiled at her stupidity and shook his head.

Women. Again he prepared to charge. In a hand-to-hand fight he would have a good chance of overcoming her.

If he could only trust his legs. They seemed incredibly heavy. His hands too. Weak and numb. And why could he not feel his feet? He looked down to be sure they were still there.

They were. He just had to move fast. He decided to pounce. He set his mind to jump, but his legs simply were not there to obey.

The strange thing was that his thinking was perfect. He knew exactly what he had to do.

His stupid body just wouldn't cooperate. He sank to his knees, then rolled to the floor,unable to move legs or arms.

Then the breathing. His chest seemed too heavy to expand.

Now the woman moved, put the pistol in her purse, and spoke to him from what seemed a great distance. Her image blurred and began to lose focus.

"I am Rhee Sung. I work for General Kung Shinwa. We do not tolerate betrayal. You are feeling the effects of VX and will be dead in a few seconds. I may use other techniques for your ex-wife, son, and father, but they will die as surely as your friend Dmitri did. Thank you for hitting your head. It will appear you fell and bled to death in a drunken stupor."

She kicked his incision. "Do you understand?"

He could hear perfectly but could not speak or move any part of his body. She shrugged and bent over his head again. He could feel her fingers moving on his skull.

"Now you will really bleed," he heard her say as she unrolled the gloves and placed them with care in a jar in her purse. He felt drowsier, could not keep his eyes open. Blood cascaded down his face and neck. He heard the door close. Breathing became too difficult. He gave it up.

CHAPTER TWENTY

PYONGYANG

APRIL 5

Dr. Ahn's jaw and neck muscles tightened into a tension headache.

How could he obey Kung's command to find the best management of a hypothalamic hamartoma? He could not consult with another physician and had no personal knowledge of possible international centers for treatment.

Only the internet could help.

He needed access to the web with time and freedom to search it in depth. He could not get that on Kung's computers. He could not go back to the hospital library, where Comrade B would block every move.

He had heard that there were mavericks in Pyongyang who could arrange a VPN link that allowed internet searches. He tracked down the putative location of one such site and convinced himself that his cause justified using this resource. He figured he needed three hours of uninterrupted time.

He found himself in the poorest part of town as he searched out the address he had been given.

It seemed like some kind of alternate reality.

Shapes flitted like wraiths in and out of the shadows. No light came from the buildings, and the fecal stench that erupted from their doorways and the piles of trash made him wonder if they had plumbing. Occasionally he could distinguish features of an emaciated face, hollow eyes, cheeks caked with grime, swollen lips with rotting teeth. Trash lay everywhere in the streets, and the shapes would pause, paw through garbage, and melt away as he came near.

Many of the apparitions seemed to be children, as young as six or seven. He called to a boy kneeling to drink from a puddle of water, asking him for the street name he had been given.

The boy turned away, at first ready to run, then walked hesitantly toward him with an outstretched hand. "I'll tell you for one hundred won," he said in a wavering voice. He apparently expected negotiation, but Ahn reached into his pocket to get the money. He felt another hand as he did so, whipping around to see another boy, as undernourished and dirt-caked as the first, about to remove Ahn's wallet.

The thief whipped his hand back and cowered like an abused animal with his arms protecting his face, waiting for the blows to land. Ahn pulled out another hundred-won bill and handed it to him.

"Who are you?" Ahn asked the boy. "Shouldn't you be with your family?"

"We have no families," the first boy said. "Our parents were killed years ago. We live here." He spread his arms out toward the filthy street. "The place you want is straight ahead three blocks, then one to the right." Both boys melted into the chill April night.

Several wrong turns later, Ahn saw one of the boys again, waving at him from a doorway. He headed for it to find a twenty-something youth standing beside the boy.

"Not a very fancy neighborhood for your shop," Ahn said.

"The police don't spend a lot of time nosing around this neighborhood. I don't think they want to see the terrible conditions here. It's a pretty good cover. What are you looking for, comrade?" the young man asked.

"Three hours of medical search on the internet," Ahn said.

"Internet access for a medical search, not pop singers or western movie stars?" the youth asked. "Don't they have computers at the hospital? How do I know you're not government?"

"Hospital computers don't have unrestricted internet search access, and I wouldn't be in this neighborhood at this time of night if I were a government worker. Trust me on that."

The young man snorted. "You're right. And besides, my street buddy here says you're OK. His approval is enough for me. It's going to cost you two thousand won."

"That's my salary for a week," Ahn said.

"It's two weeks salary for most people. That's the charge for the risk I take. No negotiation."

"How do I know my use won't be traced?"

"The transmissions are routed through Seoul and then through a VPN browser. Not even Russian hackers can follow them."

Ahn sat entranced in front of the computer screen. He read about therapeutic options available to treat hypothalamic hamartomas and the results of each treatment, stretching his understanding of written English. He had not used his English since medical training. When the English words were too hard, he resorted to Google translate.

A website provided free by the National Institutes of Health of the United States of America provided more than he could comprehend in one sitting. *Why would such a resource be supplied by a government whose main goal is atomic war with the DPRK?*

His new friend helped considerably. He showed him the website of the Hope for HH society, which had a patient's view of this tumor. He punched in Google search, PUBMED, and NORD, and smiled with delight as he watched videos of the surgery on You Tube. Along the way, he also peeked at Brittany Spears, Lady Gaga, and Gangnam-style dancing. He felt like a king surfing a world that was larger and more beautiful than he could ever imagine.

"Time's up," the youth said as Ahn realized he had spent more than three hours staring at the computer monitor. It was cold and dark when he stepped outside the ramshackle flat that housed his new window to the world. He would have to return to get more information the next day.

CHAPTER TWENTY-ONE

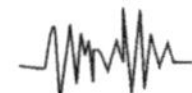

PYONGYANG AND DEMILITARIZED ZONE

APRIL 6-7

The next night, Ahn retraced his steps to the computer haven in the poorest part of Pyongyang. He didn't see his young friends as he trekked to the shop he had visited the night before.

There was no answer at the door when he knocked. He leaned on the bell. Nothing. He pushed at the door. It yielded without any resistance. He stepped into the room and flicked on the light.

He saw an empty table and chair lying on its side. Ahn shook his head, wondering what was going on.

"They came this morning," a familiar voice said. Ahn turned around to see the waif who had introduced him to the computer owner. He stood in the shadow of the door, barely visible.

"Who?"

"The police. They came and took him away."

"Where?"

"I don't know, but they beat him up bad before they left

here. Look, you can see the blood." He pointed to a stain on the cement floor, barely illuminated by the incandescent bulb. "They wanted to find out who had been using the place, but he wouldn't tell them. They cut his tongue out."

"What's going to happen to him?"

The boy shrugged. "If he's lucky, he'll just die. Otherwise, re-education camp. He won't be coming back here, that's for sure."

"Did they threaten you?"

"They didn't know I was watching."

"Will you be OK?"

"As OK as anyone can be here. Maybe I'll swim across the river to China when it gets warmer." And he was gone again, a shadow merging with the blackness of the night.

Ahn decided he had better flee. The police would almost certainly be watching this place, and he didn't want to be associated with it. He ran down the street, taking a different way home than he had come and stopping frequently to be sure no one was following him.

He again passed a sleepless night, feeling doubly distressed. The underground internet surfer would die a terrible death because of the assistance he had provided, and Ahn had no further access to the internet.

He decided that human consultation would be necessary, that he would not involve any other clandestine web surfer. For him, that meant meeting with one person —his cousin Dr. David Ko, staff neurosurgeon at Seoul National Hospital.

When he got to Ryongsung Palace later that morning, he sat without an appointment outside General Kung's office. After waiting an hour, he heard the invitation to enter.

"I am allowing you to see me without an appointment this one time, but it will not happen again," Kung said. "What is the reason for this interruption?"

"I need outside advice about the Supreme Leader's problem."

"Are you incompetent at your job?"

"The only way I will be able to give you good advice is to have a full conversation with someone who has access to all the medical information required to make a decision."

Ahn saw something new in Kung's eyes—perhaps respect. "Who do you have in mind?"

"David Ko, my cousin."

"And how do you propose to meet with him?"

"That's why I am talking to you. I have no idea."

Kung paused for a minute, then said: "Be here at 0800 tomorrow."

Rhee Sung stood at the entrance to Kung's office when Ahn returned the next morning. Kung appeared only for a moment. "Do everything she says today and you will survive," he said. "I will not join you; I must oversee military exercises."

They climbed into an army jeep and headed southwest, Rhee driving. This was most unusual in Ahn's experience. The freedom of a woman driving without an official chauffeur emphasized Kung's power.

"Where are we going?" Ahn asked as the vehicle passed over the Tedong River into the plain outside Pyongyang. He had never ventured into this part of his country.

"Kaesong. The Demilitarized Zone," she said. "Since 1953, when we won the war against the Western invaders, a band four kilometers wide has divided our homeland. We will meet your friend in the Joint Security Area at Panmunjeom."

"Is that safe?"

"Our military keeps it safe. The United Nations patrols the region as well. You must not wander or ask inappropriate questions about our countries while you are there. Soldiers are everywhere, as are listening devices."

"Any other advice?"

"You must not mention the patient's name or any identifying feature."

"Of course not."

The freeway shot straight as an arrow through the countryside, well-paved, with trees separating the two directions of traffic.

Except there was no traffic in either direction. They passed hills on the left with budding spring shrubs. April rains had left some areas of pure mud, but the rocks and vegetation made the hillsides particularly beautiful as they reflected the morning sun.

"These mountains have more than fifteen hundred long-range artillery emplacements hidden in them," Rhee said, her voice resonant with pride. "They could wipe out Seoul in a minute. It's only sixty kilometers to the south, you know. And that region"—she pointed at a verdant swath across the horizon—"is dotted with land mines. Do not leave this vehicle at any time. My uncle is responsible for all these security precautions. He has made this country safe, of course at the Supreme Leader's request."

The speedometer read one hundred fifty kilometers an hour as they sped through the countryside. By nine a.m. they were in a plain dotted with occasional villages. As more houses accumulated, bicyclists joined the traffic.

Just beyond a sign saying "Sariwon," a family sat on a blanket in the middle of the highway, apparently having breakfast. Rhee swerved and passed them without honking.

"Isn't that dangerous?" Ahn asked.

"Not really," she said. "There's never much traffic on these roads. That's one of the great features of our country. In other countries, roads are congested and unpleasant. Ours are beautifully isolated. Some of them are widened to allow airplanes to land."

She loosened her hair band, letting long black hair cascade around her face. "Superhighways such as this are like missiles aimed at South Korea. That's why we call this the Reunification Highway. Someday it will join us once again with our cousins in South Korea. Of course, we will overthrow their political system first."

The cultivated central plain morphed into a verdant forest ahead of them. "This is the demilitarized zone. Because there is no farming allowed here, it is one of the great natural preserves in the world," Rhee said before Ahn could ask. "It is a great example of our noble wish to preserve nature."

She slowed before a gate of stone with a large signboard that read, in Korean and English, "North Korea Demilitarized Zone." A uniformed guard checked their identity papers and waved them through as soon as he saw Kung's signature on the document.

In the distance Ahn saw brightly painted buildings rising high on the horizon on the right. "That looks like a city. What is it?"

"Kijong-dong, Peace Village."

"The colored buildings look very nice, not like the grey cement of Pyongyang. Can we visit it on the way?"

"No time to stop, but the road passes very close."

As they rocketed past, Ahn saw no cars, no bicycles, no people at all in the complex of structures said to be the city. The houses had no windows, just holes in the wall staring at the passersby.

"Is there something wrong with the city?" he asked. "There don't seem to be any people. The only structure that seems alive is that flagpole. And the voices coming from loudspeakers everywhere. Sounds like the same message we get in the *imimbahn*. Why would the government create such beautiful buildings with no inhabitants?"

"Sometimes better not to ask questions," she said. "Look ahead."

She slowed past a clump of roads laid out in a grid, but with no buildings left on it. "This is Panmungak, or was until our enemies destroyed it. Only this Peace Museum remains."

On the left of the road sat a small, brightly colored structure with a curved roof. Representations of flags, which Rhee identified as Swiss, Canadian, Turkish, American, English, Australia, French, and German, were displayed on the frieze.

"These are the countries responsible for the peacekeeping

mission to keep the South Koreans in check, but soldiers from these countries are not allowed on our soil."

She pointed to a three-story grey concrete building with a concave top. "Welcome to our Freedom Center. Our country welcomes visitors here who can look across at the oppressive American army and the vile South Korean countryside."

The car pulled to the side of the road and they stepped into a cool spring day. The DPRK guard in front of the pavilion demanded their papers and this time kept the packet, saying they would be returned at the end of the encounter. Ahn saw no visitors in the Center.

The strident sound of North Korean propaganda blasted from loudspeakers as the soldier, dressed in the brown wool uniform and hat of the People's Army, led them across the plaza.

"Is that broadcast every day?" Ahn asked the guard.

"Our great country tells its stories twenty hours a day," the guard answered.

"And is there no similar broadcast from South Korea?".

"We do have to put up with their lies for three hours every afternoon," the guard said. "We put plugs in our ears to stop hearing their propaganda."

He led them toward seven one-story huts, the middle three painted a bright blue, which stood in a row before them.

Four-meter wide patches of crushed stone separated them, and half-way along one patch ran a concrete ridge half a meter high.

"That ridge is the border between the DPRK and South Korea," Sung said. "Step across that line and you will be shot immediately. You will note that on this side the ground is crushed rock, on the other concrete."

"No barbed wire, no guard post?"

"No, but the bullets in the guns these sentries carry are real, and they will shoot to kill."

Ahn shuddered. So apparently peaceful, yet so deadly.

The guard directed them to building three and opened the door. A dozen mahogany tables filled the room, each with six leather chairs around it. The UN peacekeeping flag flew at each table. Four soldiers with the UN peacekeeping symbol on their helmets stood around the room.

At a central table a thin bespectacled Korean man of about thirty-five rose to his feet as Rhee and Ahn entered the room. He was dressed in a grey suit with a white shirt and thin brown tie. The soldier in front of the door leading to South Korea turned the lock and stood at attention. The three were now the only civilians in the room.

"My congratulations to your uncle, Rhee," the man said. "Getting a permit to meet here on one day's notice is unbelievable."

"He is a powerful man," Rhee said. "This is Dr. Ahn Junsu, a physician with a great interest in the case under discussion."

"I'm Dr. David Ko," the man said, extending his hand to Ahn. "I believe we are cousins."

CHAPTER TWENTY-TWO

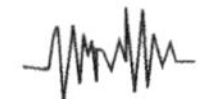

DEMILITARIZED ZONE

APRIL 7

"I suggest we get to the matter at hand," Rhee said. "The family reunion can wait."

"Right." Ko beckoned them to cluster around his open laptop. "I have already classified the treatment options for a hypothalamic hamartoma and relevant papers for each one. We can explore any of them in detail as we wish.

"First, what happens if we do nothing?" he began, scrolling through a list of fifteen articles. "We have a lot of data on that, since it used to be the only choice. The results can be summarized simply. The laughing seizures become shaking seizures; these increase in number and intensity and ultimately kill the patient."

"Not a good option," Ahn said.

"If our patient has another seizure, it is you who will likely die," Rhee said, staring at Ahn.

"So option two. What if we just treat with anti-seizure medicine?" Ahn said, trying to ignore Rhee's aggressive tone. He found it difficult to keep his eyes away from her.

Her abrasive comments both frightened and fascinated him, and she was very beautiful.

"The medication doesn't work very well," Ko said. "It's like trying to treat a sore foot with aspirin pills when the problem is a rock in your shoe. Sooner or later the rock pain will break through. For the hamartoma, you have to go through many different medications to stop the seizures, and in the end, they don't help much."

"Two other problems with that approach," Ahn said. "Our patient may not take his medications as prescribed, so it's risky to rely on them. Not only that, but the possibility that seizures might occur any day is too hard on everyone."

"You people are like our military," Rhee interrupted. "You blather about this and that as if we aren't in crisis. You must make the possibility of a seizure disappear completely. My uncle can't schedule any public or televised event until this is taken care of. Body doubles can only go so far."

"It's not our fault he has this," Ko said.

Ahn shrank back at Ko's effrontery. Criticizing General Kung's representative invited serious reprisal, perhaps even death.

"But it *is* your fault if you don't take care of it," Rhee continued. "And fast. My uncle has given you a drop-dead date of October 10. Both of you might think of taking the drop-dead concept literally."

"That's a very tight schedule," Ko said.

"Live with it," Rhee said.

"The third option is radiation for the mass," Ko said.

Ahn was glad for the change of subject to defuse the rising tension in Rhee's tone.

"Radiation?" Ahn said. "Radiation is for cancer. This is a benign growth. Some people don't even want to call it a tumor."

"Radiation can help control a benign tumor."

"As in, destroy it?" Rhee asked.

"More like, moderate its effects," Ko said. "There's a way of focusing the radiation that targets only the mass. It seems appealing at first. It doesn't require cutting the skull, but it does require a frame to be fitted to the head, and the powerful radiation beam could damage vision and other vital functions."

"I know my patient. No way he would tolerate a frame, even for ten minutes," Ahn said. "And imagine if someone took a picture of him with it attached to his head and leaked it."

"Would radiation have to be done outside the DPRK?" Rhee asked.

"Yes," Ko said.

"Out of the question, then." Rhee slammed her fist on the table. "Anything we do has to be done in Pyongyang where my uncle can control the situation. And what do you think the chances are of getting our patient to allow radiation of any kind to his brain?" She made a circle of her finger and thumb. "Zero. Complete zero. He would freak out at the idea. Knowing him, he'd worry about alien probes." She shook her head.

"What are the other options?" Ahn asked.

"Both surgical. One involves endoscopy, where the surgeon puts a tube though the brain into the hamartoma and tries to scoop it out."

"I don't like the sound of that," Ahn said. "How can he be sure of what he's seeing? And how can he stop bleeding if it happens?"

"Both excellent questions, which are being worked out," Ko said, scrolling the computer display to a new page.

Rhee stood again. "Now you're talking about sticking a tube through this man's brain and trying to take out a tumor through it? Whoever does that better be damned good and have done hundreds of those cases."

"There's no one like that," Ko said nervously. "As I mentioned, these techniques are just being developed."

Rhee put her hands on her hips. "Are you jerking us around here? You say doing nothing is bad, then you start blabbering about radiation beams and tubes through the brain. Do neurosurgeons have any real idea how to treat this?"

A soldier came toward her. "Ma'am, please keep your hands down at all times. And try to control yourself."

Ahn thought he saw a flicker of something in Rhee's eyes that chilled him. Was she really going to attack this man and cause an international incident?

Ko put a hand on her arm.

She twisted his wrist hard and hissed, "Never touch me," but sat down.

"Is there another surgical option?" Ahn asked in his most conciliatory voice.

"Microsurgery," Ko said, shaking his hand and rubbing it where Sung had grasped it. "You're very strong."

"What is microsurgery?" Rhee asked, ignoring his comment and becoming increasingly confrontational in her tone and attitude.

"Surgery through a small skull opening using high magnification."

"Do we have the equipment for that in Pyongyang?" Ahn asked.

"You have a good operating microscope, but you don't have anyone who knows how to use it. It's more for show."

"And what's the likely outcome of this microsurgery?" Rhee asked.

"Should remove the hamartoma and cure the seizures," Ko said.

"Risks?"

"The hypothalamus is an incredibly delicate area of the brain. In the wrong hands, the risks are enormous,"

"And in the right hands?"

"The hamartoma can be removed without any complications."

Sung moved around the table to a spot in front of both men. "You've made our decision easy. Surgery will have to be done. Who has the right hands?"

"I have no idea," Ahn said, shrinking away.

"Did you see me looking at you for advice?" Rhee said. "Ko, that's why you're here. Who should do this surgery?"

"There's no one in my department who could do it," Ko said.

"We wouldn't ask them anyway. We're not going to get someone from an enemy nation to do a procedure like this."

"That's a problem, then," Ko said, "because the hands-down best person for this surgery is an American neurosurgeon, a man named Duncan MacGregor."

"An American?" Rhee said, smashing her hand down on the table. "No way."

"I'm sorry; my friend gets very emotional," Ko said to the guard heading toward them again.

"One more fist like that and you will have to leave," the guard said. Ahn and Ko nodded in agreement.

"What about someone from Russia? Don't they have good neurosurgeons there?" Sung asked as if nothing had interrupted her.

"Even the Burdenko Institute, one of the greatest neurosurgical centers in the world, doesn't have much on this tumor," Ko said.

"China?"

"Same thing. I knew you would be upset, so I specifically scoured the literature to see what results Chinese surgeons have reported. They have more cases than the Russians but the results are not great—continued seizures, paralysis of an arm or leg, even prolonged coma as a result of their surgery."

Ahn entered the fray. "Not even Beijing or Shanghai?"

"A hospital needs both epilepsy and surgical sophistication to treat this problem. Neurosurgeons must work with neurologists and other doctors and become known as specialists for this rare condition. Neurosurgeons in other countries haven't developed collaborations long enough to have a track record. As a result, their surgery has a ten percent likelihood of some major debilitating problem."

"Can you imagine what would happen if our patient ended up with a problem like that? We'd be assassinated," Ahn said. His tension headache was back and his anxiety grew greater and greater as he listened to the conversation.

"Three generations of your family would be assassinated as well," Rhee replied. "I would probably see to it myself."

She looked into the distance for a moment and cocked her head to the left. "I would be killed too, for being part of the team that chose the incompetent surgeon. But they might wait until I had wiped out all your ancestors." She wasn't smiling.

"I've looked into more than published papers on this topic," Ko said. "I've reviewed the lectures neurosurgeons have given over the last two years on this disease at professional conferences around the world. MacGregor has by far the best results."

"How do you know this?" Rhee said.

"Here's an example. One of his online lectures had PowerPoint slides that I copied."

He offered her the chair in front of his computer. "One misstep in any part of the procedure and you risk disaster," Ko said as he flashed one slide after another. "Just to summarize the point, I made a graph of MacGregor's complications—that's the one percent here. Here are the complications from ten other centers. As you can see, they range from five to thirty percent of cases, and the numbers of cases are much smaller."

"Could MacGregor be lying about his results?" she asked.

Ko sat back. "I don't think so. In the American system, there are checks and balances on what a neurosurgeon reports—quality assurance conferences, vetting of data by residents, screening before someone is allowed to claim expertise. One of the strongest signs to me that MacGregor is telling the truth is that he doesn't go around boasting. His results speak for themselves."

"There's only one real way to check," he added. "We would have to visit MacGregor and watch him at work. That, of course, is impossible."

Rhee looked at Ahn. "You're going to have to be the one to tell General Kung about these conclusions. They're clear, but they're not pretty. Your life may not be worth shit after this."

CHAPTER TWENTY-THREE

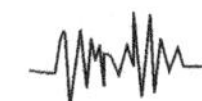

PYONGYANG

APRIL 8

Kung commanded Ahn to report first thing the next morning. Ahn arrived ten minutes early and was ushered in the moment he got there.

"What did you decide?" the general asked, leaving Ahn standing in front of his huge desk. Ahn's heart did not pound as rapidly as usual. It seemed to him that Kung felt uncomfortable, that Kung did not like things he could not control. A brain tumor that produced unpredictable seizures was high among those things.

"There are four treatment options for hypothalamic hamartomas," Ahn began.

"And?"

"We eliminated three, leaving surgery as the only real option."

"Surgery would have to be done here, in Pyongyang."

"We know. That's what gave us great trouble."

"Why?"

"Only one name keeps coming up as the best surgeon to do this."

"That name?"

"Duncan MacGregor at Harbor Hospital in Boston. He appears to be the world expert in this tumor."

Kung made a fist with his right hand and punched it into his left. "No Chinese or Vietnamese or Russian neurosurgeons?"

"No."

"Can you be sure MacGregor is that good?"

"We don't know. David Ko says he's seen the other potential surgeons operate, and they are not spectacular. He has never seen MacGregor at work."

"Sounds like you need to visit Boston." Kung picked up a glass with brown liquid and took a swallow. "Rhee Sung told me all this last night. I wanted to see how closely your story matched hers."

"And?"

"Exactly the same."

Ahn stood, fidgeting with his hands, while Kung watched him with narrowed eyes. After what seemed an eternity, Kung said, "Sit down. I want to tell you a story."

Ahn sat.

"You hear each day about the United States as the great aggressor, the power that waits to pounce and destroy our noble country. I want to convince you now that this is one hundred percent true. The facts of the case are much worse."

Kung moved to a drawer of his desk, unlocked it, and handed Ahn a faded and tattered photograph. A man, woman, and child, faces distorted in terror, ran with fire bursting from their clothes and the fields around them blazing.

"My grandfather and his family. They died of their burns shortly after this. We were the main landowners in a northern village of our country with a very proud lineage. When the war started in 1949, we had no idea what the United States or any other country was."

He took a long swallow, contemplated something that seemed internal, and continued. "Our entire district was destroyed by American airplanes bombing and burning. Day after day the B-52's dropped hellfire. We had no food, no shelter. My father, only a year old then, was rescued from a cradle in a root cellar by neighbors foraging for food. He was almost dead from malnutrition and dehydration, but they got him to a house for war orphans."

Kung began to pace. "I won't go through the whole story, but he grew up to reclaim our proud family name and serve the dynasty that has produced the Supreme Leader. He and his younger brother were part of the North Korean delegation in Hanoi during the Vietnam conflict. I began my studies in the Vietnam-DPRK Friendship Kindergarten in Hanoi. My father became a valued adviser to the Great Leader.

"His brother was not so lucky. He began to consider the American way more favorably. We think he became a double agent. Twenty-six years ago his house was torched and his wife's charred body was found beside his. Both he and his wife had been beaten as well as burned. We believed this was payback by the CIA for treason that could not be proved."

He put the photo back in the drawer.

"His two-year-old daughter Rhee Sung was visiting my father at the time. She became an orphan overnight, and after he died I raised her as my own daughter."

Kung pulled a chair to sit across from Ahn, who felt increasingly anxious at this story of violence and betrayal.

Kung waved a fist as he spoke now, but did not seem out of control. Ahn noted that the pulsation of the temporal artery increased with each sentence. Kung's cold fury frightened Ahn more than an angry outburst would have. His heart pounded and he could smell the alcohol on Kung's breath.

"Know two things, Junsu."

Ahn startled at the sound of his first name, never before used by this terrifying man. "First, America continues to be our great enemy. Individual Americans may be charming and skillful. The system that lies behind them is brutal and aims at the destruction of everything we believe in. Second, our surveillance systems stretch across the world. No matter where you are, we can watch you."

Ahn leaned forward. "Why are you telling me these things?"

"Day after tomorrow you will join Rhee Sung and David Ko on an assignment to Boston. I know I can rely on them. I want to be sure I can trust you."

"Boston? Why am I going to Boston?" Ahn felt terror at having to set foot in the country he had learned to hate.

"You need to watch MacGregor operate and see what he is like. If he is as good as they say, you will convince him to come to Korea."

"Why me?" The words escaped before Ahn realized how much out of line they were.

"Because I order it." Kung leaned forward and stabbed a finger toward Ahn. Ahn shrunk back with wide eyes and pounding heart. Was he going to be the scapegoat on the trip if anything went wrong?

Kung shrugged his shoulders and sat back again. "I always try to have three people in this kind of delegation. One alone can become a turncoat, two can make a pact. Three will report on each other if any of them misbehave. Besides, you know the Supreme Leader better than anyone else."

"But how can we possibly convince an American neurosurgeon to come to the DPRK if MacGregor is the person we want?" Ahn said, dropping his obsequious attitude as fear gripped him. "Why? To operate? No way that's going to happen." He put his hand over his mouth and looked away, realizing he had dared to challenge a man who brooked no opposition. He bowed his head, waiting for the blows to fall.

He watched Kung out of the corner of his eye. The general opened and closed his fists as his facial expression transformed from a violent scowl. "I wouldn't expect you to know how to make it happen," he said.

He looked at Ahn with a tolerant gaze. "David Ko will explain the plan in detail. We'll bribe MacGregor and his family with travel money from The Korean-American Friendship Association, whose funds I control. His need for recognition and concern for his family will be our levers. You don't need to know details beyond that."

"But what about the Supreme Leader? Why would he agree to have surgery by an American neurosurgeon?" Ahn had no idea how he had the courage or stupidity to continue his questions, but he seemed driven by a force he had not before experienced.

"Because he will know nothing about the surgeon. Wouldn't you agree that he deserves the world's best care?"

"Yes."

"And didn't you just tell me MacGregor was the surgeon who can provide that?"

"Yes, but—"

"Then shut up and get out. I'm the only person who needs convincing. The Supreme Leader does what I tell him to do."

He stood to end the discussion. "You leave in two days."

PART 2

CHAPTER TWENTY-FOUR

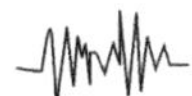

BROOKLINE

APRIL 8

Despite a grueling professional schedule, Duncan MacGregor tried his best to have dinner with his family every night. Life and death decisions peppered his day. Supper conversations with his children helped him to remember the real world outside the hospital.

"Yuck. I don't want any more of this. Can I do best and worst things of my day instead?" his eleven-year-old daughter Maggie said as she pushed her broccoli rabe away.

"Only if you take at least three more bites," Lauren said. "That's a Whole Foods vegetable creation of the day you're rejecting. Peter, will you get us started while your sister eats?"

Seven-year-old Peter hesitated for a moment, then began with a sing-song rhythm. "My best thing was that at Assembly one of the boys wore a T-shirt. The worst thing was that he got sent to the principal's office."

"What did the shirt say?" Mac asked.

"Make America Grate Again—G-R-A-T-E," Peter said.

"What do you think offended the principal more, the spelling or the politics?" Mac asked, looking at Lauren.

"You know, dear, sending him to the office was a violation of his civil rights," Lauren said.

"Boys are supposed to wear a tie to Assembly. That's one of the reasons we sent Peter to Brookline Latin, remember? I expect his friend got disciplined because he didn't wear a tie, not because of his T-shirt," Mac said.

"I know how to spell great. G-R-E-A-T, great." Maggie said with the defiant look of a champion speller.

Mac said, "I have a best thing."

Conversation halted. He felt three pairs of eyes staring at him.

"Dad, you never have a best thing. You always complain you can't talk about what happened at work because of HIPAA, whatever that is." Maggie said.

"This doesn't involve neurosurgery," Mac said. "It's about an email I got today."

He waited.

Peter took the bait after a few seconds. "Well, what did it say?"

"First, guess where it came from," Mac began.

"Africa," Peter said.

"Nope."

"The IRS," Lauren said.

Mac shook his head.

"Yay."

"The space station?" Peter asked.

"Do we still have astronauts up there?"

"Of course—both Russian and American," Peter replied.

"No." Mac said.

"What do you mean, no, Dad. Honest, we do have astronauts up there," Peter said.

"I believe you. I meant that's not where the letter came from."

He looked around the table at three faces now challenged and expectant. "I'll give you a hint. This country has both North and South parts."

"The United States," Maggie said.

"I know you've studied the Civil War," Lauren said, "but it's unlikely your father would find a letter from the United States unusual."

"No, it's not from any place in the Americas."

"Sudan?" Lauren asked.

"No, not in Africa either, but your mother is pointing out that Sudan now has two parts." He looked at each child to acknowledge his wife's grasp of current events. Lauren smiled.

"Vietnam?" Peter said.

"No, but you're on the right continent."

"I know! I know!" Maggie's hand shot up.

"Korea," Maggie said as she jutted her chin out in victory. "We're learning about Korea in civics class. The teacher says it's the smallest important country in the world."

"That would be Scotland," Lauren said. "Or Israel."

"Thank you, darling. Of course, I agree with you about Scotland," Mac said. "But Maggie's right about the source of the email."

Lauren raised an eyebrow. "Why would someone from Korea be emailing you? Isn't that a worst thing, not a best thing?"

"Apparently a group called the Korean-American Friendship Association has become aware of my work on hypothalamic hamartomas," Mac said. "They want to sponsor a neurosurgeon to attend the World Federation Meeting in Seoul in August. They're sending a delegation to Boston with the idea of potentially paying for us to go."

"Isn't that the meeting that has already rejected you?" Lauren asked. "And who's included in 'us'?"

"That's what makes it a best thing. All of us. If I am selected, they'll pay for everything. We'll all get ten free days in South Korea. And I'll deliver a keynote address right at the beginning of a meeting that includes neurosurgeons from the whole world."

"I could bring some stuff back for show-and-tell," Maggie said.

"August would work," Lauren said. "Preparation for the next school year will just be starting. What's the weather like?"

"I have no idea," Mac said. He smiled. "You'd consider it, then?"

"Maybe," Lauren said. "What happens next?"

"The letter said the delegation would arrive in Boston on the tenth. Two of the visitors are doctors, and I've already given them permission to watch me operate. The third is an administrative person—she's going to spend the day in museums and such."

"Could we meet them?" Maggie asked. "I'd love to meet real people from Korea."

"They have a busy schedule," Mac said. "They'll only be available the eleventh. And that's a school night." He looked at Lauren.

"It would be OK if we made it early dinner here," she said, answering his unasked question. "I could cook a typical American meal. If we ate at six we'd be done by eight thirty. That wouldn't interfere too much with homework."

"Assuming everyone finishes the broccoli tonight," she added.

Mac envied Maggie, who only had to eat three bites.

CHAPTER TWENTY-FIVE

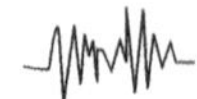

PYONGYANG

APRIL 10

Ahn and his colleagues had to hustle to get on the flight from Pyongyang to Beijing, knowing it operated only twice a week. Ahn felt like a terrified puppy at the immigration procedures in Pyongyang. He believed officials looked at him as if he were trying to escape even with Kung's personal signature on his letter.

His traveling companions seemed unperturbed. Perhaps one day he would be able to lose his fears and travel with assurance.

He gripped the arms of his seat throughout the entire two-hour Koryo Airlines flight. He decided he must have been drugged during the trip to Vladivostok, because this was much worse. The bumping and shaking of the plane terrified him, the cabin was cold, and the metallic smell irritated his nostrils. There were only six other passengers. He could not understand how they could be so nonchalant.

In Beijing airport, however, he stepped into a world beyond his wildest imaginings. Travelers of every shape, color, and size streamed through spacious and spotless hallways. Shops that actually sold the merchandise they displayed offered items he never knew existed. People wove in and around in such endless confusion he wished he were tied to his colleagues to keep from getting separated from them.

Ko and Rhee dragged him past dozens of stores, pushing to connect with their next flight, trying to find their airline. It had a small presence in the huge airport, and finding the gate created a challenge even for Rhee Sung. Ahn calculated he had walked at least a kilometer before they got to their gate.

Once he was on the plane bound for Boston, the flight experience enthralled him.

Not only were there beautiful women serving food and drinks, but the entertainment module far exceeded anything he had seen in the DPRK. His slight frame sank into the seat with room to spare. Even in economy class, he could skip between movies, television shows and music. He listened to programs to learn English and used some amazing movies as an excuse to test his comprehension. Meals were delicious and abundant. He remained awake the entire fourteen hours it took to get to the USA.

When he stepped into the immigration line at Logan airport, he could not at first comprehend what he saw. People didn't look at all like him. Their faces differed, but their relaxed demeanor and brightly colored clothing stood in great contrast to the listless bearing and drab uniforms of the citizens of Pyongyang.

Some women had very short skirts and no one had a military uniform. People with black skins and yellow skins and tan skins and white skins chatted together amicably. Men had long hair, blond hair, curly hair, dark hair, ponytails.

Women had the same, and some even had shaved heads. Men and women had tattoos on arms, neck, scalp; and some had piercings in the ears, nose, or lips. None of this would be possible in his native city.

The trio arrived at the immigration window faster than he expected. They all had South Korean passports in their own names. Ahn had no idea how that happened. The officer behind the window seemed to want to help rather than obstruct his entry. There was no body search, no peremptory demand to see all documents or mandatory ten-minute wait while they were processed.

They walked through the gateway to America one minute after the border official welcomed them to the States. In ten minutes, with no further barrier, they exited the customs hall with their baggage.

A Chinese man in a blue suit met them as they entered the reception area of Terminal E. "Welcome to America," he said in perfect Korean. "I'm Tu, stationed with the Chinese consulate here. Please consider me your USA connection. Was your flight from Beijing satisfactory?"

Rhee Sung answered, "Yes."

Ahn said "Amazing. So many well-dressed people. There were—"

"You'll find Boston very different than Pyongyang," Tu interrupted. "General Kung has arranged everything through our consulate. You will be staying in separate rooms at the Weston Waterfront Hotel, a recent Chinese acquisition."

He looked at a sheet of paper with names and photographs on it. "Dr. Ahn, you and Dr. Ko must arrive at Harbor Hospital by seven a.m. tomorrow if you want to watch Dr.

MacGregor operate. I will be in the hotel lobby to escort you at 6:30. Rhee Sung, you have the morning free to shop or visit museums. A woman from our consulate will call at ten a.m. with a car."

He led them to a section of the curb where they boarded a bus.

"Normally we would have a limousine meet us, but the rush hour traffic is tiresome and I thought it would be good to see Boston from the Harbor. Have you been here before?"

All three shook their head as the bus left the curb.

"The bus is half empty. Why is it leaving? And how are those other people around us getting to their destinations?" Ahn asked.

"Most have their own cars. That causes a lot of congestion, which is why it's faster to get to your hotel by boat."

"Normal citizens in the USA have cars?" Ahn asked. "I thought that was propaganda."

Sung and Ko looked at Ahn as if he were a child, throwing him a look that said stop talking. Tu hurried them out of the bus as it got to the water's edge. "I think we can just make this shuttle," he said as he steered them toward the dock where eight passengers dismounted from a covered boat. They found seats together.

"Here most people have not only cars but homes and several children," Ko said. "In Seoul it's the same."

Ahn stared at the seascape while he considered this astounding fact. Cars and houses for each family seemed wasteful, and having several children? How did the parents keep the children fed?

The water taxi chugged across Boston Harbor. Seagulls

swooped and eeped at each other, airplanes took off and landed at Logan, and ferries discharged their passengers in jovial clusters. Crystal-clear water splashed on the gunwales to meet the fresh spring air. Ahn saw no garbage or waste and smelled no hint of rotting fish and debris. What kind of place was this?

They disembarked at the World Trade Center, where a driver met them in a limousine and delivered them to the hotel within a few minutes. They made a plan to meet in two hours for dinner, suggesting to Ahn that he rest in his room until then.

From his room overlooking the harbor, Ahn surveyed the water traffic, airplanes, and buildings that dotted the Harborfront. They created a delightful tableau. He tried to pinpoint his distress, put a name on his emotions.

He flipped on the television, surfing the 126 available channels. He noted that they all broadcasted without apparent censorship. He delighted at the marble majesty of the bathroom, unlike anything in Pyongyang. He flopped on his bed, luxuriating in its firm but flexible mattress and soft linen sheets. He walked around the room looking for water leaks and roaches and found none. It was then he recognized what he felt.

Anger. Anger that such an evil country could seem so beautiful and pleasant.

All his life, teachers and colleagues had warned him of warmongering Americans.

Streets filled with blood and criminals. Merciless owners oppressing the workers. A rapacious economic system.

What did he find when he got here? Friendly people and a style of life that seemed magic. Was this some kind of performance to throw him off guard?

His experience thus far began to dissolve the hatred he was supposed to feel for all Americans. And that to him spelled danger. He remembered Kung's comments. Was Ahn betraying the government that had sent him here by his positive reaction to the USA?

A folded note slid under the door interrupted his musings. He ran to pick up the slip of paper. By the time he had fumbled with the security chain, he saw no one in the hall. A letter with his Korean name on it. Who knew he was here?

He snatched the folded sheet from the floor and flipped it open, reading the scrawled Korean text: *Meet me in the bar in ten minutes. Do not tell anyone where you are going. I will identify myself to you there.*

He glanced at his watch, confirming he still had an hour before dinner. He considered the implications of meeting with a stranger. In Pyongyang he would be arrested immediately. Would it be treason to have such a meeting while he was out of his native country?

This was not Pyongyang. Kung had not prohibited him from encounters with Americans. Was he just paranoid? Besides, he really wanted to know who this person was.

He arrived at an empty hotel bar ten minutes later.

He had not seen such a luxurious room anywhere. Mahogany furnishings, leather seats, and a dazzling display of alcohol forced him again to ask whether this was a false front, an elaborate show for visitors. Nothing real behind it.

He sat in the corner and ordered a glass of single malt scotch because he remembered Pavel's rhapsodic description of the drink. He half expected the waiter to say they were out of it. Instead, he was given a list of twenty-six varieties. He randomly picked the fourth.

The beverage had a richness of taste and smoothness of texture he had never experienced. It made the so-called whisky of the DPRK seem like turpentine. And that was not the only remarkable thing. He only had to give his room number to pay for it.

As he rolled the liquid around on his tongue, luxuriating in the slight burning and peaty aroma, a Korean man in his forties approached him. He wore blue jeans, a Boston Celtics sweatshirt, and earbuds.

"You're Ahn?" he asked.

"Yes. Who are you? How did you know I was here?"

"My name doesn't matter, and I can't tell you how I knew you were coming. Can I speak with you a minute?"

"Why?"

"I have a story to tell you."

"Go ahead."

"Not here. Will you walk with me?"

They exited the hotel and headed across the overpass that stretched toward the Harbor. For a few seconds Ahn wondered again what he was doing. In his home country, a walk with a stranger would be met with imprisonment. He seemed to be in some kind of dream world, where he felt safe despite the strangeness.

"Your accent sounds like you're from the DPRK," Ahn said.

"That was my home," the man said, "until I escaped."

"Escaped? No one has ever left the DPRK permanently. People don't escape. People don't want to escape."

"I did. I was a college teacher and started to teach Shakespeare to my students. A parent reported me to the police. It was considered an example of English decadence. I was arrested in the middle of the night, taken to a so-called rehabilitation camp, and tortured. My family was split and sent to several different camps. I think they're probably dead, including my parents."

They descended a staircase and sat on a bench at the edge of the harborwalk. The man moved several feet away from Ahn and talked straight ahead as if they did not know each other. "They'll think I'm talking on my cell phone if they're watching," he said. "Even in Boston there are people who report back to the DPRK, and I am sure they will be keeping you under close surveillance."

The man continued "There are more than two hundred thousand political prisoners in camps like mine. We had to work twelve hours a day with scraps or nothing to eat. My fellow prisoners ate rats if they could catch them. I preferred to starve. Some prisoners talked of escaping—swimming into the Sea of Japan or trying to cross the Tumen River into China, but the risks seemed too high. I saw several who tried to escape that way executed in front of us as a warning."

Ahn looked out at the sailboats and ferry boats and the young people jogging along the water's edge. The worlds seemed completely incompatible. He wondered if this man were some kind of spy sent to test Ahn's loyalty to the government. He would be sure not to say anything compromising.

The man continued. "After two years I volunteered for a work force to do construction in Belarus. The conditions in that compound were no better than the detention camp, but we were outside the reach of the DPRK army. One night a friend and I escaped. I am not going to tell you how, but I will say it was the best thing I ever did."

He displayed deep scars along his forearms. "In case you wonder whether I am telling the truth, these are the love notes my time in the detention camps left me with."

"Why are you telling me this?" Ahn asked. At the edge of his vision, he noted a burly Asian man moving toward them.

"At some point you may have a choice to leave the DPRK. No matter what the risk, take it. I now spend my time beaming internet messages to our countrymen. I track down tourists with Korean names arriving on international airlines and tell my story. I send American dollars to colleagues in Seoul who ship them in balloons to be dropped within our country."

His companion stood up and faced Ahn. "You don't see the suffering of the common man, the man who is not a soldier or a diplomat or a professional. The very fact you are here means you have resources far beyond the normal."

The stranger stepped in front of him.

"Is this man bothering you?" he asked Ahn in Korean.

Ahn looked as wide-eyed and innocent as he could manage. "I don't know him at all. He was just asking me some directions, but obviously I can't give him anything. Are you a policeman or army officer?"

"No, just an interested citizen." He looked at the man in the blue jeans. "I suggest you move along."

"This is a free country," the ex-North Korean man said.

The thickset stranger grunted and walked away from them, looking back every few feet.

"As you can see," Ahn's companion said, "the DPRK has spies watching even here. They can't really do anything while we're in full view."

"May I give you some advice?" Ahn said as the man turned away.

"Of course."

"Don't talk to David Ko or Rhee Sung, the two Koreans who flew in with me. You'd be wasting your time. David is already a South Korean, and Rhee is tightly linked to the leadership of the north. Talk with them and you will likely die, even in Boston."

The man got up and said, "Thanks, and good luck with whatever you're doing here." He did not offer a hand to shake or indicate in any way he had been in conversation. In seconds, he had melted into the shadows.

Ahn did not know what to make of the encounter. Was the man's story true? He hurried back to his hotel room, lay on the bed, and fell asleep. He awakened to David Ko calling his name from the corridor.

"Let's get some American steak," David said. "And then we should go to bed. Remember, we have to observe Duncan MacGregor operating first thing tomorrow."

CHAPTER TWENTY-SIX

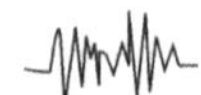

BOSTON

APRIL 11

Drs. Ahn and Ko met in the hotel lobby exactly at 6:30 the next morning. Ahn had gone without breakfast because he didn't know he could order it so early. He had stayed up until midnight practicing his rusty English with randomly chosen movies and TV shows. He hadn't had the opportunity to speak it since medical school, but it seemed to rush back. He found he had little trouble understanding.

He wore the official People's Party tunic of the DPRK and tried to flatten the wrinkles that had accumulated on the trip. He thought Ko, sporting chinos, blue button-down shirt, and blazer, did not understand the seriousness of the occasion. On the other hand, Dr. Ko was not officially representing the DPRK. Dr. Ahn felt he was.

The representative from the Chinese consulate picked them up in a black Mercedes limousine and drove the six blocks to the hospital, pulling into the front entrance ten minutes after they left the hotel. "As you can see, it's not far to your hotel. You can see it from here." He pointed toward the convention center where the words WESTIN loomed on the skyline. "A member of MacGregor's team will meet you here at seven."

They stood in front of the hospital looking up at its imposing façade. A middle-aged woman drove up, got out of her car, and looked with a friendly expression at Ahn. She handed him her car keys. "I'm already so late for my doctor's appointment. I'll be back in one hour. Can you park it nearby so I don't have to wait too long? I'll give you a nice tip when I come back."

Ahn looked at her disappearing back, then down at his uniform. "But..." he stammered in Korean.

Ko pointed to a valet parking attendant beside the entrance. "She thought you were a parking attendant because of the uniform," he said, smiling as he moved them both toward the rotating door into the hospital. "Just give them to the real valet over there. Next time we'll get you a suit. And I suggest we speak in English as much as possible. Tell me if you need help with it."

An African American man in scrubs and white coat headed toward them as they entered the hospital foyer. He looked about thirty years old.

"Are you the visitors for Dr. MacGregor?" he asked with a smile.

"Yes. I'm Dr. David Ko, and this is Dr. Junsu Ahn," Ko replied.

"Jacob Ray," he said as they shook hands.

"Are you a neurosurgeon on Dr. MacGregor's team?" Ko asked.

"No, I'm a scrub nurse in the operating room."

Ahn frowned. "Nursing is not a suitable profession for men."

Ray stepped back. "Excuse me, but in this country,

nursing is a good job for anyone, especially OR nursing. It also lets me use my experience as a military medic."

"It would not be allowed in my country," Ahn said, puzzled. "And who is this place really for?" he asked with suspicion in his voice as he looked at the spotless corridors and soaring lobby skylights. "Is it a showpiece only? Reserved for military leaders?"

"Nope, it's for everyone," Ray replied, appearing annoyed by the question.

"In my country hospitals are different. The buildings are older and more crowded. Families are everywhere, including the lobbies," Ahn said, then caught Ko's warning look.

"I thought South Korea was more sophisticated than that," Ray said. "We've had some people here from the Samsung Hospital in Seoul who say this reminds them of their own place."

"I know that hospital; it's beautiful," Ko said, putting a restraining hand on his colleague's arm. "My hospital, the Seoul National Hospital, is also big, with over two million outpatients and sixteen hundred forty beds. My colleague was talking about hospitals in some rural areas of South Korea."

"Oh yeah, I get it. There are some places in the USA like that too."

"Parts of the Ponghwa Hospital are similar to this," Ahn said, "but it is only for political and military leaders."

Ko almost slapped his hand over Ahn's mouth. "Of course, that again is in a very rural part of South Korea," Ko said. As they walked toward the elevator, he whispered in Ahn's ear, "You idiot; we're supposed to be from South

Korea. Do not mention anything about your home or institutions in the DPRK."

Ahn looked back at him with raised eyebrows, then frowned as he realized his mistake.

Jacob Ray looked at the ceiling during the brief elevator ride. Ahn felt relieved. He had no idea what to say.

At the operating room floor, Ray led them to the visitors locker room, provided scrub clothes and shoe covers, and demonstrated how to put on masks and hats. A few minutes later they stood with six other observers at the edge of MacGregor's room. "Just remember, no talking during the surgery," Ray said as he left them.

The surgical assistant, a woman, had already draped the patient and stood at the side of the table. At 7:25 a thin man about six feet tall entered, gowned, and stood in a position of repose at the operating table. The scrub nurse connected suction tubes and cautery and finished the sponge counts. With the preparations complete, the man turned to the onlookers, showing deep blue eyes above his mask.

"That's Duncan MacGregor," Ko whispered with quiet excitement in his voice.

Ahn sensed that they were in the presence of a person whose authority came naturally, not by bullying or wearing a uniform. The ten-thousand-kilometer trip was already quite instructive.

"Thank you all for being here," MacGregor began, speaking with his mask still up but projecting his deep voice to the edges of the room. "First, let me introduce Dr. Julia Pedroza, our neurosurgical resident; Susan Danby, our scrub nurse; and Jacob Ray, our circulating nurse. Neurosurgery is a team sport, and I'm fortunate to have spectacular team members."

Each member of the team nodded.

"Today we will take out a hypothalamic hamartoma. However, we have to do some extra work to get started."

He signaled to the circulating nurse, who began to unveil a small nozzle on a cable leading to a black box. "Surgeons at another hospital tried to approach this mass last year. They didn't get to it, and our patient developed brain swelling. They had to remove a large part of skull to prevent permanent damage. They replaced the bone with a titanium plate. We have to open our pathway through this. We will use a much smaller incision than they did, precisely placed."

He made a small scalp incision that seemed only a few centimeters long. Gleaming metal shone through the opening.

Jacob Ray placed dark goggles over Mac's eyes, then handed them to all the other people in the room.

"These will keep your retinas from being destroyed by the laser beam," Mac said to the onlookers. He held up the small carving nozzle. "This Neodymium-Yag laser would normally penetrate below the metal and damage the brain tissue under our opening, but we have used confocal principles to modify it. This beam will cut through titanium without heating the tissue underneath it. As my son would say, 'like a knife through butter.'"

In two minutes he had carved a rectangular opening in the plate, lifted it away, and brought the operating microscope into the field to start work on the brain itself.

Ahn felt Ko's elbow in his ribs. "Neat," Ko whispered

"We would have taken off the entire plate to expose the whole brain. It would take us two hours to open and longer to close. I'd like to get my hands on that laser. The way it cut through titanium was magic."

Over the next half hour, the muted lighting of the room, cool temperature, and gentle sound of Bach partitas playing in the background lulled Ahn into a near-trance.

Video monitors demonstrated the pulsating brain surface in high definition. MacGregor opened the path between the cerebral hemispheres, dissected through the corpus callosum, and emptied cerebrospinal fluid from the ventricles. The muttered phrases "choroid plexus, foramen of Monro, mammillary bodies" appeared to have meaning to Ko but left Ahn searching his neuroanatomy memory for details. He did understand the phrase "our target" and gaped at the monitor when a smooth hillock bulged from the brain surface.

"Amazingly fast," Ko said, "but the real test comes now."

For twenty minutes Mac prodded, dissected, gently persuaded the brain to yield its foreign mass without complaining. He passed a nodule the size of a peanut to the scrub nurse with the comment, "This should be the whole hamartoma. Let's get a scan while we're waiting for pathology."

He turned to the visitors. "Fortunately for us, titanium is not ferromagnetic, so it doesn't distort the MRI. If this were a steel plate we would not be able to scan."

The lights burst on and visitors were ushered into the corridor outside the operating room. After the circulating nurse ticked off items in a safety checklist, Ahn watched with fascination as one wall of the operating room opened to reveal an MRI scanner. Suspended from a rail on the ceiling, it glided forward smoothly and silently to encircle the head of the patient.

"How do they get such a large machine to move so quietly?" he asked Ko.

"American know-how," Ko said with a shrug.

MacGregor joined them. "We have a few minutes for questions while we wait for the scan results and the pathology," he said. "Perhaps one of our guests from Korea would like to go first?"

"Did the patient have gelastic seizures?" Ko asked.

"Yes, but they progressed to grand mal epilepsy, and the generalized seizures got worse after the attempt to operate last year. Her aggressive behavior made her miserable. And medications could not control the seizures. Her life was ruined."

"What are the main risks of the surgery?" Ko continued.

"There's a lot of important brain in this area. The optic nerves are just under it and movement fibers are beside it. A center for heart control is just behind it. The surgery can affect any of these functions. This is delicate territory, even for the brain."

Ko began to speak again; MacGregor held up his hand. "Does anyone else have a question?" he said.

"How do you know you have taken it all out?" a young woman asked.

"The main test is the sense of touch and the surgeon's experience. To be certain, we do an MRI scan during the surgery. That's what's happening now."

"Is the scanner always on?" a student asked.

"Yes, but its magnetic field is shielded until it comes through the doors."

Dozens of questions followed. Ten minutes later the machine returned to its shielded cage. Visitors filed back into the room, the lights dimmed, and the surgeons returned, newly scrubbed, to the operating table.

"Radiology here," the intercom crackled. "The mass is gone and the hypothalamus looks intact." A moment later the pathologist reported that the tissue Mac had removed was in fact a hamartoma.

"Let's finish," Mac said.

The closure of the brain covering, reattachment of the titanium disc with mini-plates, and suturing of scalp layers took less than half an hour. Ahn watched in silence as Mac and his assistant worked almost as a single surgeon with four hands. He noted that Ko craned and stretched to see each move, often jotting notes as he observed the final stages of surgery.

To signal the end of the procedure, Mac put a small strip of gauze on the small linear scalp incision and addressed the audience. Three hours had passed since the case began. "Are there questions while the patient wakes up?"

Every observer but Ahn raised a hand.

"What will she be like now?"

"How long will she be in the hospital?"

"Will she need radiation therapy?"

Mac smiled and answered each in turn. Ahn was impressed as much by his calm demeanor as by his graceful surgery.

"Do you really need the MRI machine to do this surgery safely?" Ko blurted out.

"Not at all. The texture and appearance define the tumor margins. I've had the extra benefit of checking my impression against the actual intraoperative imaging for the last ninety cases, however. I think it's fair to say I'm getting pretty good at making the distinction. The MRI is just an extra benefit."

"Isn't it risky to have an MRI come into the operating room? What about metal instruments?" Ko continued.

"Yes it's risky. That's why the circulating nurse did that checklist before the MRI could enter. A ferromagnetic object can become a lethal projectile once it's exposed to that strong magnetic field. It'll rocket into the center of the machine. A few years ago, a hospital in another city had a death when an oxygen tank ripped loose from a patient's stretcher. The aides brought the tank too close to the machine. Fortunately, we've never had such a tragedy."

The anesthesiologist cleared her throat loudly. Mac looked over at the patient. "Please excuse me; our patient is waking up." He moved back to the OR table.

"MacGregor has great hands," Ko said as he turned to Ahn. "I would let him operate on me in a second."

They heard a cough and looked over to see the patient awake and without an endotracheal tube. Mac stood beside her holding her hand. She appeared to be speaking with clarity and energy.

"Is this really the patient whose open brain we saw half an hour ago?" Ahn asked, unable to hold back his wonder at this scene.

"Yes, that's the magic of this procedure when it's well done," Mac said. "It doesn't go through any important brain. If it's done perfectly, there are no side effects. You just have to be careful as you remove the actual mass."

"I don't see any incision," Ahn said.

"It's small, and he left enough hair in front of it to conceal it." Ko said. "That's another reason we want this surgeon. A hidden incision may be the most important aspect of surgery for the Supreme Leader."

MacGregor returned to the group of spectators. "She seems intact," he said with a smile. "We'll watch her overnight in the intensive care unit and I expect she'll go home in three days. Thanks for spending time with us."

The audience dispersed. Ko and Ahn lingered behind. "A couple of questions about the technique?" Ko asked. "We were impressed—"

Mac put up his hand. "I wanted to wait until everyone else left. Would you like to discuss the case over dinner this evening?"

Ko and Ahn looked at each other with puzzled expressions. "Dinner? With you?" Ahn asked.

"Actually, with me and my family. At my home."

Even Ko looked puzzled. Ahn was thunderstruck. To be invited to a family dinner at someone's home was unheard of. And at the home of someone as exalted as this man? Both physicians stood without answering.

"Good," Mac said. "I'll pick you up at five-thirty at the hotel. Your entire group is welcome."

CHAPTER TWENTY-SEVEN

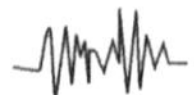

BROOKLINE

APRIL 11

Four at six?

Lauren smiled as she read Mac's text on her smartphone. She thumbed *OK*. Her feminist friends might be offended by a husband's expectation to entertain professional colleagues on short notice. She had a different attitude, saw this as an affirmation of her abilities. Life with Mac was sometimes annoying—the Valentine's Day fiasco, for example. More often it was exhilarating and unpredictable. And she could handle anything he dished out.

But what to eat? Not hamburgers or hot dogs. They might be typical American, but the visitors could get those at Burger King.

Steak? Boring.

She decided on beef burgundy, a dish she had not thought about since Valentine's Day.

She left her office early, purchased the ingredients she needed at Whole Foods, and arrived home ready to attack the recipe. Ten minutes later she found herself humming as she quartered mushrooms, diced onions, simmered meat, and collected bay leaves. She had not had the challenge of cooking a real meal for guests for some time.

She smiled with pleasure as Maggie bounced in, throwing her school bag on a chair. "Guess what, Mom! Today I got to write a letter to a school friend in Seoul." She headed for her room.

"An actual letter?" Lauren asked, thinking of pen pal days of the past.

Maggie turned and paused. "Yep. The teacher agrees with you and dad that we shouldn't use Facebook or Twitter or Instagram, so we got names of students from a South Korean class and wrote a real paper letter asking about life there. The teacher will send them all to the teacher in Seoul."

"Would you like to talk directly with someone who lives in Korea?"

"You mean Skype or FaceTime? That would be great."

"No, I mean right here. Tonight. Like you asked to do."

"Really?"

"Yes, really. Your dad has arranged to bring home three guests from Seoul."

"Awesome."

"Could you set the table to help get ready?"

Maggie took a handful of flatware from the drawer. "Do they speak English?"

"I don't know. We'll need seven settings."

Maggie placed two knives down, then said, "Mom, I better get my homework done before they come." She left the rest of the silverware in a pile.

Lauren shook her head with a smile, arranged the

flatware and plates just as her own mother would have done, and returned to her cooking.

Half an hour later, Lauren opened the door to Mac, followed by two Asian men in dark suits and a young woman in a red flowered silk dress.

"Lauren, these are our Korean guests, Dr. David Ko, Dr. Junsu Ahn, and Ms. Sung Rhee."

"Welcome," Lauren said.

"These gifts are for you and Professor MacGregor," the shorter man said with a substantial Korea accent, extending two boxes toward her. He appeared thin—chronically malnourished, she would say—and wore thick wire-rimmed spectacles.

"Thank you, Dr.—Ahn, is it?"

He nodded, blushing.

She opened the smaller gift first. It contained three tubes of face cream with the label *Unhasu*. Dr. Ahn answered her unspoken question. "This a special cream from my country that you will find soothing and restorative for your skin, especially the face."

"Thank you," she said and moved onto the next package, much heavier.

"This is gourmet kimchi," the taller man said in perfect American. Lauren wondered how fermented cabbage could be gourmet no matter what was done to it, but smiled and said, "We can try it with dinner."

"Speaking of which, something smells really good. Could it be your fabulous beef bourguignon?" Mac asked as he cast her a look that made all the preparation worthwhile.

Lauren led them through the home, beginning with the dining room with its linen tablecloth, silver place settings, bone china plates, and silver candelabra. The visitors gawked at everything they saw: the Brazilian hardwood floors; oil paintings and family pictures on the wall; music room with grand piano holding Bach and Chopin folios on the music rack and photographs of happy children and relatives on its lid; sunken living room with Persian rug, fireplace, studded Chesterfield couch and blue accent chairs.

They stopped in their tracks, however, as they entered the family room with the sixty-five-inch 4K UHD smart TV. Peter was sprawled on the floor talking to the television control device. They watched as he called up one YouTube segment after another with his young voice.

"Peter, can you say hello to our guests?" Lauren asked.

He looked around, apparently unaware that they had been watching him.

"Want to watch *Transformers* with me? Or make them?" he asked. He picked up a plastic truck from the floor and with a few deft moves created a robotic creature that stood defiantly in the middle of the rug. "This is Optimus Prime."

"Does this television respond only to you?" Ahn asked, losing his reluctance to talk when faced with a seven-year-old.

"Nah, you can do it too." Peter handed the control to Ahn, who looked at the device as if it were going to bite him.

"Go ahead. Just talk to it," Peter urged.

Lauren observed the proceedings with interest from the patio door. Her son usually had difficulty with strangers or anything that was not anticipated. He did not seem to be shy in front of Dr. Ahn.

"Maggie, our visitors are here," Lauren called, and a few minutes later Rhee and Maggie sat in a corner discussing Gangnam-style music and what the latest rage was in Korean rock.

David Ko and Mac slouched in overstuffed armchairs, deep in conversation about the exact steps in the surgery Mac had done that morning. Lauren heard questions like: "What setting is the bipolar on? How do you make sure you're not retracting the cortex too hard? What sutures do you use for the dura?"

She smiled as she returned to finish dinner preparations. Seven people living thousands of miles apart finding they had more in common than they ever thought. Where else in the world would this happen?

At dinner, the visitors ate with gusto, complimenting Lauren so effusively she blushed. Conversation included Samsung smartphones, Red Sox baseball, Korean barbecue and beer, and the emerging importance of China in world politics and the economy. As ice cream was being served, Sung Rhee asked for everyone's attention. She spoke English effortlessly, with no sign of an accent.

"On behalf of all of us, I would like to thank you for your hospitality and wonderful food. I also wish to reveal the main reason for our visit."

Expectant silence.

"We are members of the Korean-American Friendship Association, a group which makes grants to outstanding Americans to foster collaboration between the cultures. We have followed Dr. MacGregor's work in hypothalamic hamartomas with great interest. In four months, Seoul will host the World Congress of Neurosurgery. We would like to invite all of you to attend that meeting at our expense."

"But my paper has already been rejected," Mac said.

"That has changed," Dr. Ko said. "I sit on the program committee, and we were simply unaware of the progress you have made in surgery for this problem. Having watched you operate and hearing about your results, I believe the world needs to know what is possible. We have given you a featured speaker slot in the opening session. It's the most prestigious and prominent place we can arrange on the program."

Mac looked at Ko with a puzzled expression. "Just like that?"

"Once my fellow neurosurgeons understood what you have done, there was no problem."

"And what do you mean by 'all of you'?"

"Just that," Rhee said. "We will provide first-class travel for the whole family as well as a hotel suite at the Coex Intercontinental Hotel, right beside the convention center."

"Please, oh please, can we go?" Maggie shouted.

"Will we have to go to the boring meeting?" Peter asked.

"Not at all," Rhee answered. "We'll have a lot of fun excursions, and I hope we might be able to show you Jeju Island for a few days too. It's a part of South Korea most visitors don't get a chance to see. Really beautiful."

"But I was going to go to summer camp in August," Peter said. "To do tech stuff."

"We have some great technology in Korea," Ko said.

"What do you think?" Mac asked Lauren. "You're the critical decision-maker."

"I'm not teaching this summer," Lauren said. "I have some new classes I have to prepare, but I can do that anywhere." She paused. "Might work."

"Let us think about it," Mac said. "And perhaps this would be a good time to get you back to the hotel. I know your flight leaves early tomorrow morning."

CHAPTER TWENTY-EIGHT

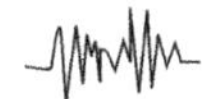

SEOUL

AUGUST 21

The Korean-American Friendship Association had made luxurious travel arrangements for Mac and his family. They stood in sharp contrast to Mac's usual trips for the World Federation of Neurosurgeons. Those often involved crowded economy airplane cabins redolent with the odors of fellow passengers. Overworked attendants and long security and passport control lines at the destination made them unpleasant necessities for his international work.

Not so with the flight to Korea. A limousine collected the family from their Brookline home. They arrived at Logan to find they had already been checked in, sped through the security fast lane, and enjoyed lunch in Delta's spacious first-class lounge. An attendant accompanied them to the Atlanta-bound plane. Two hours later they landed in Atlanta, passed through the transit lounge there, and boarded their Boeing 777 headed for Seoul. No delays, no hassles.

The MacGregor family occupied the entire front row of the first-class cabin. As they entered the plane, a smiling attendant hung their coats and offered them champagne or orange juice. Mac noted just six other first-class passengers, all Korean. Heavy curtains isolated them from the noise of the coach and business class cabins. A fresh pink rose marked each seat; its fragrance pleased the nostril as much as the petals pleased the touch.

"Seats" hardly described the units they occupied, Mac thought. More like cocoons of luxury. Each had a computer port with USB and plug outlets, touch-screen entertainment system, light source, a shelf for books and electronics, a set of pajamas and slippers, and a vanity kit. The chair reclined, had an adjustable leg rest; the attendant announced that when he wanted to sleep, she would transform the commodious chair into an even more comfortable flat bed with fresh linen.

Attractive flight attendants hung their coats and guided them to their seats. They were particularly attentive to the children. Maggie opened her vanity kit immediately, trying on the mask to block out light, slipping on the sox, applying the lip balm and face cream. "I can't wait to use this," she said as she figured out how to put the two parts of the toothbrush together.

After they reached cruising altitude, Mac slapped on the wireless Bose noise-canceling earphones, modulating the whining of the plane's engines to a whisper. With them, he could immerse himself in the latest piano albums of his heroes: Yuja Wang, Daniil Trilonov, and others while he refined his PowerPoint presentation for the conference. The lighting on the plane changed to perpetual twilight and air with a distinctive metallic tinge filled his lungs.

Lauren hauled out a pile of business folders. "I haven't had fifteen solid hours to prepare lessons since I started my job," she said as she put on her earphones. "And with the onboard WiFi, I can email the lesson plans to my secretary as soon as I finish them."

Peter played video games.

Maggie watched the informational videos on Korea in preparation for her class project.

Mac began to feel less guilty about his work and travel schedule. *This isn't coaching soccer, but I hope it counts as a parental bonding,* he thought as he looked at his family enjoying themselves.

They entered a temporal no man's land in which Mac knew their daily rhythm pattern was being reset. On the plane, everyone pretended it was early afternoon, not one a.m. Four hours after takeoff, a chef appeared with a rolling cart, creating Korean cuisine, including the small appetizer dishes he distributed to each passenger. Maggie took notes on each food item and asked Mac to take pictures of some for her classroom presentation when she returned.

Dinner, bathroom break, movie, sleep, breakfast, bathroom, lunch, nap; the fifteen-hour flight became a world in itself. To Mac's surprise, the children slept without difficulty and awoke in good humor and ready to continue their activity. Every couple of hours they would run back and forth in the cabin to keep their legs stretched, but they seemed as happy to sit in their seats and play as Mac and Lauren were.

Except for the popping ears as they descended from 29,000 feet, the family's arrival at Inchon International Airport in Seoul occurred with as much elegance as their flight. The flight attendants gave them each an extra amenity kit as they left the cabin.

The first thing the children noted as they entered the terminal was the date. It was two days after they had started.

"What happened to yesterday?" Maggie asked.

"It's just math," Peter explained. "I studied it on the way over. Two hours to Atlanta, two hours waiting, fifteen hours to Seoul, and a thirteen-hour time difference. That adds up to thirty-two hours of time difference compared with Boston time. We lost a day and a half, but we'll get it all back when we return. That'll be the longest day we ever had."

"Not only that," Mac added, "but it's only six a.m. in Boston. Your classmates aren't even awake." He paused. "You know, I've never really understood how that works. Will our used-up sunlight arrive in Boston in thirteen hours?"

Lauren said, "Look over there. I think Dr. Ko and his colleague are looking for us." She pointed to the Customs exit.

"Welcome to Seoul. How was your trip?" David Ko smiled as they approached. "You remember Rhee Sung? Now that we are in Korea, I am saying her name in the traditional order, with the family name first. She will be your guide while you are here."

"Call me Sung," she said, and beckoned them to follow her.

Thirty miles later, sitting in a Kia SUV, they crawled their way through downtown Seoul traffic. It was worse than Manhattan at rush hour. The honking and slow progress didn't seem to faze the driver, and the family gawked at every storefront and pedestrian as they inched up the main street of Seoul. Rhee and Ko kept up a tour guide banter that had the children enchanted.

Mac had never seen a Kia this luxurious. With leather seats and wood finishes, it reminded him of Lexus and Mercedes machines. It seemed to handle the traffic effortlessly, even with its sudden stops and accelerations, and the sound system rivalled the speakers he had seen in high-end American cars. He sat back and luxuriated in his welcome to South Korea.

"What's that thing that looks like a space station?" Peter asked as they saw a gleaming metal and glass structure ahead.

"That's where we're going," Ko replied. "The Coex convention center. If you think it is impressive above the ground, you should see the tunnels under the streets around it. It's like a whole other city."

They pulled up to the Coex Intercontinental hotel rising twenty stories above the exhibition hall. Ko and Rhee took them immediately to the concierge floor, where their keys were waiting.

"Take half an hour to unpack your clothes," Rhee said. "Then I want to show you something really special. I'll wait here; David, you might as well go back to the hospital."

Entering the suite of three rooms reserved for the family, Maggie broke away and ran from one to the other through interconnecting doors that had been left open. "I call this one," she said as she got to the last of the three.

"Dad and I will be in the middle room. Maggie, you can have this room if you want it. Peter you take the room on the other side. We'll leave the doors unlocked so you can come in any time."

Maggie disappeared, then bounced into their room two minutes later.

"Mom, Dad, come look. The bathroom!" She dragged them to a tiled palace the size of her bedroom at home with a large air-jet tub, a walk-in shower, and two sinks. "And the toilet seat is heated," she announced with delight. "This is the neatest hotel ever."

After they had unpacked, Rhee picked them up and they wandered under the streets of Seoul, awestruck at a complex of shops and corridors that seemed to run for miles. Nothing at street level suggested the collection of noodle houses, Korean pastry shops, restaurants, and clothing stores that packed together in the underground maze.

"This is not at all like the shopping malls at home," Maggie said.

"So refreshing not to have chain stores," Lauren agreed as she tasted a kumquat.

"There are Hermes and Dior shops at street level, but this is the real Korea," Rhee said. "It's a traditional Korean market, underground. Stick together, though; you can easily get lost."

"That's why we're glad to be with you," Maggie said, putting her hand in the Korean woman's.

Back in the hotel, the family gathered while Rhee presented the children with beautifully wrapped gifts. Maggie tore through them, holding up each item as she unwrapped it: Korean soft drinks, Korean candy, a CD of Gangnam-style pop music, a fan, and a silk shawl. Peter got a PlayStation.

"I hope you don't mind the soft drinks and candy," Rhee said to Lauren.

"It's vacation," Lauren shrugged.

"I really like this country," Maggie said.

"Dr. and Mrs. MacGregor, we have gifts for you as well, but we'll get them to you later," Rhee said as she stood in front of the gathered family. "In the meantime, I have a proposition. Dr. MacGregor, you will be the hottest commodity at the meeting after your lecture Monday. Your old and new colleagues will keep you busy for several days."

"As they should, considering all you know," Lauren said, hugging Mac.

"You will be invited to dinner, asked to comment on new instrument development, the works. I expect you might even feel a little guilty because you will also want to be with the family."

Mac nodded with a slight frown. "Usually I do these meetings alone and don't have to think about that."

"For the rest of the family, that means there won't be much to do," Rhee said. "It only takes a day to see most of the notable sights in Seoul. There is a limit to how fascinated you are by spa treatments or laps of the swimming pool at the hotel."

"Are you suggesting an alternative?" Lauren asked.

"The most interesting part of Korea is in the south."

"Maggie actually read that from the guidebook today," Lauren said. "Are you suggesting a day trip?"

"More than that," Rhee said. "I suggest we spend tomorrow touring Seoul, then leave for Jeju Island the day after—that is, on Sunday. We can spend a few days at the amusement parks, on the beaches, walking in the forests. It's really beautiful, and it has nature reserves on it that will make you all very happy. And it will leave Dr. MacGregor to do what he wants at the meeting."

"What about the hotel rooms here?" Mac said.

"We'll keep them open for the family's return. Just take play clothes."

"Bathing suits?" Maggie asked. "Can we swim?"

"Yes, and sneakers and tennis shorts and sun hats. It's a paradise island."

Lauren looked at Mac. "What do you think, Mac? Is this OK?"

"Sure," Mac said. "The few times I've gone to a convention with you, I've always felt guilty because I haven't spent enough time with you. My job is to learn and teach, and there aren't many family events listed in this meeting. Jeju Island sounds like a great side trip, except I will be jealous every minute."

"I don't want you to think we want to leave you."

"I can stand it for five days. Every day is jam-packed with lectures and other sessions. Each night has medical events that would at best be boring for you and at worst not even available to families."

"But will you promise to have a good breakfast every morning?"

Mac laughed and put up three fingers of his right hand. "Scouts' honor."

"I think we'll do it," Lauren said as she looked back at Rhee.

"Great. Throw some light things into a bag tonight. We'll tour Seoul starting early tomorrow, then get the plane to Jeju tomorrow evening. It's only an hour plane ride."

"This way I can concentrate on the lecture and not worry about entertaining you," Mac said. "Thank you, Sung; you guys think of everything."

CHAPTER TWENTY-NINE

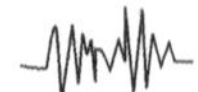

SEOUL

AUGUST 22

The next morning Mac left the hotel before Lauren and the children were awake. He felt relaxed in the knowledge that they would be in good hands, and he wanted to get a sense of the meeting before he gave his keynote address.

The organizers had placed him in the perfect time slot, the last presentation before the morning break. By that time, any glitches in the audiovisual equipment would have been fixed and all latecomers would have arrived. He could extend the lecture into the break if he had to speak longer than his allotted time, and there would be an opportunity to answer informal questions from the attendees.

He registered at the VIP desk and proceeded to the speaker ready room to upload the slides and videos for his presentation. The technological sophistication of the Coex Center impressed him. No need to lug a laptop to the podium to give a lecture. Instead, all speakers had to upload their data to a central computer that redistributed it. He noted that this also allowed his hosts to study the data and keep copies.

Two hours later he stood at the podium of the main lecture hall about to give the lecture he had been preparing for five years. Feeling his heart race, he surveyed the audience—three thousand neurosurgeons from every part of the globe waiting to hear his comments about surgery for hypothalamic hamartomas. He smiled. This was his dream, a culmination of his work.

His hands sweated a bit as he began the lecture. As the PowerPoint images flashed above him, he hit his stride like an Olympic champion. He discussed the symptoms of hypothalamic hamartomas, the tendency for their seizures to progress over a few years, the possibility of surgery in their treatment. He used carefully selected video clips of his own surgical approach to illustrate his points. He talked about complications and their avoidance. At the end, he felt exhausted and exhilarated, as if he had just finished a marathon. He looked at the timer—five minutes to spare. Prolonged applause erupted, but the moderator stopped it with a wave of her hand.

"Dr. MacGregor has done such a great job, we will actually have time for questions," she announced.

A young man in his thirties walked to one of the microphones set up in the aisles. "Dr. MacGregor, thank you for this amazing talk," he said. "I'm Dr. Foche from Paris. Can you tell us how someone can train to know as much about this as you do? We have to learn by our mistakes, and there is no margin for error here."

"Mentoring is the answer; you must watch, then assist, before you can try this alone. If you really want to focus on this type of surgery, do a fellowship with someone expert in the field."

A second questioner. "Dr. MacGregor, in our series we have noted psychological changes after surgery that might not be evident in the immediate postoperative period. Have you found a similar result?"

"This part of the brain balances emotional tone. We have come to realize there can be personality changes, usually to a more generous and understanding attitude. We're evaluating the reasons for this now."

"Dr. MacGregor, you use the intraoperative MRI for your cases in Boston. Is it necessary to have such a device to do this surgery safely?"

Mac smiled as he recognized Dr. David Ko at the microphone. No antagonism in Ko's voice, only admiration. "The intraoperative MRI is only a help, not a necessity," Mac said. "The texture and appearance of the tumor are distinctive enough to guide the resection. Of course, it helps to have had the added benefit of a hundred cases where my clinical impression was confirmed by actual imaging."

The moderator of the session thanked Mac again and announced the coffee break. Mac left the stage with applause thundering in his ears.

Young neurosurgeons swarmed around him as he entered the exhibition space outside the lecture hall. He waded through requests for clarification of one point or another, for his autograph, and for photos to be taken with surgeons from Korea, Africa, Europe, Asia, America. He felt wired by the time he moved toward the exit of the hall. He'd done the only thing he had to do at this meeting, and he had done it well. He felt a little sorry that his family could not have seen this, but the public never got to observe professional lectures anyway.

"Professor MacGregor, that was a spectacular lecture," Ko said as Mac reached the end of the line of admirers waiting to see him. "I have some colleagues I would like you to meet. Could you join me for a moment?"

Mac shrugged and followed. He did not really need anything from the coffee break. The adrenaline of his lecture and the enthusiasm of the young people would keep him going all day.

He followed through the crowded exhibition area displaying the latest advances in technology to enhance neurosurgery. They skirted around lasers and virtual reality equipment and MRI machines to a remote area of the room.

"It's through here," Ko directed toward an exit.

Puzzled, Mac followed, but with an increasingly hesitant step. This was taking him away from public space. As he left the exhibition hall, he felt his shoulders pinned back by powerful arms, smelled the sweet aroma of something he remembered from his past.

"Ether!" he shouted as he began to struggle, then sank into darkness.

CHAPTER THIRTY

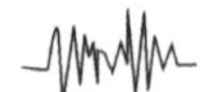

PONGHWA CLINIC, PYONGYANG

AUGUST 22

Mac tried to open his eyes, finally got them to slits. *In a bed. Hospital johnny. Bag of sterile saline on pole.*

He shook his head to clear the disorientation and help his headache. *Left hand IV. Groggy, confused.*

He pushed himself toward consciousness. A nightstand, dresser, and mirror. A large photograph of the Supreme Leader of North Korea dominated one wall.

Must be a hospital room. But the room smelled different than an American hospital—more disinfectant.

A hospital? What the hell? He jerked upright, palpated his arms and legs and head. No tenderness and no bandages. *Have I had an accident*?

He realized he was not alone and felt the heat of apprehension start to melt the semi-stupor that enveloped his senses. A soldier in a green uniform stood at attention at the door with a rifle in his hand. A large, muscular Korean man with an oblique scar on his forehead observed him from an armchair at the side of his bed. The man, elegantly dressed in a dark suit with a starched white shirt and silk tie, sat in silence.

Mac shook his head to clear his mind. He again felt his arms and legs for bruises. "Where am I?" he croaked. "Where is my family?" His voice sounded unnatural, guttural.

"Ah, Dr. MacGregor, you are awake," the thickset man said in perfect American English. "Let me help you get your bearings. You are in the Ponghwa Clinic in Pyongyang."

"Pyongyang? North Korea? How is that possible?" Mac felt agitated now. "Who are you?" he asked, forehead furrowing and eyes squinting as he tried to understand his position.

"I am General Kung Shinwa. This clinic is a medical and surgical center for government officials. It is as well-equipped as any American hospital." He leaned forward. "As you can imagine, it is also very secure."

Mac rested a moment to consider the implications of that last statement, then croaked in a thick voice. "Why am I here? Where is my family? My wife?" Energized briefly, he lifted himself in the bed. "Did I have a seizure?"

"I will explain everything in due time. Meanwhile, please relax and enjoy your luxurious surroundings." Kung did not move from his chair.

"Take me back to the hotel." Mac's voice became strident. "I want to see my family."

Kung signaled to the soldier at the door, who slung the gun over his shoulder and moved to the bedside to block any attempt to get out. The general pulled the armchair closer.

"We would prefer you to stay where you are. Are you fully awake? I want to be sure you understand your situation."

Mac nodded, although his head still felt fuzzy and his thinking was clouded. "I didn't have an accident? What happened?"

"First, let me apologize for the unorthodox methods we have used. We had to transport you into our country without you or anyone else knowing we were doing so. You have had no accident and no injury. I can assure you your family is safe and we do not mean to harm you. We wish to make you a once-in-a-lifetime proposition."

Mac felt completely awake now. "You kidnapped me and brought me across the border to the DPRK? How is that possible? I'm an American citizen. Why would you do this?"

Kung leaned back in his chair and put his fingertips together. "We have admired your work on hypothalamic hamartomas for some time. You have developed surgical techniques unique in the world. I congratulate you on a superb lecture yesterday presenting your data. You should know that we had already identified you as the world's best neurosurgeon for this condition."

Mac drew back. "So what?"

"We have an official with this problem. He's booked for surgery tomorrow, and you will be the surgeon."

Mac looked around the room, shook his head. "You drugged me and transported me here so I can do surgery?"

"Correct."

"On a patient I have never seen?"

"Also correct."

"In an operating room I have never been in?" Mac felt his jaw tighten with indignation.

"I think you will be pleased once you see it. But yes."

"With staff I have never met or worked with?

"Yes."

"And me feeling as if a truck ran over me?"

"Unfortunately, yes."

Mac looked at Kung as if the man were crazy. He sat up and twisted. "That's insane. Even if the operating conditions were ideal, I don't know enough about the patient to know he needs surgery. Is the patient even a man? How old?"

"It is a man."

"But I don't know his history." Mac almost shouted again now, felt his pulse and breathing increase. "I haven't seen his MRI. I don't know the size or shape of the hamartoma or whether it is operable. I don't know whether his general physical condition is good enough for surgery. I don't know if he has other medical problems that might make the operation too dangerous."

"You'll have the opportunity to assess some of these. Our physicians have decided that surgery is the best option and have not found any—what do you call them—*contraindications* to surgery. The patient is in good general health. You will see his MRI in a few minutes. You will not be given his name."

Mac looked at Kung with narrowed eyelids and a voice as menacing as he could make it. "There are a thousand reasons not to do surgery on a patient I am not familiar with. I don't know the operating team. I don't know your instruments. You have no idea of the potential risks. You can't just take a surgeon and—"

Kung put up his hand. "We expected you would feel this way. Let me describe the situation both for you and for us."

He sent the armed soldier back to the door. "We know this man has a mass in his hypothalamus. Our own team has considered all the options. They agree that this tumor is operable, that it needs to be removed, and that you are the best person in the world to do it safely." He spoke in such a low tone that Mac had to hang over the edge of the bed to hear him.

"But you don't understand," Mac said, as if trying to explain something to a child. "The preoperative evaluation takes weeks and must include hormone, neuropsychological, and visual studies. I see my patients two or three times preoperatively and at least twice in the month after surgery."

"You will not be able to get those studies and you will not be able to talk to the patient either preoperatively or postoperatively. But we will show you his MRI."

Mac shook his head, still trying to understand what was happening. "This is not acceptable."

Kung called out, "David, come in please."

Mac's eyebrows shot up and his stomach sank to the floor. Dr. David Ko appeared in the doorway, carrying a computer and CD case.

"What the hell are you doing here? I thought you worked in South Korea," Mac said.

"I do. That allows me to keep up with medical advances and Seoul politics. I still have family in the DPRK."

Kung interrupted. "Let's just say David has strong reasons for helping me—the strongest we could create."

He turned to Ko. "Show our surgeon the MRI scans."

For several minutes Ko and MacGregor went over the images together.

"What do you think?"

"I need to look at them alone. I have to visualize them in my head and consider how to approach the mass."

Kung looked at Ko, who shrugged.

"You have ten minutes."

Mac flicked through the images again, creating a three-dimensional model in his brain that would be the guide for his surgery. He decided that this hamartoma could be operated on, was in fact rather favorable for surgery.

He returned to the beginning of the scan and realized there were images from another patient on the disc as well. He initially thought all the scans were of the same person, but this patient did not have a hamartoma. What he did have, and Mac gasped as he realized it, was a basilar tip aneurysm. This weakness in an artery wall could rupture at any time, causing sudden death.

He looked at the patient's name, which had not been hidden. Kung Shinwa. He closed his eyes and leaned back. If he could raise Kung's blood pressure, perhaps he could cause the aneurysm to explode.

But there was no way to raise the pressure.

Should he tell Kung about the aneurysm? No point. Mac's goal was to keep his family alive. That meant safe surgery on the Supreme Leader. Nothing in the deal involved the medical care of the chief of staff.

Ko and Kung re-entered the room. "I assume that you agree with our consultants that this is a hypothalamic hamartoma and can be removed surgically," Kung said.

Mac nodded.

"Then let me explain the arrangement." Kung crossed

his arms and spoke loudly now. "After you have removed this successfully, we will deposit one million U.S. dollars to a newly-created Duncan MacGregor fund, half on the first postoperative day and half after one month."

"I don't care about money." Mac clenched his jaw and spoke as savagely as he could. "Where's my family?"

Kung continued, ignoring his question. "We will also, through the Korean-American Friendship Association, deliver a seven-tesla MRI to your hospital. We know you have repeatedly petitioned for such a machine and gotten nowhere. The gift will allow Harbor Hospital to become the premier institution in Boston for brain imaging and will help your own work. It will also make you—how do you Americans say it—a big man on campus. It will prove that you are a valuable resource. I believe you could use that kind of affirmation right now."

Mac felt like a player hit by a side blow. "How do you know about the relations between me and my hospital?"

"I know the moves you make, the sentences you utter. I know about you and Whitemore and Knight. In brief, I know everything about you."

"And right now," Kung said with a look that made Mac's heart gallop, "your ass, brain, and everything in between are mine."

"I said, where is my family?" Mac's head seemed to pound harder with each racing heartbeat.

"Ah yes, your family. There may be thousands of reasons not to do the surgery, but there are three big reasons to go ahead with it. Their names are Peter, Maggie and Lauren." He looked at Mac from the corner of his eye. "I can assure you that they are safe at the moment, but disaster can occur at any time in this complex world."

Mac slammed his fist on the bed. "This is crazy. You can't do something like this in the twenty-first century. Not to an American. I'm out."

"Out?" Kung laughed, then continued with his face a few centimeters from Mac's. Mac could smell his bad breath, see the pulsating forehead scar turn purple, look into those dead black eyes. "Shall I tell you what will happen if you refuse?"

He looked up to be sure Ko was listening. "The most pleasant result for you personally would be torture and relatively quick death. A more likely outcome would be several months of slow deterioration in one of the camps we have arranged for dissenters. No one would know you even existed there."

"But—"

"But more important," Kung continued, "your children and your parents will be tortured and killed as well. This is what we call our three-generation rule. I believe David has some experience with this."

Ko nodded his head, said in a quiet voice. "My family—"

Kung ducked to miss the right-handed blow Mac aimed at him, caught his wrist in mid-air. "Careful. If you hurt your hands, that makes you useless. That's the equivalent of refusing."

Mac sat stunned. He realized now the enormity of his predicament. His body trembled, with sweat drenching his back. His mind seemed to be clouded and his headache overpowered his anger. He decided to try a different tactic, to make these people realize how dangerous the situation was. "What if there is a problem with the surgery?"

"A big problem? That's the same as refusing."

Mac stared at Kung with hatred and disbelief. "How do I know you haven't killed my family already?"

"They're en route to Jeju Island for a five-day excursion as planned. They have no idea anything unusual is happening. Their guide Rhee Sung is my employee—my niece, actually."

He took a smart phone from his pocket, punched a few keys, and said a few words in Korean. For a flashing moment Mac could see Lauren and the children in an airplane cabin with Rhee smiling and playing Mahjong with them. They did not look up.

"Of course, even on an island like Jeju there can be accidents. The lava tubes, the volcanic ash, the terrible traffic... Nowhere is safe anymore. A shame. We should really try to make our environment more people-friendly."

"I need to talk with them."

"That is impossible." Kung flicked off the screen. "Until the work is done, we can allow you to observe them for two minutes a day to be sure they are alive. No direct communication." He paused. "And, of course, you understand that any future discussion of what you have done here would have extremely severe consequences."

"Meaning?" Mac had given up anger. Naked fear now took over his mind.

"The same result I described for failure. We are good at adding special twists to eliminating someone in the USA. No one ever knows we had anything to do with the disappearance."

Mac shook his head in disbelief.

Kung cupped Mac's chin so he looked straight into his eyes. "You must not talk about this to anyone, including your wife. You must tell anyone who asks that you have spent the next five days at a neurosurgical conference."

Mac yelled at Kung. "I'm an American. You can't do this."

"We just did," Kung said as he moved away and turned toward the door. "Your country has no idea you are here. I doubt they could do anything even if they knew. David will show you the operating room in a few minutes. Surgery is booked for eight tomorrow morning."

Wrapped in a hospital dressing gown, Mac stepped into the corridor ten minutes later. Ko led the way and a soldier followed them with his QTS-11 assault rifle at the ready. No one disturbed them as they made their way to the elevator and surgical floor.

Ko flipped on the lights of the operating room. Mac drew back with a gasp. A full-size reproduction of his own Boston surgical suite dazzled before him. Brilliant lighting. Spotless floors. The smell of the same disinfectants the Harbor Hospital cleaners used. Operating microscopes, anesthesia machines, drills, ultrasonic aspirators, and navigation systems duplicating his equipment precisely. Only the high definition monitors were different. These were better than his.

Mac felt a deep anxiety. Whoever his patient was, it was someone for whom an entirely modern neurosurgical operating room could be created. And his family provided the collateral to guarantee the surgery went well.

A million-dollar surgical procedure. What official is

worth that? Mac remembered the face smiling at him from his room and from the poster on the elevator wall, then scanned the same face hanging on the OR wall. Only one person in North Korea is worth a million dollars.

"What do you think?" Ko interrupted Mac's musings.

"I think you are a North Korean agent."

"Not an agent. Just cooperative."

"Why?"

Ko turned away. "I can confirm that there really is three-generation retribution." He swept his arm toward the room. "But I meant, what do you think about your operating room?"

"Impressive, but equipment is only one part of the requirement for good surgery. What about nurses and surgical assistants?"

"I will be your assistant. I have been studying your operative videos and surgical papers. I know you open with a five-centimeter incision a finger breadth behind the hairline, that you do not shave the hair, that you follow a transcallosal approach to the ventricle, that..."

Mac held up his hand. "OK, OK. I assume the scrub nurse has been similarly well prepared. I should thank you for your help, but to tell you the truth I can only think of one thing. Your boss has the power to kill my family. That'll make me do my best, but I cannot tell you how much I despise you and what you are doing."

"We thought you would feel precisely that way," Dr. Ko said without a smile. Trudging back to his room, Mac felt an invisible shroud surround him.

CHAPTER THIRTY-ONE

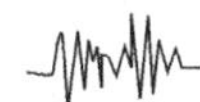

PONGHWA CLINIC, PYONGYANG

AUGUST 22-23

Mac stared at the ceiling as he tried to get to sleep. He had one goal—to save his family's life. He had a major barrier to that goal— General Kung Shinwa, powerful and ruthless chief of staff to the Supreme Leader. No way of reconciling the two. If he refused to do the procedure, he and his family would die terrible deaths. If he did the surgery, he could not guarantee it would be complication-free. He and his family would be murdered if there were any problem.

As he followed his thoughts further, he came to believe that he would probably be killed even if the surgery went perfectly. He would have too much information about someone important in the government. He was a dead man either way.

If I could only get away. Perhaps pretend to have a headache and send one of the guards to get help. It shouldn't be hard to convince them. They were just teenagers. Once they left their post, he would run to the window, lift it, and jump out.

He got up and tiptoed to the window, moving as quietly as he could to avoid alerting the soldier on the other side of the door. Pulling with all his might, he found he could not budge it open.

Even if he smashed it, the drop to the ground appeared to be at least six floors. If he survived the fall, what would he face? A six-foot wall with barbed wire defined the perimeter of the lawn, hidden from the street by tall trees but visible from his room.

Suppose he could climb over the walls. What lay on the other side? Could he make a commotion and expect to be rescued?

Idiotic. No one in the streets would help, and even if they would, there was no United States Embassy to run to in the DPRK. He would have to rely on the Swedish Embassy, and he did not know whether they would protect him. They might have more questions than he could answer about why he was there.

He had decided that trying to escape would be suicide when a rap on the door interrupted his musing. He raced back to bed.

Kung entered. "I wanted to be sure the operating theater met with your approval,"

And to be sure I was here. "What guarantees do I have that my family and I will be able to leave this country if I do successful surgery?" Mac asked.

Kung stood and straightened his back. "I am a man of honor. I will personally make sure you get back to Seoul safely if you carry the surgery out well."

He reached into his jacket. Mac thought for a moment he was going to pull a gun to emphasize his point. Instead, he punched on his phone and displayed a video of Lauren and the children listening to someone with rapt attention. "Your family had a wonderful time in Hallasan National Park today. Rhee Sung is taking good care of them and assures me they are—what do you say—having a ball."

He dropped the phone back into his jacket and marched to the door, turning as he was about to exit. "The guard will wake you at six-thirty. We expect you in the operating room by seven."

For the rest of the night Mac tossed in his bed, trying to remind himself that he needed sleep to be at his best for surgery. All he could think of was his family, apparently enjoying a holiday but closely monitored and in grave danger. By two in the morning his sheets were soaked with sweat. He had gotten up to pace a dozen times. The atmosphere in the room seemed impossibly close; the air conditioning was not functional; the windows were sealed closed, and the door was locked with a guard on the other side.

He considered the options available as he paced. He was now convinced that his patient was the Supreme Leader of North Korea. He stopped to look at the portrait smiling down at him. The inappropriate laughter, outbursts of violence, weight gain, and irrational behavior were all compatible with a hypothalamic hamartoma.

Refusal to operate would lead to assassination of everyone he held dear in his life. Having a bad outcome would have a similar result.

What if he just accepted these possibilities as inevitable and killed or permanently incapacitated his patient? He was going to be manipulating the hypothalamus, the most delicate area in the brain. A few wrong sweeps of the suction could cause permanent coma or death.

Could he do such a thing? It would violate his Hippocratic oath—do no deliberate harm.

And there were practical issues. David Ko would be "assisting." Mac knew Ko was there not only to assist but to monitor and prevent dangerous moves. If Mac veered from the protocol Ko had seen in Boston, his "assistant" would take over and keep the patient safe.

The option of disabling his patient was both immoral and impractical.

As he stared at the portrait, he thought of Mrs. Clark, the patient whose personality had been changed by hemorrhage behind her hamartoma. Would it be possible deliberately to destroy just enough tissue to obliterate the Supreme Leader's aggressive behavior and make him a kinder, gentler chief of state? Remove the same brain tissue that changed Mrs. Clark?

"What do you think, Your Excellency?" he muttered at the portrait hanging on his wall. "Would you like to be more humane?"

He followed through the logic. The violent outbursts and laughing seizures probably resulted from damage to the Supreme Leader's brain caused by the hamartoma. If Mac really wanted to achieve equilibrium, to return the patient to his "real" self, he should remove both the hamartoma and a few millimeters of tissue behind it. That would restore the natural balance.

He returned to the bed, struck by a further thought. If the operation changed the leader's personality, Mac and his family might be spared. In fact, such a personality change might provide the only hope they had of staying alive. It could also help thousands of North Koreans who suffered under the status quo.

The idea seemed so crazy he dismissed it at first. Too risky. Dr. Ko would see what was happening and would stop him. But why would Ko see anything but a few more strokes to get the tumor out?

Mac held his head, now pounding with pain and blocking coherent thought. He looked at himself in the mirror, hardly able to make his face out in the dim light. A two-day stubble of beard, hair matted, face worn. *Did the person reflected there have the guts to change his patient from a belligerent person to a kind one?*

Of course he did. The anger and frustration of the kidnapping burned within him, forging an iron resolve. The only questions were tactical. How much tissue should he remove? How would he avoid detection on the television monitors? Would the personality change occur soon enough to keep his family alive?

The more Mac thought about the possibility, the more convinced he became that taking a small bit of extra tissue was the only way to save him and his family. That concept did not make his sleep any easier. He tossed and sweated through the night.

CHAPTER THIRTY-TWO

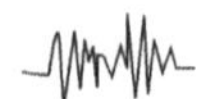

PONGHWA CLINIC, PYONGYANG

AUGUST 23

Mac was roused at six a.m., prodded by the soldier assigned to his room.

After a cold shower he attempted to shave. The dull razor blade only scraped his stubble. He gave up after a few strokes and returned to his bed to find a dish of rice waiting for him.

He could not eat. He did, however, ache for coffee. He called the guard and ten minutes later had a lukewarm cup of a preparation that at least smelled like coffee. It tasted stale and bitter. He swallowed two mouthfuls, put on the set of surgical scrubs laid out beside his bed, and planned what he was about to do.

Dr. Ko met him at six-forty and took him to the surgeon's waiting area, a bare room with four chairs and a table. A television played the one channel available to North Korean citizens. Pictures of troops marching and infantry in various maneuvers recycled over and over. He searched for coffee and found none.

A thin man about fifty years old introduced himself as the chief of anesthesia at this clinic. Ko translated his rapid Korean effortlessly, including details of drugs and technique. The anesthesiologist outlined his plan for fentanyl and propofol, precisely what Mac used in Boston.

"I trained in the Burdenko Institute in Moscow," the chief said proudly. "They are very up to date. The only potential risk to such a light anesthesia would be an intraoperative seizure, but that should be easy to handle if it happened. And of course, the advantage is that you will know right away whether there is a problem from the surgery as he wakes up. Now please excuse me; I will prepare the patient."

Mac looked at Ko. "I don't get to talk to my patient preoperatively? How can I be sure he has been informed? How do I know for sure it is the right patient?"

"You will not see his face. I will have him prepared by the time you come in. You can rest assured he has not been informed at all. He expects to have a short nap, then awaken cured. I'm sure you can arrange that."

He did not smile. His piercing gaze projected a very different man than the easy-going surgeon Mac had previously seen. "Be ready to scrub in five minutes."

As Mac stood at the scrub sink, his hands were sweating and his heart pounded against his ribs. The worst sensation was a kind of anxious emptiness in his stomach as if his whole gut was falling away. The bizarre setting, the unfamiliar features behind the masks, and his own nerves made him curse the day he first heard about hypothalamic hamartomas.

He moved to the operating table. The patient had a surgical towel hiding his face and Ko was preparing the scalp with antiseptic solution. Mac parted the hair and applied Bacitracin ointment to keep strands out of the way. He did not shave the hair and marked the incision behind the hairline, so no one from the front would know anything had been done.

As he looked up, he realized a camera was broadcasting his moves to a monitor presumably visible from the OR door. He assumed Kung would position himself there to watch the procedure throughout without having to be in the OR.

Ko asked Mac to turn away while he replaced the temporary towels covering the patient's face with the sterile drapes necessary for surgery. Mac stood with his back to OR table; head bowed, but side vision fixed on the monitor.

"Shit," Mac heard Ko say. He resisted the urge to turn around, but for a second could see the patient's face in the television monitor.

He had been right. The face on the screen was the face that smiled from banners and framed portraits everywhere around him, the face of the Supreme Leader of the DPRK.

He now understood the elaborate arrangements and high stakes, felt like a bird in the mouth of a ferocious dog.

"Everything OK, Dr. Duncan?" the scrub nurse asked in halting English. "My name Ji-Woo. I hope assist expertly."

"He's fine—just getting used to the idea that this is really happening." The voice came from the operating room door. Mac looked up and saw General Kung, even more threatening than usual, standing with his arms crossed and a surgical gown wrapped around his bulk. "I'll be just outside if there is any problem."

Mac saw Ko and the anesthetist staring at Kung; they were clearly trying to assess whether the general had seen the slipped sheet. He did not give any indication he had, and the rest of the skin preparation and draping went smoothly. As the patient was covered with sterile drapes, Mac felt his pulse and breathing calm. This was no longer an individual person; it was a body to be returned to health, an anonymous brain to be cured.

As the actual surgery began, MacGregor hunched over the surgical field, focused completely on the anesthetized patient on the operating table. Only the cardiac monitor broke the silence. He incised the scalp, removed the bone, cut expertly through the lining of the cerebral hemispheres, and gently opened the plane between the two halves of the brain.

Moving the already-draped operating microscope into the field, he sat and adjusted the video display to show the pulsating surface of the cortex.

Ko was as good an assistant as Mac had ever had. He anticipated every move, was deferential but competent, moved with confidence. As a scrub nurse, Ji-Woo also seemed to understand just what was needed. Mac could ask for anything and his translated request was immediately fulfilled.

Under high magnification he retracted the right hemisphere from the fibrous falx and released cerebrospinal fluid to allow the brain to relax. He incised the glistening corpus callosum fiber tracts that connect the two halves of the brain. Spinal fluid cascaded into the field.

He placed retractors against the Foramen of Munro and looked into the hypothalamus where a mound of glistening tissue covered the tumor. The muscles of his forehead tensed as he began to divide tumor from normal brain tissue. Normally he would have pathological confirmation of the abnormality, but he could not rely on a pathologist he didn't know.

"Can you tell it's hamartoma just by the feel?" Ko asked.

"Yes." Mac exposed the posterior aspect of the mass, the region whose injury creates a gentler patient. He increased the magnification of the microscope and paused. His plan seemed simple last night: remove the aggression region of the Supreme Leader's brain. But could he really do this? And could he do it without raising suspicion?

The tool that would allow Mac to remove the requisite brain unnoticed was a one-millimeter diameter suction device he used for dissection. The force of suction increased when a small release hole in the hub of the instrument was closed. Normally the surgeon maintained just enough power to aspirate excess fluid out of the field. When full suction kicked in, brain tissue got sucked away as well.

He noted only five people in the room beside himself: the anesthetist, scrub and circulating nurses, Ko, and Kung. They could only observe the surgery through the television monitors posted around the room. Ko had a direct view through the microscope, but he was not familiar with this surgery in detail.

Mac adjusted the operating microscope so the tumor mass filled the screen, blocking any video record of what he was going to do next. He feared his pounding heart would be easily heard by everyone, felt as if he was going to faint as he tried to control his breathing and the urge to run.

"Ji-Woo, could you please get me a two-millimeter cottonoid patty?" he asked in a strained voice. He knew that the nurses would have to open a new pack and turn their attention to counting out the cottonoids rather than to the operative field. He was gratified that Ko looked over at them to be sure they had picked the right size.

He rolled the mass forward, put his sucker tip behind it and released the control to allow full suction force. Over the lip of the tumor he could see a three-millimeter gap appear in the brain tissue. In one second he had removed a lifetime of his patient's aggressive behavior.

He let the tumor mass fall back into place. "Wait a minute," Ko said. "What was that?"

"Huh?" Mac said. His head throbbed with a screaming arterial pulse and sweat soaked the back of his surgical scrubs.

"Can you pull the mass forward again?" Ko said.

His hand now trembling, Mac tilted the tumor to show the region behind it. The brain had already closed in to fill the space.

Ko stared at the area of brain resection for several seconds. Mac closed his eyes, tried to quiet his racing heart and panicked breathing, fumbling at what he would say if Ko accused him of removing extra brain deliberately.

"I guess it's nothing," Ko said. "I thought I saw a little bleeding, but everything looks just fine."

"Would you like the cottonoid now?" Jin-woo asked.

"Perfect," Mac replied. "I'll hold it against the brain surface for a moment to be sure there is no bleeding."

"Sounds good. You're doing a fantastic job, by the way. So smooth. I love to watch you work." Mac could see genuine admiration in Ko's eyes over the mask.

"Only a couple of minutes more," Mac said. "We have one area of attachment left."

He passed his dissector under the mass, freeing it from the brain it adhered to, and delivered a pea-sized mass to the scrub nurse.

"I'll take that." Kung's voice blasted in Mac's ear. The general moved to the OR table with a specimen bottle and watched as Jin-Woo dropped the hamartoma into it, then exited without another word. Mac pretended he was surveying the operative field for any bleeding as he tried to get his breathing, heart, and muscle control regularized.

CHAPTER THIRTY-THREE

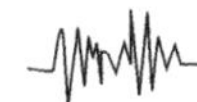

PONGHWA CLINIC, PYONGYANG

AUGUST 23

Mac finished the surgery two hours after he had started, record time even for him. He closed the incision with suture material that would dissolve, making stitch removal unnecessary. As was his habit, he then thanked Jin-Woo and Ko and the circulating nurse for their help.

Before the drapes were removed, Kung reappeared and ordered Mac to leave the room. In the corridor outside the OR, Mac dissolved into panic. Had he been insane to add the removal of the brain around the tumor itself to the plan? Would his patient wake up? Would the seizures stop?

"You should go back to your room," Kung said as he barged through the OR door and blocked the line of vision back into the OR. "Your work is done."

"But I want to make sure the patient—"

"Dr. Ko will take care of all that. We'll call you if we need you. You should hope you don't get called. That would mean a complication, which would be unfortunate."

"But I have to see my patient, make sure he—"

"You don't have to do anything but shut up and wait. Follow this man." Kung pointed to a guard.

Deciding that resistance would be unwise, Mac followed the soldier to the hospital room—that is, to the detention cell assigned to him. He should have been elated by such a smooth procedure, but instead he felt only anxiety, compounded by the inability to talk to his patient. Had he taken out too much? Had the removal of the tumor itself created any problems?

For the afternoon he lay in his room, staring at the ceiling, longing for a computer or television. Over and over he reviewed the circumstances that had conspired to bring him here. If only he had not become the world's authority on hypothalamic hamartomas, if only he had refused the too-good-to-be-true offer to attend the World Federation meeting. If, if...

At six o'clock a soft knock on the door roused him from his self-incriminations. He expected dinner. Instead, he opened the door to one of the doctors he had met in Boston.

"Hello," the diminutive physician said, looking at the floor. "I am Ahn Junsu. I met you in Boston. I brought a cell phone for you." He extended the device toward Mac. "Not to call, of course; just to observe your family. Rhee Sung is transmitting the video feed now. I think they're at dinner."

Mac looked at Maggie on the tiny screen, struggling with chopsticks while Peter used a fork to move various appetizers from the dish to his mouth. Lauren looked on with an encouraging smile. The image cut to the clock to show the time and faded away.

Mac lifted his arm as if he were going to smash the phone to the floor. Ahn rushed to restrain him. "Don't do that, please."

"You think General Kung might be upset? Well, I'm more than a little upset right now myself. I'm being held prisoner. My family is being kept hostage." He clenched his fists and began to pace.

"I'm sorry. It's for a good reason," Ahn said.

"A good reason? Is helping a dictator a good reason?"

"He's a human being."

"Stalin was a human being." Mac paused and looked at Ahn more carefully. "Why do you care anyway?"

"I'm his personal physician."

"Oh, so I guess the 'good reason' is to save your own skin. Why weren't you at the surgery?"

Mac noted the dance they both performed; no mention of the Supreme Leader's name, but both knowing the other knew who the patient was.

"General Kung wouldn't allow that. He said the less I knew about the technical details the better. I've been right outside the patient's room since the surgery finished, however. He seems perfectly OK. In fact, he seems to be a lot nicer than he used to be."

Mac hesitated. "What do you mean?"

"Well, for one thing he said I could get something to eat after I saw you. He would never have considered my comfort in the past. Maybe the experience of surgery made him more thoughtful."

"Sounds hard to believe," Mac said. "But on the other hand, I'm still alive."

"Precisely," Ahn said with a piercing look. "I'll plan to come by about six each evening to show you the family. They really look happy, by the way. I think they're having an enjoyable time in Jeju."

"It would be a lot better time if I were with them," Mac said, but the door had closed

CHAPTER THIRTY-FOUR

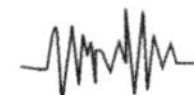

PONGHWA CLINIC, PYONGYANG

AUGUST 26

"When do we eliminate the American and his family?" Kung asked the Supreme Leader as they sat in the hospital room finishing their daily discussion. Three days of smooth recovery had passed without missing an administrative beat in the country's governance.

Kung had been ready to take over the formal direction of the state if necessary, but his boss had seemed competent and even more forceful than he had been in the past.

"I'm sorting that out," the Supreme Leader answered.

"Rhee Sung is ready to eliminate all of them when you give the word. None of them should leave Korea alive."

"Even if that means assassinating United States nationals on Korean soil? That could have serious political repercussions."

Kung answered with the speed of someone who had considered all options. "We can make it look like a hostile group struck them down while they were far away from protection—perhaps a band of militant Indonesian Islamists."

"What about the other people involved in the surgery? Would you kill them?"

"Of course, as soon as they are unimportant for your recovery. The two nurses will be first. They'll be redundant after you leave the hospital for home, which will be tomorrow."

"So soon? Is that what my doctors say?"

"It's what I say. Keeping your presence here a secret is complicated. Soon the country will want to know the identity of the mysterious patient who took the whole top floor of the Pongwha Clinic for himself."

"I enjoy the mini-vacation I'm having right now," the Supreme Leader said. "No aides pounding on my door. No crisis of the day."

"I'll be happy to intervene to take care of that for you."

"We'll discuss this further. Anything else before you go?"

"We're arranging for you to appear before the United Nations to proclaim the DPRK's unremitting objections to the warmongering of the United States."

"Fine."

As Kung opened the door to leave, the Supreme Leader called out, "One more thing. I was talking to the soldier doing night duty. His son is sick, and I told him he could come in late so he can watch over the child. Dr. Ahn will be with me from ten p.m. to two a.m."

Kung frowned. "I have the responsibility for the guards' schedules. You shouldn't have bothered yourself. I could have arranged something."

"I have taken care of it," the Supreme Leader said, and turned away.

CHAPTER THIRTY-FIVE

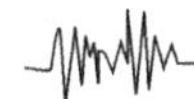

PONGHWA CLINIC, PYONGYANG

AUGUST 26

That night, like every other evening in the DPRK, Mac tossed in bed trying to get to sleep. He had never thought he would have a period in his active career when he slept too much. In Boston he had learned to function on four hours sleep a night, figuring he could make up his sleep deficit when he got old.

He had spent the last three days in bed or pacing his hospital room. Without books, television, or computer, he was left to talk to himself. Not a good companion. Nightmares, back and neck pain, self-incrimination, fear, all plagued him. He felt more agitated and less rested than he did when he stayed up all night with an emergency surgical case.

Being kept apart from his family was particularly hard.

Dr. Ahn had been a godsend. Each of the three nights since the surgery, he had appeared at six p.m. to show Mac the proof that his family was not only safe but enjoying their time on Jeju Island. Mac longed to be with them again.

When he heard knocking during his nocturnal fretting,

his first instinct was to check the time on his watch. Eleven p.m. Who would be looking for him at that hour of the night? Trembling, he fumbled into a bathrobe and approached the door.

Ahn stood there, short, thin, blinking repeatedly through his thick lenses. Alone. No soldiers in sight.

"What are you doing here at this hour? Where is my guard?" Mac choked out, a trickle of alarm running down his spine.

"He's taking a break."

Mac remembered Kung's chilling words: *You'd better hope you don't get called.*

"Is there a problem?" Mac's stomach sank as he realized his limited ability to cope with any complication. He didn't know the resources, the personnel, or the diagnostic tools available to him. If there were a significant postoperative issue, he would pay with his own life.

"Has our patient had a seizure? Stroke?" Mac asked, voice quivering.

"No, no; nothing like that. Just get dressed."

"But it's eleven o'clock."

"There's a reason for everything. Now please hurry. I told the guard to take an hour off—that I would be covering for this time."

Mac climbed into his surgical scrubs, deciding they would be quicker than his street clothes. In two minutes he crept behind Ahn along the deserted hospital corridors, onto the elevator, and up to the top floor.

No guards along the corridor. Ahn knocked three times

on one of the closed doors, listened for the invitation to enter, and opened.

The Supreme Leader sat in a chair facing the door. He did not rise as Mac entered. "Dr. MacGregor, I presume," he said in slightly accented American English.

Mac nodded.

"Ahn, please sit in the anteroom to be sure we are not disturbed."

The Supreme Leader and Mac faced each other alone. The leader searched Mac's face as if he were trying to read something in his eyes.

"So you are the surgeon who saved my life. My father would not have imagined having an American do this surgery, but I think we made the right decision. I feel quite well. Is the hamartoma completely gone?"

"Y-Y-Yes, sir. It is." Despite his anger, Mac could only stammer.

"Am I on a path to complete recovery? No complications likely?"

"I believe that's correct, sir."

"And I'm not going to have any more, uh, episodes?"

"No patient of mine has had a seizure after the hamartoma was removed."

"Do I have limitations on what I can do?"

"Begging your pardon, sir, but didn't Dr. Ko talk to you about all these issues? I understood from General Kung that he was providing your postoperative care."

The Supreme Leader leaned forward. "It's one thing to have a junior team member give his opinion. It's another to talk directly to the surgeon. I'm only sorry I could not see you each day. General Kung felt it was too risky. He did not even want me to know you were my surgeon. He thinks I have no insight into the way he runs my life."

"Yes, sir. To answer your questions then. You can do anything you want, but you're likely to feel tired, so you should plan to take it easy in general. Keep the incision dry for five more days. The stitches dissolve, so you don't have to worry about removing them."

The jangle of a cell phone shattered the quiet discussion. The Supreme Leader looked at the caller name and did not answer. He redialed a few seconds later. Mac could not hear the other end of the conversation but assumed General Kung was the caller. Mac had the impression his patient was not pleased with the conversation.

Hanging up the phone, the Supreme Leader said. "That was General Kung just checking on things. Sometimes there's a thin line between being concerned and interfering."

He turned again to Mac. "Far from feeling tired, I feel invigorated, that I can see things as they are and make decisions more easily than I could before the surgery. But I wanted to discuss you, not me."

He sat back in his chair.

"First, I apologize for the tactics we used to get you here. It was apparently the only way."

"What can I say? I just don't want my family to be hurt."

"I understand. I believe they are safe, but that takes me to the second point. I am extremely grateful for your skill. I assume General Kung has described the rewards we will bestow on you, your family, and your hospital for your surgical expertise."

Mac's eyes widened as he heard this. Nothing he had read about the Supreme Leader suggested that he would ever say he was grateful for anything.

He sat with his mouth open, then realized an answer was expected. "Yes, sir," he said.

The Supreme Leader smiled, seemed to have made up his mind.

"My third and last comment is the most important for your future. I expect complete discretion about this episode. There are ways to assure this, but I will only ask for your word that you will not speak with anyone about what you did here. Do I have that?"

Mac said, "Yes."

"You will not discuss this with anyone in your group or family, not even your wife?"

"I promise."

"You must know that we have a very long reach. If it ever comes to my attention that you have broken this oath, what I am now about to say is nullified."

Mac held his breath.

"I am ordering your release tomorrow. Your family will join you in Seoul in the afternoon with tickets to return immediately to Boston. As long as you maintain silence, I will not harm you."

The firmness and warmth of the handshake surprised Mac. "I trust we will not see each other again," the Supreme Leader said as he ushered Mac out of the room.

CHAPTER THIRTY-SIX

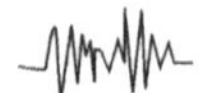

INTERCONTINENTAL HOTEL, SEOUL

AUGUST 27

Mac woke in his Intercontinental Hotel room, sprawled on the bed in the street clothes he had worn when he was abducted five days earlier. He had no idea how he had gotten there. He remembered Ahn approaching him in his hospital room in Pyongyang with a syringe, a cool feeling in the arm with the intravenous catheter, then nothing.

His watch agreed with the television clock. One p.m. He swung around to sit up but still felt drugged. On the nightstand lay a sheaf of airline tickets, one for each member of the family. Departure time tonight, nine-thirty. Beside them, a note.

limousine front lobby five p.m.

He shook his head to clear the fuzziness. It didn't work.

A key fumbled against the electronic lock. The anxiety he had felt during the surgery did not compare with the anticipation now. Was this the DPRK police, coming to haul him away to a re-education camp? Had the Supreme Leader changed his mind? He held his breath, felt his heart pound mercilessly against his chest wall, thought he might faint.

The door burst open. Maggie catapulted through. "Daddy, we saw spotted seals and shrews and dolphins," she said as she jumped onto Mac, pushing him back onto the bed. "And we hiked and shopped and swam and everything."

Peter followed, a little more subdued as he clambered onto them. "I got to try the new Samsung voice-activated gaming controller. It's awesome. You just speak orders to your character and it follows your commands. You don't even need a joystick. It hasn't come to the USA yet. And we got to do some great rides at the fun park."

Lauren entered third. She looked puzzled at the passionate embrace she and the children received from a husband on the verge of tears. Mac did not usually show emotion. "We missed you too," she said as Mac pulled her onto the pig-pile on the bed, "but we had a wonderful vacation. This is the first time I've gone to a medical meeting where we got to do something we like separate from medicine."

"How was your meeting, Dad?" Maggie asked as the family disentangled.

Mac thought about being forced to operate to save his family, sitting in terror in his hospital room, feeling fear every moment of his day. Then he remembered the Supreme Leader's warning and assumed the hotel room was bugged.

"I had a totally boring time," he said after a pause. "The meeting didn't have that much new stuff but at least I'll get my continuing medical education requirements for this year."

"Do we have to go back to Boston tomorrow?" Maggie asked. "I still haven't gotten the souvenirs for the show-and-tell that I promised the class."

"In fact, our plane leaves tonight," Mac said. He looked at his watch. "A limousine will pick us up at five o'clock."

Maggie began to pout.

"Maybe we can buy something for you in the hotel shop or at the airport, pumpkin," Mac said. "Now we have to get ready. Pack all your things and meet back in this room."

Mac's heart skipped a beat again when a loud knock at the door interrupted the family preparations. It took him back to the panic of his time in North Korea. Had General Kung, who Mac did not trust at all, taken matters into his own hands?

Mac peeped through the security port in the door. David Ko stood on the threshold balancing several packages in his arms. Mac considered Ko a cipher, a man with loyalties hard to gauge. Although he lived and worked in South Korea, he appeared to have strong ties with the DPRK and particularly to Kung. He was certainly not a simple friend.

Mac hesitated, then realized he had no choice. He swung the door open.

Ko entered with a flourish, piling boxes on the chair beside the door. Mac and the family sat on the edge of the bed. He thought of the similar occasion that Rhee Sung had suggested a fun outing for the family while Mac attended the meeting. What was Dr. Ko going to suggest?

Ko began by giving a box to Maggie. "For the Korea scholar," he said.

She ripped off the flap, lifting out a twelve-inch computer. "This is the latest Samsung hybrid tablet, meant for teenagers, with direct satellite internet connectivity, Kindle and

Nook and other reading programs, and a host of creativity apps. I hope you'll get to use it on the plane ride home," Ko said.

From the next box, Maggie extracted thirty full-color booklets on South Korea and an equal number of notebooks and pens with the logo "I heart Korea." Under them lay a pile of unisex children's T-shirts of every color with *Gangnam-style* printed on them. She squealed with delight. "This is enough for all the kids in my class. My show-and-tell's going to be the best ever."

"Next, for the techie," Ko said to Peter. The boy's eyes widened as he opened his container and took out the exact Samsung controller and play box that had enchanted him during the Jeju visit. "You'll be the first kid in the USA to have one," Ko said. "It has a twenty-hour battery life and complete voice control. It comes equipped with over a hundred games. You might have to use the hand controllers during the airplane ride, though."

Ko opened the third box and extracted half a dozen silk scarves from it, passing them to Lauren. Probing deeper, he pulled out a deep blue silk dressing gown with a golden dragon on the back and handed this to Lauren as well. "Rhee Sung said you liked this when you were shopping on Jeju Island."

"I did, but it seemed too expensive," she said as she wrapped it around her and blushed.

"There's only one set of gifts left." Ko handed a big box to Mac, who passed it on to Maggie. He could not trust his emotions. This ostentatious distribution of gifts made him angry, as if the whole week had just been a big happy party. He felt like walking over and strangling Ko.

Maggie pulled out layer after layer of tissue paper from Mac's box. "There's nothing in it," she said as she came to the bottom of the box.

"Look harder," Ko said.

She finally produced two envelopes and looked quizzically at her father and Ko.

Both nodded and she extracted one letter.

"IOU one seven-tesla MRI scanner," she read. "What's that?"

"Just a gift we promised your dad," Ko said. "Let's just give the other one to him directly." He handed the envelope to Mac, who put it in his pocket without looking at it.

Ko looked disappointed that Mac kept silent about the letter's contents, but recovered quickly and opened the final box himself. "This may be the most important gift of all," he said, and pulled out a fiberglass suitcase with all-direction wheels. "It should hold all of these things and anything else you had that was making your packing too tight. I want to wish you bon voyage. I hope we'll meet again sometime."

Mac sat immobile, staring at the floor. Lauren waited for him to say something, then shook Ko's hand when Mac remained fixed in place. "Thank you for all of these mementos and for the wonderful experience your colleagues provided on Jeju Island, David. This was a truly memorable vacation."

On the airplane back to Boston, each member of the family stretched out in First Class luxury once again. Mac remembered the letter he had shoved in his pocket. It was a note from the Korean-American Friendship Association establishing the Duncan MacGregor Foundation Trust with Mac as the sole trustee.

Through the in-flight internet, Mac could access the account to find a balance of five hundred thousand dollars U.S. This would support his research for years. And another five hundred thousand in a month? He could stop writing grant proposals and just do research.

He felt too emotionally drained to be excited. Part of him did not believe it was real. He tried to blot the complexity of the situation out by watching a movie.

Lauren occupied herself finishing preparation for the fall semester.

Peter played several of the new games on the computer Ko had given him.

Maggie spent her time learning about her new tablet.

As they exited the customs line at Logan airport, Maggie gushed. "This was the best vacation ever." Peter and Lauren agreed enthusiastically. Mac said nothing.

PART 3

CHAPTER THIRTY-SEVEN

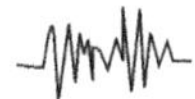

PYONGYANG

SEPTEMBER 3

Rhee Sung emptied the nurse's lifeless body from the bag onto a trash pile. She moved quickly. A car in the Potongan district of Pyongyang might be remembered even at midnight.

The killing had been easy. One well-placed knife wound from behind, then a body-sized plastic bag to keep blood from staining the trunk of the car as she drove to this remote corner of Pyongyang. Her victim had exsanguinated en route; now Rhee kicked the corpse several times and took the cash from her purse to make it look like a robbery gone bad. The investigation would concentrate on why a respectable Pongwha Clinic nurse was found dead in the most violent quarter in the city in the middle of the night. The attack that killed her would not be interesting. Death was an occupational hazard in this district.

"Four left," she said as she drove off.

She found the opportunity for the second nurse two days later. Her uncle General Kung Shinwa had told her that the

Army left keys in the glove compartment for vehicles in the short-term lot. She commandeered a jeep and drove to a parking place a short distance from the Pongwha clinic. As her target bicycled past on the way home, Rhee slid into the empty street behind her.

The chosen moment came in an area with deserted buildings in the center of the city, an area which had been built to be a center of commerce. At the moment, it had no occupants or pedestrian traffic. With no cars in either direction, Rhee raced toward the bicycle and hit it with such force the rider flew several meters into the air, then collapsed in a heap beside a pile of bricks and building debris.

Not bothering to confirm what she knew was certain death, Rhee sped off and had the jeep back in the lot within an hour of its loan.

She read the news of the fatal accident in the hospital bulletin the next day. It seemed to be the work of a hit-and-run driver, and the focus was on finding the responsible vehicle.

Unfortunately, there were no eyewitnesses or clues to identify the perpetrator. The investigation started at a dead end and would probably stay there.

No one seemed to connect this event to the other nurse's death, nor was there any reason to do so. The link with the Supreme Leader's surgery was known to only one man in the hospital, and he would not be alive for long.

Rhee entered the Pongwha Clinic at five-thirty the next afternoon. Surgery had finished for the day and the operating suite was untended. She slid into the women's dressing room, changed into surgical scrubs, added a hat and mask, and stuffed a pair of latex gloves into her pocket.

She knew her target usually stayed late to get ready for the next day's cases. His meticulous care of antiquated anesthesia machinery was one reason for his success. She spotted him through the door to the main operating room, confirming that he matched the face and name her uncle had given her. He had definitely been the Supreme Leader's anesthesiologist.

She entered the OR with a wave. He appeared to be inspecting the anesthesia machines in an otherwise deserted space. "I'm Mia, a new operating room assistant," she said. "I'm surprised to see the chief of anesthesia working so late."

He smiled. "It's what keeps me chief. I never know whether these machines are going to work, so I check them before every case."

She moved to a position beside him and gave him her most innocent look. "Why? Are there things that might go wrong?"

"Anything and everything can go wrong," he said. He seemed to be glad for her company and the opportunity to expound on a topic he felt passionate about. "To begin, there may not be enough anesthetic gas in the cannister to finish the case." He pointed at the machine he sat beside. "This one is full."

"Or there may be a leak in the system." He turned a valve on the machine and let her sniff the pungent odor of the gas. "Smelling that odor during the case means there's a leak."

He blocked the tube leading to the mask. "Stressing the

system by blocking the flow and seeing if you smell that gas the night before is better than trying to look for a loose connection or leaking gasket during a procedure." He put the tubing down. "This circuit is tight as a drum."

"Is there ever a problem with the mask itself?" she asked, pretending to be interested in every aspect of good anesthesia.

"Of course. It can be stiff or unsuited for the face of the patient. It has to fit snugly."

"Can you show me how it should be?" She moved behind him to examine closely the ideal conjunction of mask and face. He placed the mask over his nose and mouth. Her gloved hands moved toward him as stealthily as a snake.

He turned suddenly and lifted the mask away. She pulled back. Did he suspect her?

He shrugged and explained, "It's important to take away anything that will prevent a tight fit." She nodded. He removed his glasses, put them on the anesthesia machine, and placed the mask on his face again.

With lightning speed, she clamped her left hand onto the mask, pressing it tight as she released the anesthesia knob to its full opening with her right hand. This time there would be no interruption.

He turned toward her with a puzzled expression in his eyes, then began to reach for the mask, shouting something muffled like, "Take it off; I can't breathe." Perhaps realizing this was not a mistake after a few seconds, he thrashed his arms and legs to twist away, but she could now use her full strength to contain him.

It took only twenty seconds for the anesthetic to have its effect. He slumped into her arms. She turned off the oxygen and maintained the inhalational anesthesia at full strength. Ten minutes without oxygen would destroy his brain.

As his body relaxed, she let him slide to the floor. His limp body rested against her legs, head lolling to the right. She palpated his weakening carotid pulse intermittently. When his lips were blue and she had felt no pulse for five minutes by the OR clock, she knew he was dead. She readjusted the settings, allowing oxygen to flow again with a very low concentration of anesthetic agent.

She slipped out from behind him and arranged his body as if he had been in the chair and slumped to the floor, mask in place. She checked her arms and legs to be sure she had left no blood and looked for strands of her hair. Finding none, she stood back like an artist admiring her creation.

She shook her head."So sad, the way some anesthetists sniff gas as their drug of choice. Who knew that would be true of the chief here? You would've thought he could titrate the dose better. What is the world coming to?"

She turned, confident there had been no witnesses and fully aware there were no monitoring cameras in the operating theater. She discarded her scrubs in the hamper and placed her hat, mask, and gloves in the trash. Ten minutes later she was on the street and far away from the murder scene.

Two to go. Tricky, because they live outside the DPRK and are surgeons. One would be eliminated despite the order of the Supreme Leader to keep him alive. *Oh well, life is just one challenge after another.*

CHAPTER THIRTY-EIGHT

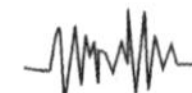

SOUTH KOREA

SEPTEMBER 5

Dr. David Ko shuddered as his bus arrived at the DMZ. He remembered only too well his previous meeting there. So much had happened since he reviewed the Supreme Leader's MRI scans and established the diagnosis of hypothalamic hamartoma.

Today he had a different mission—to obtain news of his family.

Ko's mother and younger sister had visited the DPRK to spend time with their relatives five years ago, leaving Ko and his father in Seoul. When they tried to return to South Korea, their birth papers and passports had been confiscated. After three years of futile effort, Ko's father had remarried and told David to treat them as dead.

Ko could not bring himself to do this. Realizing that General Kung was the ultimate decision-maker in the DPRK, he had personally petitioned the general to allow his family back into South Korea. With the promise of releasing them some day, Kung had recruited the young surgeon into clandestine service.

In the two years since then, Ko had seen no progress in their release and felt increasingly indentured to Kung. Fortunately, an agreement between the two Koreas allowed separated relatives to meet occasionally in the no-man's-land of the DMZ. His mother and sister were not allowed to join him. Instead, an aunt spoke on their behalf.

His aunt seemed thinner and more anxious than he remembered as she took a seat across from him under the watchful eyes of the guards.

"Is my family all right?" Ko asked.

"The same," she said. "Everything is always the same. They survive."

"Please give them my best. And you?" he asked. "Is the Pongwha Clinic still treating you OK?"

"It's a job. I get up in the morning, go to my *immamban* meeting, do my clerk work at the clinic, and go home. But we've had some trouble. The city's not as safe as it used to be."

"Trouble?"

"Jin-Woo, a nurse friend of mine from the clinic, was murdered last week. And a second OR nurse died a day later. Car accident." She shook her head. "Too many deaths in one week."

Ko felt an uneasy sensation spreading through his gut. Jin-Woo was the scrub nurse who had helped in the Supreme Leader's surgery. "What was the name of the other nurse?"

His aunt named the nurse who had circulated in the surgery. "But why do you want to know?" she asked, turning toward him with narrowed eyelids.

Despite his mounting panic, Ko thought he had better change the subject and said as casually as he could manage. "No reason. Just curious. I brought some clothes for my family and for you."

He put three piles on the table—wool scarves, hats, and gloves. A soldier examined them, then handed them to the aunt.

"The red ones are meant particularly for mother. It's her favorite color," Ko said.

The soldier had not discovered the South Korean *won* notes sewn into the red hat's lining. They were equivalent to ninety US dollars, or about six months of wages. Ko knew his mother could get a good exchange on the black market.

"Thank you. Your mother and sister don't have anything to give you back except a wish for your success in life."

"Thank them."

She got up to leave as the guard gestured at his watch. "We had another death in the clinic too. A doctor," she said.

"Anyone I know?"

"I don't think so. The chief of anesthesiology, very respected. Apparently sniffing anesthetic gases and overdosed. Created a mini-scandal."

Ko took in a sharp breath. His heart raced as his panic mounted. "Sounds as if the Pongwha Clinic is becoming a dangerous place to work," he said, trying to force a smile.

"Hasn't affected me," she said.

"Thanks for coming today. See you next time." Ko felt choked, the atmosphere heavy.

He rushed out the door and back to the bus.

Three deaths. The three Pongwha staff who had participated in surgery on the Supreme Leader.

His gut knew that General Kung had orchestrated these deaths, probably through Rhee Sung. Confronting her or Kung would just make them more watchful and they would deny any involvement.

I'm next.

Soon.

They can track me down. Workplace. Condo.

The inevitable conclusion: he had to get out of South Korea right now. He should do it without airline travel because immigration lines and ticketing were so closely monitored.

There were two possible destinations by sea—Japan and China. Japan was safer because it had fewer present ties to the DPRK. Ko knew that a ferry ran from Busan to Fukuoka, Japan several times a day. That would be his escape route.

He had his passport and credit cards, plus enough extra cash to keep him for a few days. Of course, he could not use the credit cards now. Once he got to Japan he could work out his next steps with less fear of surveillance. He could not risk going home now.

He watched the lush green countryside give way to urban sprawl as the bus approached the outskirts of Seoul. As soon as they crossed a subway line, he transferred to the underground to get to the central train station. Within a few minutes he hopped on the fast train from Seoul to Busan. He checked continuously for anyone who looked familiar or suspicious. In his compartment there sat a fat businessman focused on the newspaper. No one else remarkable.

From the train station in Busan, he walked to the ferry terminal as fast as he could without drawing attention to himself. He doubled back more than twice to be sure no one followed him. He bought his ticket to Japan with cash. No credit card purchases, no use of his car. He was off the grid.

Perhaps he would make it without detection after all. He was not leaving an electronic trail and was disappearing fast, without any warning to anyone. The only traceable item was the passport he would need to enter Japan, but General Kung would probably not have agents in the Japanese immigration office.

He began to relax after an hour on the ferry. In the middle of a weekday, it had few other foot passengers. He stood alone on the upper deck, shivering in the cold but happy for the solitude. He congratulated himself on the resolve and speed that had brought him here.

Looking out over the Sea of Japan, he imagined a new life spreading before him. Uncertain, but exciting.

He turned as a whiff of distinctive perfume drifted by his nostrils. "Leaving the country?" A familiar voice.

His mouth gaped and muscles tensed as he looked over at the passenger who had silently joined him. "Rhee Sung!"

She stood in wool sweater and cap, looking like the quintessential tourist, hands behind her back, perfectly relaxed as she stared out at the sea.

"Wh-what are you doing here?" he stammered.

"I was going to ask you the same thing."

He twisted around and raced toward the stairway, but found a large Korean man with a woolen cap blocking the access. The thickset man looked as if he would like nothing better than to dismember Ko.

"That's Charlie," Rhee said without expression.

Ko turned to run the other way and saw a second man appearing at the opposite end of the walkway, blocking any escape.

Rhee did not introduce that thug but walked toward Ko, still hiding her hands. "All dressed up and no place to go."

"Don't come near me," he shouted. "I'll—" Charlie's huge hand clamped onto his face and he could say nothing, could hardly breathe. He began to kick and squirm, but his opponent, bigger and stronger than he would ever be, lifted him off the ground and left him kicking air.

"I'll make a deal," Rhee said. "If you promise only to listen, I will ask Charlie not to break your neck."

"What difference does it make?" Ko asked.

"Right," Rhee said and nodded to the man with the woolen hat.

Ko felt the deck under his feet again. The beefy hands repositioned to make one snapping twist.

"OK, OK," Ko said. "I promise."

"Good." Charlie loosened his grip as she approached.

"I'm sorry this has to be done," Rhee said. "I enjoyed working with you, especially our trip to Boston. Of all the people I have to eliminate, I'll miss you the most."

"You don't have to do it, you know," Ko said, struggling

in Charlie's powerful grip. "You could defy your uncle. Come with me to Japan. Start a new life."

"Why would I want to do that? I'm happy at my work and happy with my family. Rare combination."

"How did you track me down?" Ko hoped a change of topic might distract her.

Rhee's gaze fixed on his belt, on the beeper which had become such a part of him he didn't even remember it existed.

"I'd like to say we used facial recognition software and surveillance feeds from all the cameras in Seoul. We didn't have to. We just followed the bug we had placed in your beeper a long time ago. We know what a conscientious doctor you are."

Ko tried to rip the beeper from his belt, but Charlie pinned his arms even more tightly. "What are you going to do to me?"

"Give you a gift. No pain. You will just black out. Then you will disappear, but you don't need those details."

She glided toward him, close enough that he could smell her jasmine perfume and see the makeup rendering her face smooth and young. He saw her gloved hands and the syringe they held. He felt Charlie encircle his chest with a massive arm, grab his forehead to extend his neck. He felt like a toy in a monster's grip.

"An intracarotid injection will be the most humane; the drug goes directly to the brain," she said. He felt her fingers palpating and isolating his carotid artery, then winced at the sharp prick as the needle punctured the vessel.

"What are you giving me?" he said, relaxing even as he spoke.

"Fentanyl and propofol. My special ratio. You'll have it a lot easier than MacGregor. He and his family will suffer as they die. And then of course there's the bomb. You are a lucky man."

Her image, scent, and voice faded. He felt himself lose control of his body, his speech, his thinking. His world slid into darkness.

CHAPTER THIRTY-NINE

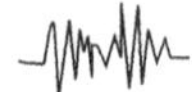

PYONGYANG

OCTOBER 10

Dr. Ahn surveyed Kim Il-Sung Square, considering the difference between this occasion and Generalissimo Day, the last time he had observed an event here. Today the square shimmered in the midday heat. Sunshine and warmth replaced the bitter cold of February.

He saw a more significant difference, however. Instead of rocket launchers and goose-stepping troops, the square sported a regulation basketball court in its center. As part of the Workers Celebration Day, the Supreme Leader had arranged an exhibition basketball game.

Large screens at strategic locations gave every spectator a closeup of the action on the court. He estimated that a hundred thousand onlookers shouted from the stands or jostled on the sidelines for a view.

The Supreme Leader sat on the viewing stand along with the joint chiefs of staff, General Kung, and a favored American basketball giant. Ahn sat nearby, but his presence at these events had become a kind of afterthought. His patient had experienced no laughing spells or anything else suggesting a seizure since the surgery.

Ahn sensed a difference in the tone of the crowd compared with Generalissimo Day. He felt an undercurrent of release, of freedom of expression bursting to escape. Perhaps he was just projecting his own feelings on the surroundings.

The game pitted an All-Star team consisting of the best current players of the NBA against the Legends, a group of senior players now officially retired. As the game began, the Supreme Leader looked out at the crowd and commented, "You see, I was right. Having this game as part of Workers' Celebration Day was a good idea. And Ryugyong Chung Ju-yung Gymnasium would have been much too small for this event."

"But a basketball game in our military square?" a general asked.

He got a tolerant smile from his boss.

That simple exchange meant something amazing to Ahn. An officer voiced a reservation about what the Supreme Leader had done. The response was a smile, not an angry outburst or instant demotion. Something big had changed in his patient.

Furious and fast action drew his attention to the court. At first, the strategic moves of the senior players matched the vigor and speed of the younger. A halftime score of 48 to 44 emphasized the similarity.

In the second half, the Legends began to show fatigue. Their shots were not quite as accurate, running not as strong. With one minute to go, the game stood at 78 to 76 for the All-Stars. Then the Legends' forward seemed to find new strength. He sliced a surefooted path through the defense and pounded a layup into the basket, tying the score.

On the next play the referee called a foul against the Legends. The All-Star forward aced the two penalty shots as the final bell sounded, giving his team an 80 to 78 win.

The crowd erupted as the opponents high-fived each other and shook hands. The Supreme Leader beamed. The American basketball ace turned to him, "What do you think, Dear Respected? Age and experience can't beat youth and energy. I'm glad I'm sitting here with you and not trying to play out there! Old guys like me belong in the observer seats."

Ahn frowned. Despite calling himself an "old guy," the speaker was younger than Kung and the generals around him. The average age of the Supreme Leader's advisers was sixty or above. Did they now belong in the observer seats rather than running the country? Ahn couldn't help thinking of Kung's claim of seniority and wisdom.

The Supreme Leader seemed energized and excited by this event. Hearing the screams of delight that came from the crowds, he turned to General Kung and his advisers. "Have you ever seen anything like that in your life?"

The advisers shook their heads, some displaying approval but a few having a more guarded response. The Supreme Leader continued, "This is going to be the start of my new sports and music cultural initiative for our country. Over the next year we're going to invite some of the world's best athletes and musicians to perform here. They will see a new DPRK, one that appreciates more than guns and nuclear missiles."

As the officials filed out of the stadium, Ahn saw Kung speak in sequence to three of the most senior generals in the entourage. They hung back, and Ahn could hear Kung's question: "What do you think?" The first replied, "I'm not sure what his father would have said." A second muttered, "Perhaps this is not the best way to proceed."

Kung touched that man on the arm, "We should meet." The remaining general took the man's elbow and moved him away with the curt comment, "It is not our place to question these things."

Kung noted that Ahn was observing. He targeted Ahn with a sharp glance. "What do you think, Doctor? Whose side are you on?"

Ahn stood motionless. There were sides? He had assumed all decisions from above came from a united position. He had been placed in the middle. If he agreed with Kung, his alliance would be conveyed somehow to the Supreme Leader and personal disaster might follow. If he said he agreed with the Supreme Leader, Kung would make his life hell.

"I'm just a physician," he said. "I don't have an opinion."

"Convenient," Kung said, but did not pursue his question.

CHAPTER FORTY

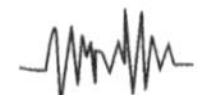

PYONGYANG

OCTOBER 11

Dr. Ahn had just reached his office at eight the next morning when General Kung's voice blasted from the intercom, "Report to my office immediately."

He headed for the chief of staff's headquarters without removing his coat, heart pounding. The corridor felt dank without the usual flow of foot traffic. The cool cement walls smelled of yesterday's cigarettes. Fluorescent lights, still flickering with the night-time power conservation schedule, barely illuminated the perpetual twilight.

Ahn wondered what could be urgent enough to disrupt Kung's morning schedule of weight training. Was there something new about the Supreme Leader's health? Had he developed a new medical problem overnight?

As soon as Ahn arrived, Kung snapped, "Leave your coat here. We're going to meet with the Supreme Leader. Your job is to sit and listen during this discussion. Say nothing but remember everything." He spoke fast, drumming his fingers on the desk before heading toward the door. He turned and answered the unasked question as they exited: "He asked that you be there for the meeting."

Ahn hustled to keep up as they headed down the corridor. He expected to be ushered into the leader's office, but instead they turned up a set of stairs that led to the palace grounds. A dazzle of early morning sun blinded him briefly and the smell of newly mown grass filled the air. They crossed the expanse of immaculately groomed lawn and courtyard to the entrance of the dining room.

Kung notified the guards standing at the door that they had arrived. Ahn could see a remarkable gathering as he looked through the open door. Twelve very tall men of every color, facial hair distribution, and body tattoo sat around a massive table with the Supreme Leader at the head. Three soldiers dotted the periphery of the room but seemed to be enjoying the scene as much as the participants.

Prodigious heaps of rice, banchan, beef barbecue, fried eggs, and kimchi were piled on the table, which was covered by a damask tablecloth. The group laughed and swapped stories, all in English. The visitors did not refuse the bottles of beer, manufactured in the DPRK, that adorned every place setting. Several impromptu toasts peppered the conversation.

The Supreme Leader looked up when the guards whispered to him. He arrived at the door looking more relaxed than Ahn had ever seen him. He beckoned them to a room off the dining room. Ahn gaped at the leather-bound books on mahogany shelves, thick oriental rugs, plush velvet chairs. He could not help thinking about the barren medical library as a sad contrast.

Three armchairs had been arranged together. Kung pulled one away and nodded to Ahn, who dragged it to the wall and watched from the edge of the room. Kung offered the larger remaining one to the Supreme Leader and pulled his own chair to be directly across from him.

The Supreme Leader began without the usual formalities. "General, shall we get to the point directly? What is so urgent that it takes me from the basketball breakfast? These guests are leaving early this afternoon and I want to spend some time with them." A trace of annoyance tinged his voice.

"Dear Respected, that's what I wanted to talk with you about," Kung began, looking at the floor. "You and I come from very ancient Korean families. Your ancestors originated from the golden egg twenty centuries in the past. My family can be traced back to the Shilla dynasty twenty-one hundred years ago."

Ahn drew his breath in and stared. What was Kung doing? Comparing ancestries was as close to heresy as the Korean system could allow. School children were raised on the unique and glorious lineage of the Supreme Leader. There was no relevant comparison with any other family.

Kung kept his gaze on the floor. The Supreme Leader fixed his eyes on him through narrowed eyelids.

"My honorable father had the great privilege of helping your esteemed grandfather create the DPRK. In my turn I, although unworthy, worked with your own exalted father to continue that tradition. I believe I have been able in some small way to help in the day to day management of our magnificent country—"

The Supreme Leader broke in, almost speaking to himself. "Especially in managing the prison camps and re-education centers."

Ahn detected accusation rather than commendation in this comment. In Boston, he had heard the media describe human rights violations in the DPRK. Reporters claimed that hundreds of thousands of citizens were imprisoned in *kwan-il-so* prison camps for political disagreement. He and his friends knew nothing of such camps and had dismissed this as Western propaganda. The Supreme Leader appeared to confirm their existence here, at the same time denying responsibility for them. Were they Kung's particular contribution to the social order?

"Yes, those have been among my special activities to maintain your position," Kung said.

Ahn drew in his breath again as he considered the implications of this comment. The general was claiming loyalty perhaps; but he implied that incarceration of dissidents had been necessary for the Supreme Leader's survival. This was not the way a conversation with the Supreme Leader should go. It should be filled with humility and oblique claims and requests. Ahn began to twist his hands together.

The Supreme Leader tilted his head. He was seeing his general through new eyes, Ahn thought. "And why do you bring these issues to my attention?" the Supreme Leader asked in a strained voice.

Kung remained silent, still looking at his shoes. After several seconds, he looked up and said, "May I be honest with you, Supreme Leader?"

"Have I ever asked you to be otherwise?"

"Our beloved country is surrounded by enemies. We have been able to continue our great Communist program only by restricting interaction with those hostile forces. Our belligerent stance has made us feared and respected as a country. That respect is essential to our national pride and continued existence."

The Supreme Leader pointed to the gathering in the dining hall. Chatter and laughter still reverberated through the morning quiet. "Do these people look like hostile forces or foreign spies? They're just basketball players."

He rose and left Kung and Ahn sitting in their chairs. "We will revisit this another time," he said as he exited.

Ahn observed a series of changes in Kung's expression that he had trouble classifying—puzzlement, sadness, and finally a new resolve marked by narrowed eyelids and clenching of fists. Kung did not comment, but simply walked away.

Ahn stayed in his chair to consider the staggering implications of what had just happened.

First, Kung had implied that his lineage matched the Supreme Leader's and that he knew best what needed to be accomplished.

Second, Ahn had witnessed revelations about the real conditions in his native country that left his heart sinking. Did this regime maintain power through brutal repression by prison camps and other limitations on freedom? Were the restrictions on information—limited radio and television channels and internet, enforcers and informants sprinkled everywhere in the city—an integral part of a desperate system trying to protect itself?

He thought of the occupants of the "labor re-education camps" he had examined after interrogations by the *bowibu.* These were emaciated and neglected human beings. He had been told that they had voluntarily undertaken hunger strikes and had been self-abusive; but were they in fact starved and beaten by their captors?

Ahn shook his head. Thoughts like these were not safe. He would have to turn them off.

His gut tightened and his hands shook as he left the palace. What was coming next?

CHAPTER FORTY-ONE

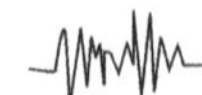

PYONGYANG

OCTOBER 12

General Kung handed his guest a glass of *inpung sul* whiskey and gestured to a leather armchair in front of the office desk. Admiral Han Dae, Leader of the DPRK Navy, lowered his ample frame into it.

"What's important enough to bring me across the city from the admiralty at eight p.m.?" Admiral Han asked. "On a night my driver is off."

Kung sat back, surprised by the antagonism of a man who he had known since military college. He had considered Han a loyal supporter and had maneuvered his rise through the naval ranks as a colleague and friend. "I wanted to review some issues with you in strictest confidence," Kung said. "Do I have your word?"

"About what?"

"About keeping this conversation confidential."

"How can I promise to keep what I don't know confidential?"

Kung looked at his whiskey, then back at Han, and raised his glass. "Let me propose a toast to the safety and protection of the DPRK."

They each took a perfunctory swallow.

"What did you think about the Supreme Leader's basketball ideas?" Kung asked, trying a new tack.

"Why do you ask?" Han's eyes darted around the room as if he were looking for something.

"Don't worry. No surveillance in this office. You may speak freely. I think I understand your opinion, however. What should we do about it?"

"There's nothing to do."

"Nothing at all?" Kung peered into Han's emotionless eyes but could not read what his colleague was thinking.

Han shifted in his chair. "Perhaps we could try to convince the Supreme Leader to change his mind," he said.

"Do you think that will work? You and I go back a long way. Surely we can be honest with each other."

"Of course it won't work."

"So we just sit and let our country and our present lives be destroyed?"

Han set down his glass. "We do not discuss policy without the full council."

"I didn't say that. I just said convincing the Supreme Leader might be difficult. Have you ever thought there might be another way?"

The admiral leaned forward in his chair and said nothing.

Kung interpreted this as interest. "My program to identify sources of nuclear warheads outside our regular channels is moving along."

"Where have you found them?"

"Kazakhstan. I have already sequestered a half dozen Scarab missiles with nuclear payloads."

"Why do you need sources outside our usual supply? Our Russian comrades give us what we ask for."

"It's important to have an independent dealer."

"Why have you not told us about this at the Joint Chiefs' meetings?" The admiral shifted in his chair as if the discussion were making him anxious.

"I wanted to discuss this with you as an old friend first."

"Does the Supreme Leader know about these extra missiles?"

"He approved the program months ago."

"What does this have to do with basketball games? I'm not sure I want to hear this." Han looked at his watch, then at the door.

Kung realized he had limited time. "We have the warheads. Our restriction is the delivery system. We don't have adequate rocket technology to reach the USA."

"For this I had to come halfway across the city? No one knows that fact better than I." Han moved to the edge of his seat, apparently about to leave.

"Suppose we choose another delivery method."

"What would that be?"

"Transport a warhead into the USA, then detonate it."

Han leaned forward. "That's insane. How could you possibly get it into the country? And why would you try?"

"I've figured out a way," Kung said. "And we should do it because would prove our power. China would protect us against retaliation."

Han shook his head, put down his glass, and lifted his bulk from the seat. "I've been worried you might consider some crazy plan like this. The Supreme Leader will never agree to such a move. You exceed your authority even to think about it."

Han stepped to the door. Kung pressed a button under the desk. "You are a danger to our country," Han said as he lumbered toward the exit.

Rhee Sung entered as he left the room. Her petite frame, downcast eyes, and conservative dress modeled the submissive Korean woman. Han paid no attention to her as he bumped her aside, did not react to her grasping of his wrists briefly or look down at her hands. He pushed her out of the way with a gruff "excuse me" and disappeared.

"He seemed in a hurry," Rhee said. She stopped and peeled off her gloves with care not to touch the outside surface. She deposited them in a Ziploc pouch taken from her Louis Vuitton shoulder bag and turned her attention back to Kung.

"What did you use?" Kung asked.

"A sedative that should take about twenty minutes for full absorption. Smeared it on both wrists. I don't even think he noticed my touch. He was in a big hurry."

"Will it be obvious?"

"Not at all. He will drive halfway across the city and his car will simply lose control." She sat in the chair the doomed man had occupied.

"I had a premonition that fox would not agree with us," Kung said. "The traitor implied he would go straight to the Supreme Leader to reveal our plan."

He swallowed the rest of his whiskey, poured another

glass, and looked at his niece for several seconds. "Admiral Han was our last chance to get support from inside the organization. It's just us from here on."

"So? Two against twenty-five million seems about right." She stared at him. "*Samchon*, why are you saying this? Are you worried about my loyalty or resolve? You are like a father to me. I owe you everything."

She sat for a moment. "But perhaps you doubt my skills?" In a split second, she had bounded to a position behind him and had her thumbs ready to gouge out his eyes. "Would you like me to blind you physically? You seem mentally blind. Remember, I have assassinated dozens of our enemies, and no one has ever touched me."

Kung put up his arms in mock surrender. "It's not your loyalty. It's whether I have the right to draw you into this fight. It may be a battle to the death."

She stood back. "This is not about what is right. This is about my family. Our family." She pointed to the palace grounds above them. "If you told me to go up there and assassinate the Supreme Leader, I would do it without hesitation, accepting the death sentence that would go with it."

"We may have to eliminate him, but not yet," Kung said. "The targets I have in mind are much easier."

"MacGregor and his family?"

"Exactly."

"Against the Supreme Leader's wishes?"

"He doesn't understand the stakes."

"I already have them in my sights, and I know their habits. But I thought you had a bigger target in mind."

"The United States?"

"Yes."

"That's still the master plan."

"So why waste time with a scum surgeon and his family?"

"Getting revenge on MacGregor is personal. Either he did something deliberately to our Supreme Leader's brain, or he's incompetent and doesn't understand the side effects of his surgery. He changed our leader's personality. For this, he and his family must die."

Kung downed the rest of the *inpung sul*, savored the burn all the way from his gullet to his belly, and slammed the glass onto the desk.

"You're certain America will retaliate with nuclear weapons if we set off a nuclear warhead?" Rhee asked.

"Yes. The president is a hothead who shoots first and asks later."

"And there may be no later for the USA," Rhee said.

"Exactly," Kung nodded. "After we detonate a nuclear warhead in Boston, the Americans will decide all our talk of reconciliation was a smokescreen. They will direct their nuclear missiles at Pyongyang and try to destroy us. Our government will be safe in the tunnels here."

"Why don't we add other targets—Washington or New York City?"

"No need. One is enough, and Boston is a perfect place. The only brains in the government seem to come from Harvard or MIT." He poured himself another glass.

"The unknown in the equation is our leader. He will have to decide whether to annihilate South Korea in the seconds before the American missiles arrive. I expect he will let go with everything we have."

"Which will make the U.S. wild. It will begin further retaliation, and Russia and China will be bound by the pacts we've made to launch against the United States. A perfect scenario of mutually assured destruction, except we will be safe in the underground tunnels."

She lifted the glass toward her mouth, raised it as if she were going to toast, sniffed, and put it down with a shake of her head. "But you don't think you can count on the Supreme Leader any more?"

Kung shook his head. "After MacGregor's surgery, he talks like a coward."

"Next steps?"

"I know he requisitioned tickets to fly me to Moscow tomorrow. I expect he wants me to witness the capitalist takeover of the city for myself and convince me that is the path we should follow. I'm going to suggest I make a side trip to Kazakhstan to see how former Soviet satellites are thriving. I'll arrange for the warhead there and prepare for a later visit."

"And me?"

"Stay here to make sure nothing changes. Our Supreme Leader will consider you security for my return. You will in fact be my eyes and ears on the ground."

After Rhee left, Kung slept on the leather couch for the rest of the night, anticipating a summons to the Supreme Leader's office early the next morning.

He woke to loudspeakers. They informed every listener that Admiral Han, a great military officer, had died the night before in a tragic car accident. A collision with a tree destroyed his car and mangled his body. The police theorized he had fallen asleep while driving. There was not so much as a whisper of assassination.

Within a few minutes of this announcement a military aide appeared at Kung's door. He announced that the military staff would meet at eleven o'clock in the situation room. The Supreme Leader wanted Kung in his office half an hour before that meeting.

Kung used the time until the meeting to make phone calls, then walked to the executive office.

The Supreme Leader looked as if he had not slept. He did not offer a seat as Kung entered and himself remained seated behind his desk. "I will miss Admiral Han," he began. "He gave good advice and was loyal to our work. That's all I ask of one of my officers. He was, however, more than just an officer. I considered him my friend."

"Mine as well," Kung said. "He and I attended the Moscow Military Academy together. He was a great asset to our armed forces."

"His death does not affect my reason for seeing you before the general staff meeting. I have been thinking about our conversation yesterday. You need to observe for yourself what I was speaking about. I would like you to visit Moscow as well as meet with some of our colleagues in the Kremlin to consolidate our relationships. I understand it is a world-class city now and would appreciate your impressions."

"I will go," Kung said with a bow of his head. "Might I suggest a brief visit to Kazakhstan as well? It seems to be the model of a progressive state emerging from Soviet rule."

The Supreme Leader looked at him with a quizzical expression. "I expected you to protest my request to leave Pyongyang, but you ask to extend it?"

"I am here to serve," Kung said.

The Supreme Leader hesitated a few minutes, then nodded his head. "I will grant your request. I've arranged for three days of official meetings for you get to know the Moscow leadership. Adding two days in Nur-Sultan would not be a problem. You leave tomorrow."

CHAPTER FORTY-TWO

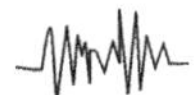

NUR-SULTAN, KAZAKHSTAN

OCTOBER 19

Kung stepped onto Kazakh soil ready to give lip service to the Supreme Leader's plan.

His major objective, however, was to implement his own.

He had despised his visit to Moscow. Following the itinerary prescribed for him, he met with a dozen mid-level officials. "We are moving toward the same kind of détente with the West you have achieved," he lied. He surveyed the capitalist success that sprouted everywhere in the revived city. He felt ashamed.

Mother Russia had birthed the DPRK. Modern Russia had betrayed its ideals. The communist system had become a capitalist oligarchy.

He saw some evidence of the same tendency in Nur-Sultan, but it lagged far behind Moscow. For the most part, it maintained the massive Soviet architectural style of the mid-twentieth century without dilution by modern designers. In the main square of the city, the opera house, ballet theater, and symphony hall rose as glorious examples of Soviet architecture.

The hotel Kung had been booked into was not the same. Shaped like a twisting pear, its façade of glass and metal contrasted with the stolid stone of its neighbors. He considered it a travesty, but the guests seemed to feel it symbolized the new Nur-Sultan.

He found the note on the desk as he checked in.

Meet me at two p.m. in the bar.

As Kung entered the bar exactly at two, the man who rose to greet him looked like a business executive. An Armani suit, crisp white shirt, red Ferragamo tie, and Italian leather shoes made him ready for any corporate board room.

He checked Kung's face against a smartphone picture and asked him to touch the pad with his index fingertip, confirming his fingerprint identity. Apparently satisfied, he ordered Kung to follow him, sweeping the room with his eyes and phone as he left.

He led Kung outside the front entrance to a large black Mercedes sedan and climbed in, indicating that Kung should sit in the back. "Don't worry about coats; it's warm in the car, and we're not going to get out. No meeting place in that hotel is secure. If someone questions you about this excursion, you can tell your Supreme Leader that a thoughtful businessman offered to take you for a ride to show you the real Nur-Sultan."

As they sped along the well-paved streets, he said, "You are right on every count. First, there are many Soviet nuclear warheads that have been unregistered and forgotten. I have made my business tracking them down and am pleased to tell you we have found what you are looking for. I'm sure your Supreme Leader would be happy to know we have what he wants. Second, there are indeed excellent plastic surgeons here who do not ask questions. Third, it is nothing to delay a shipment at the airport for a few hours if you want to add something to the cargo."

"Where are we going now?" Kung asked.

"I assume you want to examine the merchandise. I should also tell you something about it. These warheads have been removed from their rockets; they must be placed where you want them. That makes them much smaller than the total rocket dimension."

"How long are they?"

"About two meters."

"Perfect," Kung said.

"Second, their detonation mechanism is very robust. I will provide you with a trigger that looks like a watch. You can set it at the time you wish, but once it has begun its countdown nothing can stop it. No cutting a red or blue wire to"—he made air brackets with his fingers—"'save the world.'"

"Excellent. How long can the countdown be?"

"Up to twelve hours. Third, and perhaps most important, please do not think about eliminating me after we have finished the transaction. That automatically triggers a notice to be sent to the International Nuclear Regulatory agency about our arrangement, precisely which warheads you obtained, and when and how you obtained them. Blows my cover, but if I'm dead I don't really care. Do we have a deal?"

"I believe we do," Kung said, allowing a smile to flicker across his face.

CHAPTER FORTY-THREE

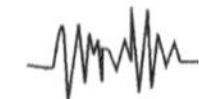

PYONGYANG

NOVEMBER 13

After he returned from Kazakhstan, Kung felt greater and greater disagreement with the direction his country was taking.

Cultural exchanges, DPRK leaders attending state events in Seoul, photographs of the Supreme Leader smiling beside the President of South Korea. These and other disgraceful souvenirs sat on his desk as a reminder of the depths his country had sunk to. There was even talk of meeting with the president of the United States.

This was more than a political sea change for Kung. It was a betrayal of all his fundamental social and political beliefs. His resentment grew at the leader of his country, at the neurosurgeon who had somehow messed that man up, at the rapacious capitalist system that seemed to be sweeping the world. Most of all, his hatred for the United States changed from smoldering coals to white-hot flame.

His discontent deepened because he now had a concrete alternative to these soft concessions to western culture. He stopped making suggestions or comments at the joint chiefs' meetings and occupied himself arranging for the change he considered inevitable. He lost no sleep over it. That was not his way.

When the Supreme Leader ordered him to clear a day to spend together, he realized his time had come.

In his underground headquarters, Kung passed the whole night preparing for the next day's meeting with the Supreme Leader. He had the premonition that it would be a difficult conversation wherever and whenever it took place. He electronically transferred ten million U.S. dollars to the fifty million he had already sequestered outside the borders of the DPRK. He arranged to have guards loyal to him accompany him all day. He felt ready for the summons just as the Supreme Leader's office ordered him to proceed to the front door of the Palace.

A White Hawk helicopter sat on the helipad ready to deploy. The sleek silhouette of the chopper, modified for quietness and smoothness of ride, drew a smirk from Kung. He had acquired it for the Supreme Leader's use and knew it well.

He also knew the guards assigned to this aircraft. All were loyal to him. One of them assigned to do security clearance took him behind a screen, ostensibly to check him. With a knowing smile, that guard slipped a Tokarev TT pistol and suppressor into the shoulder holster Kung had worn, then loudly announced him clean and ready to ride.

Kung anticipated that these men would follow onto the helicopter as security. Instead, the Supreme Leader, already strapped in place beside the pilot, stopped them from climbing in and gestured for Kung to move to the second row.

As he took his assigned seat, Kung noted three soldiers in full combat gear, including parachute packs in the plane's rear cabin space. He did not know these men, nor did he understand their mission. Perhaps the Supreme Leader was going to display some new military maneuver. They took up all the seats in the chopper, so his men were left standing on the ground.

The Supreme Leader gave the thumbs up to the pilot and the bird rose into the sky. Its modified rotors whirred in silence as they ascended. There was no need for them to shout to make themselves heard inside the twenty-million-dollar marvel.

After ten minutes they hovered over Kaeson, on the border between the DPRK and South Korea. Below them they could see the forested region of the DMZ. The south lay to their left, the north to the right. The Supreme Leader pointed to the 100× sighting telescope. "Look at the two Koreas spread beneath you. Tell me what you see."

He did not give Kung a chance to answer but continued as the general adjusted the eyepieces. "When I look through that telescope at our country, my country, I see empty roads, fake cities, and bare fields. Across the border in South Korea, I see thriving industry, commerce, and agriculture."

"We'll get there. It just takes time," Kung said.

"We've had three generations, decades in which the countries around us have become economic and social powerhouses."

"You forget that we fight crippling trade restrictions from the oppressive United States and Europe," Kung replied.

"It may be time to talk about lifting those restrictions," the Supreme Leader said. He directed the pilot to turn north, toward the Chinese border.

"That would mean changing our policies."

"Perhaps we should do that. Russia, China, and Vietnam have all seen the light."

"And have betrayed the cause." Kung begun to feel anger. He did not want to discuss this topic.

"They're thriving. We are not."

Kung took a deep breath and decided on a different approach. He used his most reasonable and persuasive voice. "Dear Respected, think of your family. Saviors of the DPRK. Your divine legacy."

"Address me as Supreme Leader." No mistaking the angry and decisive tone of that remark. "My father and grandfather thought they had the right way. It didn't work."

"Didn't work?" Kung stared, as if seeing his leader for the first time.

"The Soviet Empire showed us the way," the Supreme Leader said. "Modernizing our means of production and political system is the only way to rescue our people."

Kung turned his head away with set jaw and clenched fists. This was treason, coming from the very man who was supposed to embody the system. Out of the corner of his eye he assessed the soldiers sitting at the rear of the cabin. Could they hear any of this? Who were they? They looked like active military, but he did not know them. And the pilot? Not one of the men he had selected. *Best to back off a little.*

"I'm aware of Moscow's recent growth. I saw it during my visit."

The Supreme Leader gave him the smile that glowed from so many propaganda posters. "All right. We agree on that.

Let's talk nuclear weapons." He turned back to his MacBook Air. "Do you know the computer game *Thermonuclear War*?"

Kung shook his head in disgust. "Video games are for children."

"Adults can learn a lot from them. I've played it many times. Every scenario ends in world destruction."

"I live in the real world, not some computer fantasy," Kung said. "And you're forgetting our tunnels. They will protect us."

"I don't think so. I've just received a report from our engineering group. The tunnels are old and eroding; the consultants say they would collapse under a direct hit. They have several weakened sections. If any segment were compromised, the entire tunnel network would become a radioactive death trap."

The Supreme Leader looked out the window, where the northern border of the DPRK began to be visible. "I am now convinced that the only way to win the nuclear game is not to play it."

Kung said nothing, trying to keep the fury and disappointment from his face. His leader had become a pawn of the West.

The East China Sea appeared on the horizon. "We've just flown across our entire country. Did you notice the barren fields? The empty cities? Our productivity is far below what it should be."

"The people are lazy and obstinate," Kung said.

"And abused. I've listened to some of the broadcasts of our citizens who have escaped to the West. Their stories are terrible."

"What do you mean?" Kung asked.

"Starvation, beatings, rape while they were in re-education camps in our country. Children without arms or legs left to fend for themselves."

Kung's pulse pounded. "That's American propaganda."

"I don't think so. I'm sure you're aware of these conditions. I was not."

Kung hesitated, deciding whether this was the time. He felt for the pistol his guard had slipped him as they finished the pre-embarkation inspection. Was the DPRK ready for a coup?

He decided to provide one more chance. "What do you expect?" he said. "That's the only way to maintain order and achieve the society we want."

The Supreme Leader looked through the telescope again; "Kung, what if we are wrong? Across that sea is Japan, a country destroyed in the second world war, now one of the world's great powers."

"What's that got to do with anything?"

"Japan accepted help and emerged a big winner. Shouldn't we do the same?"

Kung put his head in his hands, then stared at the Supreme Leader. He began speaking with as much control as he could muster, but he knew his tone was louder than it should be. "I told you yesterday, and I'm telling you today. You will not be able to control what happens. You and all those around you will be killed. There will be civil war. South Korea and the USA will walk all over us."

"And?"

"And everything your father and grandfather worked for

will be lost. You will be a failure, a man who couldn't control his destiny. You will fulfill the impression we had of you in school. Weak. Pathetic."

"And the strong move would be nuclear attack?"

"Yes."

"That's insane. We just went through all those scenarios."

Kung pounded his right fist into his left palm. "Who cares about a computer simulation? This is real life. A nuclear explosion will get us back on track."

He continued in a more controlled voice. "It's that American surgeon. We never should have let him touch you. You're not thinking straight. He messed with your brain. We should have killed him and his family right after the surgery. If I get the chance, I'll eliminate him as well as the city he lives in. Boston would be a great nuclear target."

The Supreme Leader asked quietly. "And why do you think I should listen to you?"

"I know more about what is right for my country than you ever will. You've been nursed for thirty-five years in the palace or away at school in Europe. You're a child in a grown-up world."

Something snapped in Kung, an explosion of years of suppressed anger, fear, and resentment. He pulled out his pistol and aimed it at his chief's head.

"Are you serious?" the Supreme Leader said without flinching. "You won't get out alive."

"Neither will you." Kung squeezed the trigger.

A click.

Ripped from his seat and thrown to the floor, Kung found himself face down, arms pinned, back flattened by the weight of three soldiers. A paratrooper boot kept his head down, pancaked against the floor.

"You failed the loyalty test," the Supreme Leader said. "We emptied the chamber before your friend handed you the gun."

The soldiers wrestled Kung toward the doorway, which now gaped open. "You think I've become soft." The Supreme Leader gestured with a wave. "Not for some things. Goodbye, General."

Kung flailed, twisted, and thrashed, using elbows, feet, and head as weapons as the soldiers inched him toward the blue sky.

Strong as he was, he could not prevail against the combined effort of three paratroopers in combat gear. He gradually lost ground and saw the opening loom ahead of him.

At the edge of the broadening expanse of sky, he collapsed to his knees, grasped the closest soldier and, with a surge of adrenaline, propelled the man with him. They hurtled over the edge of the open helicopter door as one body.

CHAPTER FORTY-FOUR

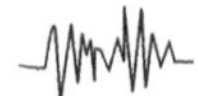

DPRK NORTH BORDER

NOVEMBER 13

Kung grabbed the paratrooper by the legs as he slammed out of the helicopter. He calculated he had ten seconds before their rocketing descent would be unrecoverable.

His weight pulled the soldier into foot-first free fall. In three seconds, Kung had hauled himself up the man's body toward the parachute pack. His victim twisted to dislodge his unwelcome rider, flailing his arms toward the parachute cord.

Bucking against the gravitational pull and hurricane-level airstream, Kung snatched the combat knife from the man's belt as he climbed. He grabbed the soldier's helmet with his left hand, held tight with his legs, and slit the man's throat with a thrust that ripped through both carotids and trachea.

Torrents of blood erupted in diminishing pulses, arcing through the air and spattering Kung's face.

As blood, breath, and life ebbed from the paratrooper's body, the soldier's chest deflated against the straps of the parachute pack. Kung rammed his left arm through the shoulder strap of the backpack, then ripped the parachute release cord with his right hand.

Before the chute opened, he worked his right arm under the dead man's right shoulder strap. He braced himself, tensing every muscle in his arms and shoulders.

The impact of parachute deployment almost ripped off Kung's arms as it arrested the fall, whipping him and the lifeless paratrooper back into the sky for a moment. His grip held. With the slowing of his fall he could hear again.

The roar of the helicopter became more distant. He looked skyward for a moment. His victim's chute had opened perfectly, but two other chutes now appeared silhouetted against the sky. At their descent rate, the other two paratroopers would hit the ground shortly after he did.

He looked downward at mountains covered with trees, and in the distance to the north, a small city. Almost certainly Sinuiju, a far outpost of the DPRK on the Chinese border. He would make that the meeting place.

With its payload weighing almost two hundred kilograms, the chute hurtled toward earth much faster than it should have. Kung knew that a jumper normally meets the ground at five meters per second. He estimated they would hit at twice that speed. An advantage, since he would outfall the other parachutists. A problem, since impact would be even more bone-crunching than usual. He could not afford even an ankle sprain.

He identified a clearing in the trees two hundred meters north of their projected touchdown. If they could not maneuver the parachute to land there, he would end his life skewered by the upper branches of a pine tree. At that velocity, a tree limb would penetrate his body like a lance.

Lesser men might imagine themselves screaming in agony as their viscera spilled onto the leafy boughs below. Kung allowed no such images. Climbing onto the shoulders of the dead soldier, he pulled back on the parachute ropes, straining to redirect his trajectory.

Nothing happened. The upper tree branches raced toward them. He mustered all his strength, bowing his body against the shoulders of the flaccid companion he rode. He could feel a gradual shift in the direction of descent.

Not enough to clear the trees.

He could pull no harder.

A gust of wind hurtling down the pass between mountains caught the parachute and lifted it at the last moment, changing its direction enough to clear the upper branches of the trees bordering the clearing. Seconds later, still riding on the paratrooper's shoulders, Kung felt the crushing force of touchdown.

The paratrooper's body took most of the impact, accordioning like a rag doll. By the time the spine had telescoped into itself, ramming vertebra into the chest cavity and collapsing the skull, Kung had already jumped, rolling as he landed.

He harvested the rifle pack, knife, and pistol from the dead soldier and left the parachute to flop and bounce.

The returning helicopter rained a fusillade of bullets into the clearing. Kung reached cover before any of them found its mark. He dove behind a fallen tree as a volley tore the parachute and dead soldier to shreds

A few seconds later his stolen AK-47 was ready to fire. He watched the two paratroopers above him reach the tree line.

One did not clear it. Kung heard that man's dying screams as the branches impaled him.

The other was luckier. He steered himself into the clearing and almost made it to the ground alive. Kung's well-placed shot though the visor blew out his brain before he landed.

No point in wasting ammunition on other parts of the body. Kung knew well the vulnerable points in the armor of his soldiers. Helmets may protect the head, Kevlar the chest and abdomen, but the eye shield was only a defense against glare, not a Type 58 bullet.

The helicopter doubled back and strafed the clearing. Kung knew it would not try to land. There was no one remaining in it who could create a ground attack. Instead, the Supreme Leader would recruit other helicopters, send reinforcements to block the border, and intensify a land and air search for his rogue general.

After two more passes with ineffective fusillades, the helicopter lifted away and disappeared.

Kung checked his body for fractures or deep lacerations. Many scrapes and bruises. One ankle pained with each step, but the tight combat boots he wore would keep swelling in check.

He diagnosed minor injuries only and set out for Sinuiji village, traveling only under cover of the tree canopy.

At one juncture he came across the two-lane highway that connected Sinuiji with the rest of his country. Newly established military barriers closed the road, with soldiers standing to intercept any motor traffic. The Supreme Leader must have already put out a bulletin for his capture.

He turned deeper into the forest. Smoke rose in the distance, perhaps two kilometers from his position. As he approached, he spotted a house hidden behind a hill. He entered the small clearing around it with caution, sidling up to a window at the back of the house. He peered through the corner of the grimy window, expecting to see a single farmer or a small family.

Two soldiers knelt on the floor going through the pockets of an elderly man lying before them. The man had a bullet through his chest, with blood pooling on the ground.

Kung smashed the window with the butt of his rifle. The soldiers looked up with expressions somewhere between annoyance and surprise. He shot the first man between the eyes and the second through the heart. Their faces relaxed into blank stares as they collapsed to the ground.

He inspected the house, establishing that he was the only living occupant, then searched the pockets of the soldiers, satisfying himself that they were DPRK army. He took their pistols and arranged them as if they had shot each other. Any investigators would not bother to match bullet with weapon.

From the nearest man he removed a cell phone, dialed a number, spoke briefly, and smashed the phone with his heel. He then sat in a corner to wait, considering the next steps of his plan. He had beaten the odds by surviving the helicopter drop, but an attempt to cross the river might well fail, as it did for hundreds of comrades each year. Failure would mean certain death. Painful death. His plan would have to be perfect.

An hour later he heard a car motor. He slid out the back door of the farmhouse, climbed the low branch of a tree at the edge of the clearing, and watched the vehicle break into the open space.

On the outside, the vehicle looked like a typical UAZ-469, manufactured by Ulanovsky Automobilny Zavod in Russia. The model was an enclosed jeep known for its all-wheel drive.

Inside, however, he knew it to be quite different. He himself had requisitioned twenty of these vehicles for use in remote areas of the DPRK.

He knew, for example, that it had centimeter-thick Kevlar chassis and fuel tank protection, bulletproof windows, and military grade run-flat tires. It could handle any terrain with ease. Best of all, it had been sealed to be an amphibious vehicle. The manufacturers claimed it could reach fifteen knots an hour on the open sea using propellers mounted on its rear axles.

Two other features made it a very special jeep. A rocket launcher filled its trunk, and Rhee Sung smiled from the driver's seat.

Kung dropped from the tree and approached, showing his pleasure at seeing his niece again.

"Where to?" she asked with a smile, as matter-of-fact as if she were a taxi driver in the center of Pyongyang.

They traveled along forest paths inaccessible to any regular car, always protected by trees and always heading north toward the river that separated their country from China. They saw no troops, but occasionally heard vehicles on a roadway in the distance. By nightfall the car crouched in the forest at the edge of the Yalu River between Sinuiju and Dandong. Kung and Rhee rested inside, ready to make their move.

CHAPTER FORTY-FIVE

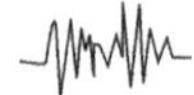

DPRK/CHINA BORDER

NOVEMBER 13

"There's a bridge at Sinuiju." Rhee Sung said as they parked in the forest fifty meters from the road. "We could try crossing the river there after dark, pushing our way through the barriers."

"The guards will be on alert," Kung said, shaking his head, "and they will not hesitate to kill first and ask questions later. We'll use Grandmother Plan instead."

He descended from the car and crawled to the edge of the road. Extending himself prone behind a small rise in the ground, he observed every movement of the guards. Despite the rock-strewn frozen ground, the rotting smell of decomposing leaves on the forest floor, and the ants that skittered over his hands and face, he remained immobile for an hour.

Satisfied that the soldiers monitoring the road passed every twenty minutes, he slithered back to the car.

When he knocked on the window and Rhee turned on the interior compartment light, he stepped back in astonishment. Even though her transformation was part of the plan they had created, she had completely modified her appearance. She had cut her hair short and changed into a white shirt, pants, and tie. She wore no makeup, and some of the acne and imperfections of her facial surface could now be seen. She looked like a young man, smooth-faced but passable.

"Good work," he said. "They probably won't have a bulletin out for you, at least for a day or so. The authorities will be watching for a single middle-aged Korean man or perhaps a young woman and older male companion."

At six a.m., just after the guards had passed, Rhee drove the jeep toward the river's edge through piles of fallen leaves and patches of snow. She flicked the lever to amphibious mode, cut the engine, and let the vehicle roll in neutral down the hill. It slid into the Yalu with a gentle splash. The current and momentum carried them toward the center of the river.

"We'll see how truly amphibious this prototype is," Kung said. "I requisitioned it from the Russians for use in remote marshes of the DPRK. I'm not sure it's been tested on an open body of deep water."

The atmosphere was foggy, and the moon seemed reluctant to show itself. A few flurries of snow and freezing rain whipped across the river. Kung thanked his ancestors that the night had decided to cooperate in cloaking them.

He hesitated to start the propellers because of the noise they would make, hoping momentum would propel them far enough into the river to be out of hearing range of the shore before they had to initiate propulsion. He realized in a few minutes that they were being swept out to sea by the current.

He estimated that three hundred meters lay between his country and the China shore, but that gap was not closing.

For sixty seconds they floated in the dark, with the stench of sewage filling their nostrils despite the cold air and icy water lapping at the car. A few meters offshore the current picked up significantly and Kung felt the car drifting toward the mouth of the river and its opening to the Yellow Sea.

Gray fingers of dawn infiltrated the darkness. He could make out an area two hundred meters ahead where cliffs replaced the gentle slope of the shore. After that they would not be able to get off the river.

"We have to start the engine," he said.

The propellers roared into action as the amphibious vehicle began to make headway across the current. The motor's whine shattered the silence of the night.

At the sound, flashlight beams from the shore played on the river but did not reach them. They could hear shouting and rifle shots, but none riled the water around the vehicle.

For a few seconds Kung thought they would make it to the Chinese shore in safety. Although he never allowed himself to be relaxed, he felt a touch of relief.

The sound of a motor on the river changed that.

It had to be a DPRK patrol boat.

A searchlight swept back and forth across the water half a kilometer away. On the deck beside the light he could make out several silhouettes as the vessel approached.

"Point the car to head directly toward that flat area on the shore," Kung said.

He climbed into the rear seat and folded down its back

to access the trunk. Fumbling at first, he identified the lid release by touch, popped it, and lifted the rocket launcher into position. His fingers almost froze in the unheated compartment.

By the time a swath of searchlight approached the car, he had the missile in the firing chamber with the muzzle aimed midships at the water line of the patrol boat.

Bright light from the searchlight spilled into the jeep's interior, throwing Rhee's face into shadowy contrast, then passing beyond. Kung could make out the patrol boat's silhouette against the increasing light of dawn.

Before the searchlight could sweep back to illuminate them again, Kung pulled the release trigger. A roar and flash erupted from the car's trunk. He could see the jet-stream of the missile as it sped toward the patrol vessel.

The rebound from the launch rocketed the car straight ahead, not toward the China shore. Rhee yanked the steering wheel to the right, almost dislodging Kung from his position.

The sound of punctured metal fractured the night. The boat's searchlight flipped into the sky and stared at the clouds, unmoving. Kung heard shouts of panicked men, then the sucking sound of water pouring into a cavity. Random shots peppered the air. All missed the car.

The shadow of the patrol vessel seemed to shiver, then slide toward the river's surface. As the patrol boat disappeared into the depths of the Yalu River, the amphibious vehicle emerged from the water onto the China shore.

They drove along a deserted street in the earliest haze of dawn, finding a suitable site where a sloping hill led to a cliff at the river's edge. Removing their belongings and any other identifying material, they directed the car back toward the river, opened the doors with the gear in neutral, and pushed. With gradual acceleration, it bounced across the dirt and rock that separated the road from the cliff and rocketed into the abyss.

Kung watched from the edge as it smashed into the water, swirled in the current, and began to sink as the passenger compartment and trunk filled. The speeding current carried it into the middle of the stream, and as the sun rose, the cab disappeared under the Yalu surface.

Two hours later a sad-looking Chinese pair checked in for the South China Airlines flight heading from Dandong to Beijing.

"I'm taking my revered grandmother to Beijing for medical consultation," the young man explained to the airline agent in perfect Mandarin. "She has an inoperable cancer."

The boy was clean-shaven, almost feminine in appearance. He appeared as mixed race as his identity papers suggested, probably Mongolian.

His grandmother was impenetrable: hard of hearing, bent over almost double with her folds of cloth and traditional head covering, unsteady as she relied on her walking stick to provide stability. Any attempt to get close to her was repelled by body odor that turned even the most determined security guard away.

They hobbled toward the door leading to the bus that would take them to the plane. Seeing a pair of soldiers standing at the boarding gate, the young man asked why there was so much security.

"We're searching for a traitor from the DPRK last seen in this area," the man said, and motioned them on. "Helping out our comrades."

In the airplane, the attendant moved them from their assigned seat to the back of the plane. Seventy minutes later, they hobbled through the Beijing Airport.

"Do we have to keep this up?" Rhee asked. "I think we overdid the body odor."

"Yes," Kung said. "Perhaps you could buy some perfume for your nose. We could requisition a jitney to take us to our gate. Walking in this position is very difficult."

"Couldn't we just be normal?"

"No. They will have circulated pictures of me and the scar is hard to conceal even with makeup. I could not get fake ID's that had a scar on them. We continue as we are until we are in our apartment in Nur-Sultan."

Three hours later, having been driven to their gate, they boarded an Nur-Sultan Airlines plane bound for Kazakhstan. There were no special guards and they passed through the immigration officials in the arrivals area without difficulty.

CHAPTER FORTY-SIX

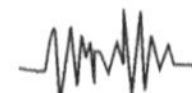

KAZAKHSTAN

NOVEMBER 19

For the first five days in Kazakhstan, General Kung and his niece remained in the apartment he had leased on his previous visit. He scanned the news daily for news about a rogue DPRK army officer and found nothing.

He decided they could proceed. On November nineteenth, Kung presented himself to a plastic surgeon known to work at the margins of the law. The doctor spoke no Korean, so they conversed in English.

"This will need repair," the surgeon said as he marked Kung's forehead scar. "Will use incisions here and here to change contour. Filler in cheeks to diminish effect of high cheekbones. Straighten broken nose. For hair, I suggest you shave head completely and use wigs."

"Fine," Kung said, practicing a new humility. His hands clenched and opened as he considered that this man would decide what changes would get him through facial recognition paradigms at border points.

"Two other things. Demeanor is as important as specific facial detail. You look like man eager to change impression you leave. I don't know why. I don't want to know why. I suggest you stop weight training, lose thirty pounds, and learn to slouch."

"The other thing?" Kung asked.

"I take payment up front. American dollars only. Fifty thousand."

"Done. Can we begin tomorrow? Here's twenty thousand to start."

The next day he lay with local anesthesia while the surgeon carved his face. He refused general anesthesia, hating the idea of losing control.

After three hours of surgery, the heat and brilliance of the operating light irritated him. Rivulets of blood dribbled down his neck. The smell of alcohol prep solution and blood filled his nostrils. The instruments created scraping and sliding noises that seemed to come from deep in his skull.

The nose was particularly difficult. Kung grimaced as the septum was broken and reset with a *crack* and lancinating pain. The surgeon appeared to take particular pleasure in this maneuver.

Kung remembered that when he watched Rhee break the surgeon's neck the next day. She came up behind the unsuspecting victim while Kung was handing over the final payment for surgery. They reclaimed the money and poured a bottle of cheap vodka into the doctor's mouth, spilling it liberally over his clothes. Kung dragged the body to the top of the stairs and pushed. They had to step carefully to avoid the twisted corpse as they walked out the door.

During the week of facial healing, Kung didn't go out in public. On the eighth day they drove to Pavlodar, a town almost on the Russian border. The journey took seven hours along highway A17, but the result was everything he had hoped for.

The man who he had met in Nur-Sultan welcomed him as they stepped out of the car. He looked at Kung's face and grimaced.

"I have heard that there might have been some complications. You look beaten up," the man said. "What happened?"

"Irrelevant. No complications. I want to see the merchandise," Kung said.

"We've been saving it for you—a warhead from an OTR-23 Oka. But I have to insist on blindfolding you until we get to the site."

Kung was not a man of deep faith. He tolerated the ten-minute blind ride poorly. It was worth it, however. When he opened his eyes, his guide stood beside a warhead two meters in height.

Kung almost smiled, went over to it, and rubbed its metal skin as if he could make it purr.

"Can you have it at the airport by six tomorrow morning along with the other material I asked for?"

"No problem. My men will be in a white Foton Tunland. The package will be in the back. They will not know what it contains."

Kung and Rhee arrived at the cargo terminal of Nursultan Nazarbayev International Airport at six a.m. the next morning. A wintry wind whipped snow along the tarmac. The sub-zero air was tainted with diesel fuel.

Rhee spotted the van first, sitting with lights off beside the main door to the building. Kung flashed their headlights, received a return flash, and parked alongside it. Rhee descended and plastered a thick envelope to the terminal door.

A new car approached. The driver got out, unlocked and opened the door to the cargo terminal, took the envelope, checked quickly to confirm its contents, and drove away. He did not look up at either of the other vehicles.

"Twenty thousand tenge?" Rhee asked Kung.

"Yes. Enough to be sure we are undisturbed for three hours."

Two men from the truck joined them to enter the terminal. Kung had already confirmed that it was located far enough from the passenger area to allow activity without suspicion. He led them to a pair of crates addressed to an imaging center in Nur-Sultan.

He tore open the smaller of the two crates, exposing an MRI patient table. "Remove the side panel," he instructed. The men did so, exposing the empty space under the table.

"Now we need to reinforce the walls." He pointed to six lead slabs on a cart that Rhee had rolled behind them. "Cover every internal surface with these panels and fix them in place. They have been cut to fit perfectly."

The men quickly fixed the lead in place with bolts.

"Now you can take a cigarette break. Come back in twenty minutes."

The men disappeared. Rhee wheeled a cart carrying a package two meters long and two-thirds of a meter in diameter. She removed the wrapping like a game show hostess, bowed, and sprang aside to reveal the Cyrillic lettering and radioactive danger label marking the warhead.

"A beauty," she commented. "Amazing such a small thing can do so much damage. Do they make it in a pocketbook model?"

Together they rolled the warhead from the cart into the space they had just lined with lead. They packed the rest of the cavity with Styrofoam and pushed the side of the table that had been removed back into place.

Rhee took a Geiger counter from the cart and passed it around the table. Only background radioactivity registered.

"Perfect," Kung said. "Now we ship it to Harbor Hospital in time for it to be our special Valentine's gift to America."

The men reappeared. "Screw the side panel on again," Kung ordered. "I don't want to see any visible sign that we've been here."

He was impressed by the result. He gave each of the men an envelope thicker than the terminal manager's. They ripped their envelopes open, looked at a sheaf of thousand-tenge notes, and stuffed them into their back pockets with wide smiles.

"Do not speak of this to anyone," Kung said.

They nodded and jostled each other in the rush to get back to their pickup truck.

"Do you trust them to stay quiet?" Rhee asked.

"Of course not."

"Good. I cut their brake cable when I brought the package in. They should have an short ride on the high-speed freeway to Nur-Sultan."

CHAPTER FORTY-SEVEN

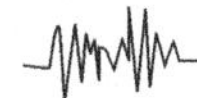

BOSTON

DECEMBER 10

Mac spent his first three months back from North Korea having nightmares about his abduction. These faded by December. The continuous challenges of surgery, teaching, research, and family overfilled his day and made sleep possible.

He even forgot to wonder about the seven-tesla MRI he had been promised. When it had not appeared by Thanksgiving, he assumed it was not coming and was glad he had not told anyone about it.

In mid-December, he was working on an NIH grant application when Tony Whitemore barged into his office unannounced.

"Guess what!" Whittemore said, looking excited and waving a sheet of paper.

"What?" Mac made no attempt to hide his annoyance at being interrupted.

"This is notification of a seven-tesla MRI machine donated to the hospital by the Korean-American Friendship Association. It will be here in ten days. The donors make a big point of how impressed they are by your research work in hypothalamic hamartomas and specifically say you should have first dibs on its use. You made one hell of an impression in Seoul!"

"What if I don't want to accept it?" Memories of Kung and the abduction rose in Mac's mind.

Whitemore put the papers down. "Are you kidding? You have no voice in this. A high-field MRI will make us the leading brain imaging center in the city. You've been badgering me for months about getting one. Now it appears, no strings attached!"

"But I don't feel right about it."

Whitemore rubbed his hands enthusiastically. "Well, I know how I feel about it. Fabulous. And it's free." He paused. "Of course, we're going to have to leave it on the loading dock for a couple of months until we find space. I will also have to push through the Determination of Need and all the regulatory stuff. I may need your help."

"It brings back some uncomfortable memories for me."

"Tough. I'll let you know when it arrives," Whitemore said and left.

Ten days later Mac watched a twelve-wheeler Peterbilt maneuver into Bay Four of Harbor Hospital's loading dock. Brian Mancuso, a slender man with thick glasses who was in charge of imaging equipment, joined him.

Whitemore arrived just as a crane lowered two boxes onto the receiving area. The skids groaned under the weight of the crates.

"Why does it come in two shipping boxes?" Whitemore asked.

"One is the magnet, the other the table for patients to be moved in and out of the bore," Mac said.

"Can our floor take the load? They look heavy." Whitemore asked.

"We'll have to pick a site that can," Mancuso answered.

"We have lots of time," Whitemore said. "The paperwork will take at least a month. While we're waiting, we can give the press weekly updates on our progress—great publicity to string them along. Speaking of which, we invited several members of the press here today, and one of our own cameras is going to record this for posterity. Shall we?"

Straightening his tie and making sure his hard hat was on straight, he moved to the center of the loading dock as the press cameras collected on the other side of the dock began to roll. He beckoned for Mac to join him.

"Good morning, ladies and gentlemen. I'm Dr. Tony Whitemore, chief medical officer of Harbor Hospital. I'm delighted to welcome you to the arrival of the newest addition to our imaging center. This high-resolution scanner will allow us to image the body with unparalleled detail."

He took off his spectacles and peered at the audience as if he couldn't see anything. "With the usual three-tesla MR imaging, the kind most hospitals use now, we can see structures maybe up to three millimeters. Kind of like looking at the world without a good set of spectacles."

He put his glasses back on. "With this seven-tesla machine our capacity to view the brain increases hugely. We can examine brain tracts, visualize brain metabolism, and use functional MR imaging to test speech and movement with unparalleled efficiency. We can also image much faster.

This device underscores the international reach of Harbor Hospital, as it is funded in part by our colleagues in South Korea. We have Dr. Duncan MacGregor to thank for this, someone whose vision and persistence we admire."

Mac didn't hear the rest of Whitemore's speech because he had already started back into the hospital before it was finished. He chuckled a little as he glanced back at Whitemore trying to locate him.

CHAPTER FORTY-EIGHT

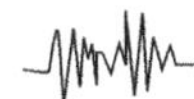

BROOKLINE

FEBRUARY 11

Mac began to have flashbacks of his North Korea experience after the new year. When he looked at his children, he thought of the video segments he had been allowed to watch while being held captive. He panicked again at how close the family had been to disaster without knowing it. And he had the premonition that something terrible was about to happen again.

He sometimes woke up drenched in sweat, and his new headaches seemed to be worsening.

At breakfast on February 11, he listened impatiently while Maggie bubbled about her Korea project for school. "Can't you think of something else to talk about?" he growled before he considered what he was saying.

His daughter ran sobbing from the table. Lauren sent Peter to be with her, then turned to Mac. "What's going on? Maggie begins an innocent conversation about Korea and you blow up at her."

"It's just work pressure." Mac could see she was close to tears.

"No, it's not. You always work under pressure. I know

you well enough to recognize that this is different. Something else is going on."

"I-I can't talk about it."

"What do you mean you can't talk about it? Remember me? I'm your wife. I thought we had no secrets from each other." She paused. "Are you having an affair?"

Mac shook his head, startled. "Good God, no. How could you ever think that? You and the children mean everything to me. Please don't even think that's possible."

"Good. Whatever it is, you need to take time off to work it out. Other staff can cover your practice. You have to get to the root of the problem."

"I know the root. It's the Korea business."

"How? You had a great meeting and we had a wonderful time. Are you angry that the family enjoyed themselves without you?" She put her hand over her mouth. "I'm sorry. It's just that everything seemed so great at the meeting. And to top it all off, you got a huge research donation and a seven-tesla MRI. Where's the problem in all that?"

"Yeah, the machine. Now that I've got it I don't want it. There's something wrong about it."

"Let the hospital administration worry about that. Your job is to get some help with whatever is bothering you." She looked at her watch. "I've got to get the children to school. Please tell me you'll think about it—taking care of yourself, I mean."

"I will."

Mac sat dazed as the family left. He had no idea how much his growing anxiety was affecting those around him.

Instead of driving directly into the hospital, he took half an hour to walk around his neighborhood and clear his head.

The brisk February air, bright sun, and melting snow soothed his spirit, made him believe spring would come again. He met several neighbors walking their dogs or just enjoying the winter sun. The sturdy homes reminded him that walls can be erected to protect what is precious to us.

He realized again, if he ever had forgotten it, that family for him was everything. By the time he returned to the house, he knew what he needed to do.

He arrived at his office ready to change. He arranged for coverage for his patients and dispatched an email memo to his colleagues announcing his decision to take a brief leave of absence.

Tony Whitemore barged through the open office door ten minutes after Mac sent the email.

"You should have talked to me before this," Whitemore said, face white and jaw jutting, as he slapped a copy of the notice onto the desk in front of Mac. "You can't abandon your patients like this!"

"Other staff have already agreed to cover me," Mac said, his voice level.

"The hospital will be getting complaints. Our referrals will diminish just as the brain tumor program is taking off, and—"

"I'd rather have complaints about scheduling than bad surgical results," Mac said. "I need some time."

Whitemore opened his mouth, then continued with a different tone. "What went on at that meeting in Korea,

MacGregor? All my reports were positive; your lecture was spectacular, and our referrals have skyrocketed. But you haven't been the same since you came back. Did something go wrong?"

Mac said nothing.

"I served in the Army Reserves in the Gulf War. A lot of my buddies couldn't reintegrate after what they saw. You remind me of them." He looked around the room as if he were waiting for an invitation to take a chair.

"Thanks for stopping by," Mac said, waving him toward the door.

Mac left the hospital at noon. As soon as he got home, he checked his computer for any news on the DPRK. Usually the bulletins parroted official propaganda—harangues against the capitalist system, strutting of military might, extravagant praise of the Supreme Leader.

That afternoon he got real news. The Supreme Leader would address the United Nations one week from today. Commentators circulated opinions that he would announce a demilitarization of nuclear capability and begin to welcome foreign travel and investment.

For Mac, the most important part of the press release lay in the pictures and videos.

General Kung, always prominent in the past, was nowhere to be seen.

At five a.m. the next morning the jangling of Mac's landline interrupted his restless sleep.

Lauren dragged a pillow over her head.

Mac stared at the caller ID scrolling on his phone to figure out who would be calling at this hour.

Unknown caller.

No one at the hospital would use his home phone number to reach him.

"Hello. Who is this?" Mac asked, irritated and apprehensive as he lifted the phone off its cradle.

"Dr. MacGregor, it's Dr. Ahn Junsu from Pyongyang."

Mac stiffened. Ahn's spoken English had improved substantially. But how could he get a high quality direct phone call out of North Korea? That alone suggested a major change in the politics of the country.

"Who is it?" Lauren asked, half asleep.

"Medical guy," he said. "I'll take it in the bathroom." He slid through the door and eased onto the chair at Lauren's cosmetic table.

"How did you get my home number, Ahn?'

"We have taken over an information system that Kung used to control."

"Is everything all right? I thought I wasn't going to hear from you people again." Mac's mouth was dry.

"I'm calling on behalf of the Supreme Leader."

"Is he OK?"

"Very well. No laughing spells, no seizures. Losing weight. Makes my job easy. I'm thinking about doing more training. But he wanted me to let you know General Kung has been dismissed."

"How? Why?"

"He had a major disagreement with the Supreme Leader, then disappeared."

"Disappeared? Is he dead? Where is he now?" Mac asked, feeling his body tense.

"We don't know exactly."

"So why did you to call me?" Mac's heart rate accelerated.

"Before he was dismissed, Kung complained that you did something to change the Supreme Leader's personality. He became obsessed with getting revenge."

"And?" Mac's head pounded.

"We think you might be his special target. We believe he plans to detonate a nuclear warhead somewhere in the USA. Claims it would restore the correct balance of power."

"Excuse me?"

"Kung is planning to explode a nuclear bomb somewhere in your country."

"Doesn't Homeland Security need to know about this?"

"We've already spoken to them, the CIA and FBI," Ahn said.

"And you think he may be heading for Boston and my family?"

"Precisely."

"You really have no idea where he is?"

"We lost him in Kazakhstan. The Kazakh government is not cooperating with our attempts to find him. They don't want their black market in Russian nuclear missiles discussed."

"Anything else I need to know?" His gut churned.

"We will try to help in any way we can. The Supreme Leader remains grateful to you."

Mac stared at his telephone after the call disconnected. Wrapping himself in a bathrobe, he crept down the stairs to the music room. As his fingers released the soothing melodies of the Chopin D flat major Nocturne, he formed his plan.

Returning to bed, he waited for dawn.

CHAPTER FORTY-NINE

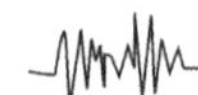

BROOKLINE AND BOSTON

FEBRUARY 12

At eight a.m., showered and suited, Mac presented himself to the Brookline Police Station. The officer on duty seemed to care more about his cup of coffee than Mac's complaint.

"Have you ever been injured by the man you're afraid of?"

"No."

"Threatened?"

"Not recently."

"What do you mean 'not recently'? In the past? Why didn't you report it then?"

Mac turned to look at the others waiting in the intake room. "Look, can I talk to someone in private? This is sensitive."

The officer shrugged and beeped for another officer to join them.

"This is Mr. MacGregor," the intake officer said. "He says someone's trying to attack him. Mr. MacGregor, this is Detective Yancey. He'll take your story in detail."

Detective Yancey was about forty, with thinning brown hair and a face still showing the scars of childhood acne. He wore wool slacks, a well-worn Irish tweed coat, and a regimental striped tie, but his shoes were those of a cop on the beat.

Mac decided he was a man who had experienced a lot, who had come up through the ranks after working the street. Mac trusted him.

Yancey led them to an interview room and sat at a small bare table, inviting Mac to sit across from him. He took out his smartphone, punched a key, and notified Mac officially that this would be recorded.

"Why do you think someone plans to attack you?" Yancey asked to start.

"I got a call from a friend."

"Could that friend provide any more information? Can we talk to him or her?"

"He's in Korea. I don't think you can reach him."

"Korea? How does someone in Korea have anything to do with you?"

"I attended a medical meeting there last summer."

"You met this friend and the man who wants to kill you while you were there?"

"Yes." Mac began to tremble as he felt himself getting into trouble.

"Why can't we reach him? International calls are easy to make."

Mac didn't answer, just stared.

The detective looked at Mac with narrowed eyelids. "Just what did you do in Korea?"

"Medical stuff."

Yancey shook his head, looked at his intake sheet. "Do you have a description of the man you're talking about? Pictures?"

"Here's a blow up of him taken from an old picture." He handed a grainy closeup of Kung's face. "I'm not sure he's the person who will be attacking. He has a team."

The detective looked at the photo, put his pen down and stared at Mac.

"This guy certainly looks mean. You confuse me, Mr., I mean Doctor, MacGregor. You seem genuinely worried, but the information you have given is very vague. Of course, we'll keep an eye out for anyone who looks like this picture. He would be hard to miss in this neighborhood. I don't think we can do much more. In case you need us, though, take my card and cell number." He scribbled a phone number. "Let me know if anything concrete develops."

Mac got up to leave, feeling more foolish than angry.

"We'll also put a patrol car on your street a couple of extra times a shift."

"Thanks."

Leaving the police station, Mac decided he would go directly to the hospital for some personal items. The MRI operating room was his home-away-from-home. In a personal drawer, he had surgical loupes, OR caps made for him by the first nurses he had ever worked with, and notebooks he wanted to preserve. He would start his leave of absence by reclaiming those items.

He checked the published OR schedule on his cell phone to be sure no one was using the room. No cases were listed in the entire neurosurgical pod. A typical Saturday. He would be left alone as he cleared his things out.

He changed into scrubs, enjoying the quiet of the empty locker room. Honoring the principle that the operating room was to be kept as clean as possible even when it was not in use, he put on shoe covers, hat, and mask before he entered.

The room was in semi-darkness, as it should have been when no one was working on a case. The anesthesia machine sat ready for use beside the patient table. The operating microscope had been covered and moved to the corner of the room along with the ultrasonic aspirator and laser. The MRI machine lay ready, always on, but cloistered behind automatic shielded doors.

He opened the drawer marked "Dr. MacGregor" and was putting his last items into a bag when a woman entered through the main doorway. She also wore surgical scrubs, mask, and hat. It was hard to make out her features in the low light, but she appeared athletic, five feet three inches, with Asian eyes above the mask. She could be one of the weekend nursing personnel except for the designer bag hanging from her left shoulder.

"Dr. MacGregor, I'm so glad to find you," she said in a soft voice with perfect American English.

Mac felt a tingle as he lowered his bag of personal effects. That voice sounded familiar. "Don't I know you?"

"I'm Rhee Sung. I met you last year. I was the person who took your family to Jeju Island. I wanted to warn you that your life is in danger."

He hesitated a moment, trying to figure out what was going on. His heart rate accelerated by instinct. Something was not right.

She moved toward him with her right arm extended as if she were going to shake his hand. As she came closer, she swerved and swiped her fingers at his face.

They caught his mask but did not touch his skin. He noted that she was wearing a surgical glove, could smell her jasmine perfume as she brushed by.

"What the—" he said, backing away.

She ripped the glove off her hand and tossed it into a far corner of the room.

Whatever was happening, it was not good. To buy time, Mac threw his bag at her.

She ducked, giving him the opportunity to flick two wall switches behind him.

Brilliant operating room lights blazed into action, dazzling his vision even though he had half-closed his lids in anticipation. The woman stepped back and pulled something from her purse, but appeared temporarily blinded by the lights.

He lunged at her arm. A pistol dropped out of her hand and clattered onto the floor.

She kicked at him, missing his face but forcing him to pull back. She yelled in Korean and assumed the attack position.

Mac noted the doors behind her pulling open. Activated by one of the switches he had flipped, the intraoperative MRI began to move slowly into the operating room on its ceiling-mounted tracks. The automatic mechanism slid it silently toward their position.

She charged, delivering a vicious kick to Mac's flank, then diving for her gun as he toppled to the floor.

He winced involuntarily with pain. When he opened his eyes, she towered over him, pointing the gun at his head.

"Time for you and your family to die, Dr. MacGregor. You now, them tomorrow."

"M-my family?" Mac stammered.

"They are accomplices. And so are thousands of others."

"Thousands of others? What are you talking about?"

"You'll find out," she said, then added, "or maybe you won't, since you'll be dead. We're going to give your city a nuclear Valentine's Day gift."

The movement of the MRI continued, silent and inexorable, behind her. Mac calculated the reach of the powerful magnetic field enveloping the machine. Three more feet and it would include her in its grasp.

"We?" he asked. "Who's we?"

"General Kung—my uncle—and me. And the people of the Democratic People's Republic of Korea we represent."

Two feet.

Mac narrowed his eyelids, trying to stall her for a few more seconds. "You're doing Kung's dirty work? You're the assassin. That's what the swipe across the face was about. Poison."

One foot. Her body was in the field, but her gun hand remained at the margin.

She smiled. "Poison is my specialty, but it doesn't matter how you die. A bullet will do. The first one will only be painful, not fatal—"

She took two steps backward to set her shot.

The pistol rocketed out of her hands, hurtling toward the MRI. She screamed, again in Korean, glanced at Mac lying on the floor, and ran after it as it slammed into the MRI bore with a loud *whack*.

For seconds she pulled ferociously to dislodge the gun from the bore of the magnet, filling the air with Korean curses.

That gave Mac enough time to race to the anesthesia machine and rip an oxygen tank from it. He chose the accessory cylinder, a green iron tube about twenty inches long and five inches wide, weighing ten pounds.

Pivoting, he sprinted back toward the MRI until he could feel the iron tank drawn into the massive magnetic field. As he felt it being lifted out of his arms, he heaved the cylinder with all his strength.

Captured by the tremendous field of the magnet, the tank shot toward the bore of the MRI with the accelerating velocity of a military projectile.

Rhee didn't realize what was happening until the last second. She turned, standing squarely in the center of the MRI opening as the cylinder rifled toward her.

It decapitated her, carrying her head through the magnet's bore.

Her body slumped to the floor. Brain and bone plastered against the scanner as geysers of blood cascaded from her severed arteries and formed rich red pools on the floor. The splattering sounded like drops of rain on a tin roof.

Then there was silence.

Mac felt his stomach churn as his heart rate decreased. He retched but had nothing to bring up. After his breathing and heart returned toward normal, he pushed the red panic button, a button intended for operative emergencies. His head, heart and flank continued to pound as security and operating personnel flooded into the room.

He realized that this was only the beginning. If Rhee was in Boston, so was General Kung. And what was the "nuclear Valentine's Day gift"? A bomb? Where? And how?

With a pounding head and pitching stomach, he prepared himself for the barrage of questions that would now be inevitable.

CHAPTER FIFTY

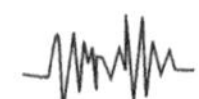

BOSTON

FEBRUARY 12

Detective Yancey extracted Mac from the operating room, then steered him into the elevator and through the crowds gathering in the hospital lobby. Members of the press shouted questions as they rushed toward the exit; Yancey ignored them all. With his car sirens blaring, he sped Mac to the precinct station in South Boston.

"This station's not as fancy as Brookline," he said as they disembarked, "but you are now in the jurisdiction of the City of Boston. I will continue as primary investigator."

"So what happened?" he asked once they were seated across from each other in the interview room.

Mac summarized the events of the day, trembling and nauseated. Yancey took notes, then picked up on one critical comment.

"She said they had a what?" he asked, mopping his brow.

"A gift. She said she and her uncle were going to give Boston a nuclear Valentine's Day gift."

Detective Yancey paused. "What kind of gift? Jesus, Doc. Are you sure you don't know this woman?"

"I'm not sure." A lump formed in his throat as he realized how complicated and impossible his story would be.

"How do you explain her wish to kill you?"

Mac shrugged.

Yancey shook his head. "Was she working for the man you described to me this morning?"

"Look, I need to talk with my wife and get cleaned up. Can you give me an hour?"

Yancey looked at his watch and nodded. "We need the time to run fingerprints and ask for help from other agencies anyway. I'm going to have a cruiser take you home and wait. You'll also have a surveillance team on your house twenty-four seven."

"What's wrong?" Lauren asked as Mac came through the door. "You look terrible."

"Do you remember Rhee Sung?"

"Of course. She was our guide in Jeju Island. Wonderful. Why?"

"She tried to kill me this morning."

"What?" Lauren said, color draining from her cheeks. She sat on the couch. "Is this a joke? What do you mean?" Disbelief and fear flashed in her face.

"She pulled a gun on me at the hospital."

"How can that be? What happened?"

Mac spilled out the entire story as straight as he dared. His kidnapping, the surgery he had been forced to do in North Korea, his terror at knowing the family were constantly in danger while they were on Jeju Island, last night's call from Ahn, today's attack in the OR. He changed one small detail. He told her, as he would tell everyone, that General Kung had been the patient, not the Supreme Leader. He said that the surgery might have changed Kung's personality, making him more violent.

Lauren sat first with a quizzical expression, then amazement, then relief. "No wonder you've been so edgy the last few months. And by the way, I believe you completely. No one could make that story up." She began to cry. "And I still thought it might be an affair." He put his arm around her.

"Are you safe now? Are we?" she asked. "Where is the general?"

"That's the big question."

She took his hands in hers and looked at him with an expression that melted his heart. Anger, pity, sympathy, love blended in a gaze only a life partner could give. "What a terrible time this must have been for you," she said. "I can't imagine what stress you've been under. I'm so sorry we couldn't help."

She hugged him hard.

"And now you know the problem." He gently detached himself. "I have to go down to the police station as soon as I've showered and changed. I don't know when I'll be back."

"Why do you have to go down there? Can't the police come to us?"

"This is way beyond the police now. I expect FBI, CIA, and Homeland Security are involved."

"Will we be OK here?"

"There'll be a cruiser in front of our house every minute of the day until the situation is resolved."

"Will that be enough?"

CHAPTER FIFTY-ONE

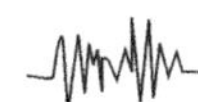

BOSTON

FEBRUARY 12

Mac returned to the interview room early that afternoon.

"Dr. MacGregor, meet James Parker from the regional FBI office in Chelsea," Yancey said as he gestured to a sandy-haired man sitting beside him. "We also have three people listening on secure lines: an Interpol agent from Lyon, the northeast regional director of Homeland Security, and a CIA agent from Washington covering Korea."

Each said hello through the speakerphone on the table.

Mac shook hands with Parker, a thin man in a blue pinstripe suit. His firm handshake and direct gaze led Mac to trust him.

Once Mac had taken a seat at the table, Yancey looked hard at him. "We've identified the woman you killed at the hospital. She's a North Korean assassin."

A voice issued from the speakerphone. "Homeland Security here. We think she was traveling with Kung Shinwa, former chief of staff to the Supreme Leader of North Korea. We haven't been able to trace him, but we have some intelligence that he might somehow have brought a nuclear warhead into the States."

"Dr. MacGregor, we need to know why this woman came for you," Parker said.

Mac said nothing.

The men stared at him.

Parker finally broke the tense silence. "Dr. MacGregor, please tell us what happened when you were supposed to be at a neurosurgical meeting in Seoul last August."

Still silence. Mac had no idea how he could explain without endangering his life and his family's. His head throbbed and his palms moistened with sweat as he tried to sort out what to say.

Parker clasped his hands together, leaning back in his chair. "Let me tell you what we know. Housekeeping at the Intercontinental Hotel remembers your family well—remembers that they went off to Jeju Island. The cleaning staff were disappointed the children left so soon after arriving. Maggie was a particular favorite. She asked about what they did with the bedsheets, how they made sure the right sheets got back to the right room after laundering, stuff like that."

"That's Maggie," Mac said with a weak smile.

"But they report that they don't remember you at all. They didn't believe you stayed in your room for that whole week. The bed wasn't slept in, the toilet paper was untouched. We ran the security tapes of the week and didn't see you ever coming in or out of your room."

Parker leaned forward. "So, Dr. MacGregor, where were you while your family was on Jeju Island?"

Mac decided that the only way forward was to tell the truth, at least as much as he had told Lauren. He shook his head, took a deep breath, and began.

"I was kidnapped by the North Koreans to operate on General Kung, the Supreme Leader's former chief of staff. He had a benign brain tumor called a hypothalamic hamartoma. I'm a world expert in surgery for that tumor."

Yancey's mouth and eyes opened wide. The Interpol official grunted audibly over the phone. Parker shook his head and frowned.

"Kidnapped?" Parker said. "How? When?"

"After my lecture Monday, the first day of the meeting."

"And when and where did you perform this surgery?"

"At the Pongwha Clinic in Pyongyang."

"And they took you to this hospital and brought you back over the border to Seoul after you completed the procedure?"

"Five days after. Yes."

"How did they get you across the border?"

"I have no idea. I just woke up in the hotel."

The CIA agent took over from Parker, transmitting his question through the intercom. "Is your surgery the reason the Duncan MacGregor Research Fund got a million-dollar anonymous gift after you returned?"

"Yes."

"How does Rhee Sung fit in?" Parker asked.

"She's General Kung's niece. I assume he wanted revenge for his dismissal and enlisted her help."

"And how would a patient behave after this surgery?"

"Hard to predict," Mac said. "This part of the brain controls emotions—hate, aggression, anger. Kung could be insanely violent. His memory, physical coordination, and thinking would remain intact."

"What exactly happened to you after the surgery?" Parker continued.

"I was held captive in the Pongwha Clinic for several days while my patient recovered. My family was on Jeju Island with Rhee Sung. They thought they were just having a vacation, but in fact were being held hostage. Thankfully, everything went smoothly. On the fifth day, I think I was drugged and transported back to Seoul. I only remember waking up in my room at the Intercontinental Hotel. My family came back from Jeju Island later that day and we left for Boston that evening."

"The North Koreans just let you go? You expect us to believe that?" Parker asked.

"Believe it or don't," Mac said. "That's what happened."

"Can you prove to us you are not a North Korean operative?" one of the listeners on speakerphone said. Mac couldn't distinguish who asked the question.

Mac laughed. "Are you kidding? But no, I guess I can't prove anything."

"Who else did you meet in Pyongyang? Who assisted in the surgery?" Parker asked.

"I can't tell you that. It would get both of us killed."

"If it was a South Korean neurosurgeon named David Ko, you should be aware that he has been missing for several weeks. We think he's been assassinated."

Mac said nothing.

Parker continued. "Dr. MacGregor, you've created an international crisis with the death of Rhee Sung, a North Korean citizen, in your hospital. You entered a hostile nation illegally this summer. By your own admission, you may have rendered a powerful international leader insanely violent. That man is here in America, possibly with a nuclear device at his disposal. I would suggest you answer our questions."

"I didn't plan any of those things. I was abducted."

"Will you excuse us please?" Parker shook his head.

Yancey took Mac back into the reception area.

Irate citizens, shoplifters, traffic violators pressed against the intake desk. The scene provided a pretense of normality. How could all of this be happening to him in a world that otherwise looked the way it always did? Had he been vaulted into an alternate universe?

After ten minutes Parker called him back into the conference room. "We're going to move you and your family to a safe house," he said. "Tonight."

CHAPTER FIFTY-TWO

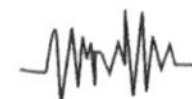

NEW HAMPSHIRE

FEBRUARY 12-14

"Tonight? Leaving in two hours?" Lauren said, her voice quavering.

"Yes," Mac replied.

"Children too?"

"Yes."

She moved her chair toward him. "What's going to happen to us, Mac?"

"I have no idea."

She put her head in her hands. "How can this be happening?"

"Let's just be ready to leave when the limousine comes."

"Where are we going, Daddy?" Maggie asked when the family clustered to hear the news that they were leaving for a vacation that night.

"I can't tell you," Mac said, then added, "not because I don't want to. I don't know."

"But I can't go. I have a lacrosse game tomorrow," Maggie said.

"I'm sure your coach will understand," Mac replied.

"Why do we have to go right now?" Peter asked.

"I can't go into the reasons, but they are very good ones," Mac said.

Maggie stood and stamped her foot. "You can't just make us do it. It's not fair."

"I know," Lauren said. "But it might even be fun. You can bring as many books and toys and dolls as you want."

"It's kind of like a special vacation. We can ski and do all kinds of snow stuff," Mac said, doing his best to make it sound promising.

"It doesn't sound like a vacation to me," Maggie said with a pout. "Sounds like jail."

During the limousine ride, Maggie and Peter watched movies on portable DVD players provided by the FBI; Lauren listened to music, squeezing Mac's hand throughout the trip; and Mac closed his eyes and wondered what lay ahead.

About an hour after they left Boston, Mac noted the New Hampshire logo on highway road signs. Leaving the highway after an hour, the limousine bounced for several miles along a potholed road, finally stopping at a high gate and sturdy metal fence. Snow was piled into three-foot banks at the edge. The driver punched in a phone code and the gates lumbered open.

A small white house to the right of the entrance displayed a large window overlooking the entrance to the compound. A guard in winter camouflage uniform stood at the road's edge, checked the driver's cred pack, then opened the back door to survey the family.

Mac started to climb out. "Not yet, Dr. MacGregor," the guard said. "Your destination is up ahead. Just wanted to make sure you got through the potholes safely. The access road to this place can be pretty rough. Everyone back here OK?"

The children waved at him.

"Just one bit of advice," he continued. "Don't try to cross the fence that surrounds the area. It's electrified and alarmed, and there are cameras everywhere."

They continued along a pathway so pitted that rapid driving would have been impossible. On either side, fields of snow lined the narrow access road. They could not see the extent of the fields in the darkness.

A quarter mile in, they spied a red barn at the side of the road. As the limousine pulled toward it, its doors opened and swallowed the car. Inside, the temperature changed from ten to sixty-eight degrees. An asphalt parking area sat in front of a wood frame house with white shingles. It looked like a New Hampshire farmhouse built inside a barn.

The driver unlocked the front door, turned on lights, and waved them in. The children ran through the house, flipping on lights and expressing their approval—fireplace, cable TV and game room, modern kitchen, good heat and plumbing. A bedroom for everyone and a study for Lauren. Refrigerator stocked with eggs, milk, meat, and vegetables. No internet connection and only a phone landline. Blocked cell phone communication.

They claimed their bedrooms and tumbled into bed.

The next morning, Mac could almost imagine they were on vacation. The bedroom window looked onto a field of crisp white snow. The bathroom had a heated floor. The air temperature was warm to the point of coziness. There was nothing much to do.

As soon as they finished breakfast, the children asked to explore the barn that enclosed the house. Mac and Lauren saw no reason to stop them.

While they were gone, Lauren started lesson preparation. Mac trekked down to the gate house and chatted with the agent on guard duty. He learned that two men stayed there at all times, alternating shifts. He used their computer to look for anything coming out of the DPRK. There was nothing new. There was also no news on the search for Kung.

Shortly after he returned, so did the children. "We found a bunch of neat stuff in the barn," Peter said. "Can we play outside now? Please?"

Mac volunteered to supervise. He found three pair of snowshoes in the barn. Wrapped in parkas, snow pants, and insulated boots, he and the children laced on the snow-walkers. The snow was soft with a firm layer underneath. The February sun bounced off with blinding brilliance. The fresh cold air left a slight ting in his nostrils but was not so cold that it hurt to breathe.

They discovered a horse barn down the hill with tractors, ploughs, and other farm equipment. They walked in the snow, fell over, built snowmen, and created snow angels all around the property.

Mac's anxiety lessened a little.

They ate, watched movies, and snuggled together for the rest of the day. The setting was lovely, almost overshadowing the reality of their situation.

The next morning, Mac rose early, wished Lauren happy Valentine's Day, and told her to go ahead with breakfast when the children were ready. He would take his morning constitutional to the guardhouse and get whatever new information he could.

She told him she had brought the ingredients for beef bourgignon and would prepare it for their family dinner.

During his stroll he could almost taste the savory beef and smell the aromatic gravy of her culinary magic. At least the family would be together this year. No surgical emergencies to interfere.

He stopped in front of the guardhouse front door. No one came out to greet him. He could not see anyone through the window. He knocked—no response. Rang the bell—no answer. Pushed the door—locked.

He cursed the rule prohibiting cell phones and walked around to the back of the house, ignoring the snow that spilled into his boots.

Snowmobile tracks ended ten feet from the house with footprints to and from the rear entrance.

He pulled at the back door, which opened easily. Fear began to nibble at him and his breathing quickened. He called into the house, repeating the name of the guard he knew was on duty. Silence.

He entered and moved through the hall to the foyer.

The guard lay in a sea of blood, throat slit open, pistol in his lifeless hand.

Mac clattered up the stairs to the bedroom where the second-call soldier should be. He found the body on the bed, skull smashed. Blood and brain soaked through the pillow and sheets. Mac felt for a pulse but knew there would be none.

My family. Are they alive?

Terror flooded his mind. He raced back down to the front path and ran for their so-called safe house.

When he entered the barn surrounding the house, silence faced him. He called for the children. No answer.

He entered the house. "Lauren, Peter, Maggie," he shouted, poking his head into the living and dining rooms, then heading for the kitchen.

On the kitchen table he saw two bowls of cereal with spoons still in them. His pulse raced and his legs felt weak. Something had happened quickly.

He ascended the stairs.

No one in the children's bedrooms.

He moved into the bathroom. *At least I know where the epipen is*, he flashed as he saw it on the back of the sink.

Shower curtains covered both bathtub and shower stall. He went for the bathtub curtain first, pulling it back with one swift move.

He felt the cold press of metal against the back of his neck. "Wrong curtain," a familiar voice said.

Mac whipped around. He hesitated. Kung's voice, but not the face he remembered. No scar, different features.

There was no doubt it was Kung, however, as the general moved the pistol to aim at Mac's chest. "Where is your family?" he asked.

Mac's body flooded with relief, "I have no idea." *Kung hasn't found them yet.*

Kung slapped him with the back of his hand.

"You don't have to hit me," Mac said, lowering his head and raising his arm as if he were cowering from the blow.

Kung hesitated. Mac erupted like a switchblade, straightening and sweeping his arm in a powerful arc that cut the gun away from Kung's hand. It fired into the ceiling.

Kung turned his head to follow it. Mac grabbed the epipen from the sink behind him and palmed it as Kung turned back.

"I don't need the gun. I'll kill you with my bare hands," Kung said with a shrug.

His massive hands encircled Mac's neck in a flash. Powerful thumbs pressed against Mac's trachea and made breathing more and more difficult. Kung pulled Mac toward him.

One chance, Mac thought as he fought for air. If he could inject epinephrine into the carotid artery, the rise in blood pressure might explode Kung's aneurysm. He could see Kung's features twisted with hatred, could smell Kung's sweat, could hear Kung's grunts as the grip tightened.

Mac raised his left hand to place two fingers in a V against the general's neck. The general did not respond to this move, continuing the throttling with both hands. Mac could feel Kung's carotid artery pounding between his fingers. With vision swimming, he positioned the epipen over the artery, then pushed as hard as he could. He felt his legs weakening beneath him as he began to black out.

He heard the pen's mechanism click to inject the epinephrine. The spurt of blood after he pulled the pen out confirmed that he had punctured the carotid. The effect should be massive and instantaneous, he thought, raising Kung's blood pressure enormously. That spike in pressure should rupture the weakness in the brain artery Mac had seen on Kung's MRI.

But Mac was rapidly losing consciousness. He kept his eyes open long enough to see a puzzled expression on Kung's face.

Mac could feel his world disappearing. He could not breathe, could not move, could barely see.

His plan hadn't worked.

Kung had beaten him.

Kung stepped back and grabbed at his head, screaming with pain. With one long intake of breath, he collapsed.

Released from Kung's death grip, Mac fell to his knees, gasping for air. He had only once before watched a patient's aneurysm burst, filling the brain with blood at impossible pressure, stopping all cerebral circulation as the brain blasted against the skull. The result was immediate respiratory arrest and death.

Which is exactly what he saw now. Kung did not writhe or groan or seize. He lay flaccid, without moving or breathing, on the bathroom floor.

Mac rested against the sink, panting. Sweat soaked his shirt and his vision swam with his near-death asphyxiation.

He felt no elation or relief, just intense fatigue. The general remained motionless where he fell. Mac pried the eyelids open to confirm the widely dilated pupils, checked for a pulse and found none.

He stared at the corpse of the man who had kidnapped him, haunted him, almost killed him.

And startled at the sound of a "ping." On Kung's wrist, a device that looked like a watch dinged once and seemed to spring into action. The dial read 119:58, counting down what appeared to be minutes and seconds.

Mac raced to the landline telephone and dialed the FBI number.

"Parker here."

"Parker, this is Duncan MacGregor. You need to get someone here now. Kung killed two of your men. He's dead, but his death seems to have started a countdown device."

He slammed down the telephone, now desperate to find his family. Kung had not known where they were, which left him hope. But where would they have gone? He searched every room and closet in the rest of the house. He returned to the kitchen, where half-eaten food meant the family had run out quickly.

Could Kung have an accomplice? Mac opened the door of the house leading to the forest, confirming only one set of skimobile tracks and footprints. He checked the coat rack. Coats and snow boots were still there. The family must still be in the building, but where?

CHAPTER FIFTY-THREE

NEW HAMPSHIRE AND BOSTON

FEBRUARY 14

Mac stepped into the shell of barn that camouflaged the house. He looked up toward the roof. Four levels of flooring stretched in a U around the open space, a bizarre variation of a hotel foyer. A rickety ladder led to the first level about twelve feet above the floor.

He mounted, catching himself several times to maintain balance. On that level, the uneven planked floor, caked with dirt and cobwebs, contained abandoned equipment. In the faint light from the central hanging bulb, he thought he could make out footprints in the dust.

Coughing and straining to see, he followed the tracks along the wooden planking to another ladder propped against the next level. He tried to call out again but the dust swirling around him choked his throat, making his voice hard to hear. He started up this new ladder. A rung collapsed beneath him. He dropped toward the floor, grabbing a rung higher as he swung over the two-story drop. He hauled himself back up, now testing each step before he took it.

He crawled onto the next floor, which had even thicker dust than the last. The ceiling was also higher, for which he gave silent thanks. He hated small spaces. He could no longer see well enough to follow footprints but could hear the scurrying of small creatures around him. He wandered the length and width of the landing, finding nothing but debris and boxes.

Above him lay the final floor. He discovered the ladder and clambered up, grimy and wheezing. The ladder seemed solid. He tried to shout again, but his throat emitted only a croak.

On this level no light penetrated. He had to pick his way like a blind man, hands before him, groping through the chilling darkness. The smells of mold and dust made every breath a trial. The rafters of the barn were so low he brushed them as he walked, with cobwebs covering his face. He bumped against something hanging from the rafter, grabbed it, and threw it against the floor as he recognized it was a bat. He heard the high-pitched squeak and ducked as whirring of wings brushed by his face. He did not think his heart could pound any faster.

Fumbling his way to the farthest corner, he felt a doorknob and twisted.

Light blinded him. He blundered through the open doorway, raising his forearm to make out what lay beyond.

The form of a woman materialized as his vision cleared, a woman lowering a flashlight in the left hand and holding a baseball bat in her right. Her face was streaked with dirt and her lips trembled, but he could recognize Lauren's features.

He rushed to her, encircled her with his arms. She

returned his embrace and began to sob. He stroked his fingers through her dust-caked hair, inhaled hints of her familiar perfume, and covered her forehead with kisses. "Everything is going to be all right now. Are you OK? The kids?"

She stepped aside to show the two children huddled behind her under a blanket, holding tight to each other.

Maggie disentangled herself and jumped to her feet. "It was so scary, Daddy. We heard a skimobile. A big man raced toward the house, but he kept falling through the snow crust. We ran."

"Peter remembered this playhouse from exploring the barn," Lauren said, "and we couldn't think of any other place to go. Thank God it was you coming up the stairs. We would be trapped if it had been the other guy." Lauren looked at Mac "Was that Kung? What happened to him?"

"I'll explain. Right now, let's get back into the house."

They descended the rickety ladders and returned to the main building. The residence no longer felt like a safe house.

"Don't go upstairs," Mac instructed. "At least not until the FBI agents get here. I called them before I came searching for you. I don't know how they're going to make it on those roads—"

A thunderous eruption drowned out the rest of his comment. Maggie ran to the window. "A helicopter!" she said, pointing to the open field behind the house.

Mac and Lauren joined Maggie. Peter still seemed too shocked to move and remained wrapped in a blanket on the couch.

A Blackhawk helicopter set down with deafening noise and a vortex that whipped snow everywhere around it. Two men emerged in black parkas marked FBI. As they sprinted toward the house with automatic rifles in hand, Mac recognized one as Parker.

"Two of your men are dead in the guard house," Mac shouted, pulling the door open to admit them. "General Kung, the guy we were looking for, killed them. He's upstairs, also dead. But he has some kind of countdown device on his wrist." He pointed to the bathroom.

The agents raced up the stairway.

"What are we supposed to do now?" Lauren asked.

"Nothing, I hope," Mac said. He sat on the couch beside her, putting one arm around her and gathering the children under the other. "I'm so sorry to have gotten you into this mess."

"This is way beyond you," Lauren said. "It's not your fault."

Mac was forming an answer when Parker appeared in the doorway. He looked worried. "Can I speak to you a minute?" he asked.

Mac joined him in the foyer. "I don't know how you did it," Parker said, "but Kung's definitely dead. We found two items of interest on him."

He held up a small object about the size of a USB stick. "This is a tracking monitor that seems to be pointing at you. I expect the North Koreans implanted something while you were out."

Mac felt the back of his head. "My headaches! And that's how they tracked me here."

"We can get a surgeon to explant it later, but right now we have to deal with this." He held up the watch he had removed from Kung's wrist. "This is the other item. As you said, a detonation countdown device. One hundred minutes to go. That's not enough time for the national units to get mobilized from Washington. We have to use this chopper to get to the bomb."

He put the countdown watch on his wrist and stared at Mac. "So where are we going, Doctor? Where did Kung hide the nuclear device that's going to annihilate Boston?"

"My bet is the MRI scanner the Korean-American Friendship Association just donated to the hospital."

"If that's your hunch, we'll run with it. You and I are going to Harbor Hospital."

Mac looked at him with dawning dread. "You and I? Can't someone else help now?"

"No." Parker looked straight into Mac's eyes. "We need you to be sure we get the right device."

"My family needs me here."

"Agent Morris will stay with them until new guards arrive. There are no other assailants. And your family won't be around very long if the bomb detonates. None of us will."

Mac paused for a moment, then strode to Lauren and the children in the next room. "I have to go with Agent Parker for a couple of hours."

"Where are you going? Can we come with you?" Lauren asked.

"No. Agent Morris will stay with you." He hugged each of the children and kissed Lauren. "Don't worry. I'll be back soon."

He hoped they didn't notice his tears as he left.

CHAPTER FIFTY-FOUR

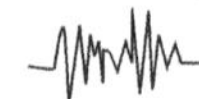

BOSTON

FEBRUARY 14

Mac clapped the headset over his ears and drew his microphone into position as the Blackhawk chopped its way into the spitting snow. He could hear nothing above the infernal roar of the rotors, punctuated by short incomprehensible phrases from the pilot.

"How long?" he shouted after the copter had been traveling for several minutes.

Neither pilot nor Parker paid any attention. They sat in front, leaving him bouncing against his shoulder belt in the rear seat. The pitching and vibration made his stomach churn and he could hardly think straight.

His anxiety, high because of his mission and his family, escalated as the turbulence increased. It seemed impossible that a nuclear explosion would destroy the world around him in less than two hours.

He tapped Parker on the shoulder, pointed at his watch, and raised his eyebrows to indicate he was asking a question.

Parker lifted one earphone from Mac's ear and shouted, "Fifteen more minutes to the hospital. I have to clear traffic from the Seaport and Logan, then sort out what we're going to do once we get the bomb. Can't talk."

For ten minutes, Mac watched the New Hampshire landscape crawl past in a monotone of white. The shrieking wind and pitching of the chopper made it impossible to think. He bounced up and down in suspended animation hell, unable to do anything about his frozen fingers and toes, sickened by the stench of oil and the churning of the rotors. He could deal with surgical disaster, physical attack, and almost anything an opponent could throw at him—if he could throw something back. He had a hard time with powerlessness.

He tried yoga breathing, checked his pulse. It continued to race despite his various maneuvers to calm himself.

Parker slapped Mac's knee to get his attention, held up two fingers and pointed to the scene below.

Two minutes to the hospital. Downtown Boston, then Boston Harbor, spread below them. Both were deserted, with no planes on Logan runways and no boats crisscrossing the water. Even the perpetually busy Rose Kennedy Greenway had no traffic. It looked to Mac as if the end of the world had already begun.

The chopper headed for the large red cross on the Harbor Hospital helipad. Moments after it touched down, a woman in Kevlar clambered aboard. Almost six feet in height, she had cropped hair and a frown.

"Meet Agent Susan Ramsdell, our unit's Bomb Technician," Parker said, taking off his headset as the rotors stopped. "She's the head of our NEST team."

"He has to go," Ramsdell said, tilting her head toward Mac.

"Negative," Parker said. "He's the only one who knows the target."

"Wrong," Ramsdell said. "As soon as you called I sent a squad to the MRI on the loading dock. They'll identify the warhead and disarm it. We don't need any civilians getting in the—" Her clanging cell phone interrupted. She listened and returned it to her pocket with a look of fury.

"It's not there," she shouted at Parker.

"What?" he shouted back.

"There's no warhead in the MRI crate. They just opened it and found nothing. Our medical consultant here must have made a miscalculation." She shot Mac an accusatory glare. "We're screwed."

"We have thirty-eight minutes," Parker said.

"But it has to be in the MRI shipment," Mac said. *A cardinal rule of neurosurgery. Always look at the situation yourself. Don't rely on someone else's description.* "I need to see what your people are looking at."

Ramsdell and Parker outstared each other a silent showdown for a few seconds. "C'mon, Mac," Parker said finally and led the way out of the helicopter.

The high-speed elevator from the hospital roof to the receiving level seemed to take hours. As the doors opened, Parker and Ramsdell followed MacGregor at a run.

At one side of the loading dock, a four-man crew surrounded a wooden container with one side torn away. It had MRI in large stencils on every side.

"We've looked through the whole crate—no detectable radiation and nothing that looks like a warhead," the leader of the group reported to Ramsdell.

Mac stepped in, inspecting the gantry and rotor exposed within the shipment. "But this is only part of the scanner.

Where's the patient table?" He looked around the dock at the blank looks from the workmen. "We need Brian Mancuso. Fast."

Brian appeared in seconds. "Meet Brian Mancuso, the master of all things mechanical," Mac said to Parker and Ramsdell to introduce the sprightly man. "He runs the receiving dock."

"You wanted the table for this magnet, Dr. M?" Brian said. "We left it in wraps."

He led the group to a long, thin crate lying at the side of the corridor. The workers ripped it open with crowbars and hammers.

The gleaming metal table sat splendidly displayed within the wooden carton. The men surrounded it, looking for some access point. They tried to lift its top, complaining about its weight. They could not budge it.

The man passed a Geiger counter over it. "Background activity. Maybe this is a wild goose chase too."

"Brian, get me a chisel, hammer, and metal shears. Please." Mac did not give Ramsdell a chance to respond.

"Got them right across the way," Brian said.

In less than a minute, Mac poised the hammer for the first blow.

"What the hell are you doing destroying one of my MR tables?" Tony Whitemore shouted from the doorway and began to trot toward Mac.

Mac closed his eyes and shook his head.

Ramsdell stepped into Whitemore's path. "Who the hell are you?" she asked as she blocked him.

"That's my line to ask you," Whitemore said, but he

stopped and shrunk back. "I'm the chief medical officer of Harbor Hospital. I heard there was a SWAT team invading our premises. That's trespassing in my hospital, and—"

"Wrong." She waved her NEST credentials in his face. "I have jurisdiction here. Now go back to whatever hole you crawled out of."

"But you can't just—"

"I forget your name but if you're still here in five seconds you'll be on the unemployment list. Now get out."

Whitemore blustered as agents escorted him back into the bowels of the hospital.

Mac had already sliced a line of chisel cuts, taking care not to penetrate deeper than the outer layer of the box.

"Non-ferromagnetic metal on the outside with a lead lining to block radiation," Ramsdell said as she watched over his shoulder. Her voice had lost its caustic tone

Mac used the metal shears to rip a six-foot-long opening in the shape of an upside down U, then prised the lead liner down with the side of the table.

The group crowded to see what lay inside.

Ramsdell's LED flashlight illuminated the object perfectly: a six-foot metal cone with a base widening to a diameter of two feet and Cyrillic lettering on its surface. The Geiger counter now rattled furiously when it was brought near.

"We got it," Ramsdell said as she mopped her brow. "Now all we have to do is disarm the goddammed thing."

"Thirty-two minutes," Parker said.

"Should I kick your ass or thank you for the reminder?" Ramsdell snapped. "Dr. MacGregor, I need a room with secure computers and video camera uplinks."

"The imaging suite down the hall. Brian can clear it for us. We can roll the table right there," Mac said, and began to push.

In two minutes the team had commandeered the computer workroom of the Surgical Planning Laboratory.

"Let's bring this baby into the light so we can show it to our experts," Ramsdell said. With three of her men she rolled the warhead out, lifted it to the mattress of the table, then arranged video cams to display it. "I'm linking to NEST headquarters to see what we're dealing with."

"Thirty minutes," Parker said and turned to Mac. "I need you to come with me while Ramsdell is finding out about the warhead."

He dragged Mac by the arm to an adjacent room and flipped on a high-definition video cam and computer used for teleconferences. Parker punched in several codes and Mac stiffened in surprise. From his chair in the Oval Office, the president of the United States faced them.

"What's the situation, Parker?" the president asked.

"We've found the warhead, Mr. President. It's from a Russian missile, but it was planted by a rogue North Korean official who was fired months ago. It was not part of any official government action. We're working to deactivate it now. In case we don't succeed, I wanted you to meet Dr. Duncan MacGregor, the man who located the warhead for us."

"Thank you for your service," the president said.

Mac bowed his head slightly.

"We need directions for action if we can't deactivate the device," Parker said.

"Our options?" the president asked.

"If it explodes here on the ground, Boston and its suburbs disappear. Harvard, MIT, and thirty other universities and major hospitals will be obliterated."

"Direct casualties?"

"At least two hundred and fifty thousand immediate deaths. A million injured. Complete infrastructure failure."

The president frowned and looked up from a pad he had been writing on. "Option two?" he asked.

"We try to get it airborne and let it explode two thousand feet in the air."

"And?"

"Less damage, but still massive."

"Number three?"

"We drop it in Boston Harbor."

"The effects of that maneuver?"

"Fewer casualties, but it wipes out the northeast coastline and part of George's Bank."

The president looked away and folded his fingers. "Parker?"

"Yes, Mr. president?"

"Just deactivate the goddamned thing, whatever it takes."

"Yes, sir."

The screen blackened. Mac slumped in his chair. His heart pounded in his chest.

"At least he knows who you are if we don't make it," Parker said as they rejoined Ramsdell.

"We've been able to get help from our Russian counterparts on Zoom as well as our own experts," Ramsdell said. "This is a Teller-Ulam bomb, a fission/fusion device. The timer ignites a chemical explosion that facilitates fission with beryllium and plutonium— "the urchin." That event in sequence sets off lithium deuteride and uranium-235 fusion."

"And then?"

"Full nuclear catastrophe."

"Can we cut the wires of the timer?" Mac asked.

"No. These warheads have a tamper-proof detonation sequence once they are activated."

"How about the chemical explosion? Can we stop that? That's what we do in seizure surgery—remove the focus that starts the seizure."

Ramsdell tilted her head. "Are you suggesting we operate to remove the chemical explosives?"

"Yes. That should abort the whole sequence. Are the chemicals accessible?"

Ramsdell looked at Mac with narrowed eyelids and what appeared to be new appreciation. "Yes, I think they are, in packets around the plutonium core that form a focusing lens. But how the hell would we get to them?"

"I think I can help with that," Mac said.

"Twenty-four minutes," Parker said.

CHAPTER FIFTY-FIVE

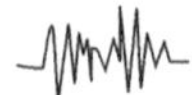

BOSTON

FEBRUARY 14

Mac surveyed a transformed operating room.

A six-foot thermonuclear warhead lay flat on the OR table.

Jacob Ray, an ex-Navy medic who had volunteered to scrub on the case, prepared the laser, diamond drill, and irrigation.

OR techs rolled away the anesthesia machine and other equipment usually critical to surgery.

Video cameras in the handles of the overhead lights, usually transmitting images to students in an adjoining room, sent them instead to nuclear emergency teams in Washington and Moscow.

Mac heard none of the usual sounds of surgical preparation: checklists, requests for last- minute supplies, machine bleeps and dings, murmurs from visitors and staff. He smelled none of the odors that signaled the start of a case—anesthetic gas, surgical prep solution. But he did feel the fear that accompanies the start of any complex surgery. That fear, and the adrenaline released by it, sometimes made the difference between success and failure.

He felt bizarrely dressed in the lead apron, thick laser goggles, and radiation badge that replaced his surgeon's uniform. No shoe covers, no gown, no hat. He did wear surgical gloves to remind him of his role.

His anxiety morphed into focused attention. He had a simple goal—remove the chemical explosive pack that would start the nuclear reaction, just as he would remove a hypothalamic hamartoma that started a seizure.

The double doors opened and Parker scuffed through, walking backwards with a platform cart in tow. Ramsdell maneuvered the other end. The cart creaked under the weight of the lead coffin on it. Two bulky pairs of lead gloves perched on its cover.

"Heavy," Ramsdell said as they parked the lead-lined container behind them at the table.

"Fifteen minutes ten seconds," Parker said, checking the device on his wrist.

"What's the box for?" Mac asked.

"Shielding," Ramsdell said. "Once you get the radioactive core exposed, we'll dump it in here."

Mac marked out a rectangle three feet by one foot on the warhead's surface. "Is this big enough?" he asked the lights.

A voice with a thick Russian accent reverberated through the speaker system: "Please make ten centimeters bigger to expose entire inner contents."

Mac extended the outline. "Will this work?"

"Yes, better."

Mac pushed his foot against the laser pedal and picked up what looked like a pen attached to a long fiberoptic cable. A red dot flickered and danced on the titanium casing.

"All set," he said and lifted his arm to begin.

"Hold on," Ramsdell barked.

Mac lowered his hand. What was wrong now? His heart rate increased despite his calm exterior.

"I want to make sure you understand what you'll see," Ramsdell continued. "First, a metal casing that looks like a five-foot-long peanut shell. The inner bomb components are inside that, surrounded by plastic packing. You'll have to open the front compartment of that casing. Inside you'll see the array of chemical explosives. If you get them out, the fission reaction should abort."

"You have fourteen minutes," Parker added.

Mac began his cut, raising smoke plumes from the incision line in the titanium casing.

The metal edges glowed red as the opening lengthened along the warhead surface. "Watch it!" A new American voice issued from the speakers. "Don't let the exterior casing heat up. We don't know what might set off the explosives inside."

Mac nodded. Jacob irrigated the field with fluid from the bag on the IV pole. Steam replaced smoke and Mac slowed the pace to lessen the heating.

Despite the mask, the smell of the dissolving metal was acrid, and irritating, not at all like the familiar odor of burning tissue. Wisps of metallic steam drifted onto his face. The laser goggles protected his eyes but made the surgical field so dark he could hardly see any detail.

"Twelve minutes," Parker said.

Mac removed a five by one-foot window from the bomb casing. Before him lay a white surface. He put his gloved hand out to touch it. Firm and crinkly.

"Styrofoam?" he asked.

"Plastic packing," Ramsdell said. "Over a radioactive casing. Get it out fast."

Using the laser beam Mac sliced chunks of the packing material, throwing them on the floor as if he were opening a box of shipped furniture.

On the fourth slice, smoke billowed from the cavity, filling the air with the odor of burning plastic. Flames licked the surface of the white material.

"Saline." Mac's voice continued steady.

Jacob passed the liter bag of saline from the IV pole to Mac, who slit it open with the laser and poured it onto the flames. Steam hissed into the air from the cavity. Burning flecks of plastic spattered over the surgical field and obstructed Mac's already gray vision.

"Chemical fire. Water's useless," Parker said as he raced to the fire extinguisher at the operating room exit. Back at the table, he released the trigger and plastered the entire operative surface with white foam.

The flames lessened, but a mixture of smoke, steam, and foam shot upward to envelop the team in a cloud of acrid emission. They all stepped backward and turned away, coughing violently. Mac grimaced in distress and put his arm over his mouth.

As the plume reached the ceiling, fire alarms began to wail and the sprinkler system poured water onto the field.

From the speaker system, the Russian voice asked. "What is happening? What is terrible sound?"

Mac ignored the Russian. "Do something about the goddammed sprinklers," he said to Jacob. He had remained calm until this, but the combination of screeching alarm, smoke, water, and darkened vision began to irritate him.

Jacob reached up to arrange the parabolic OR lights in a cluster that acted like umbrellas over the table. The torrents of water lessened to a steady drip.

"The capsule is uranium-238," Ramsdell said. "Even with these gloves, the radiation may burn your hands." He held the gloves from the lead coffin open for Mac, who shoved his hands into the rigid lead fingers and began to scoop away soggy packing material. It was like operating with a shovel. Slopping through the slurry of foam and plastic, gloves slippery from the torrential water, Mac threw chunks of the plastic packing into the coffin behind him.

He began to see a smooth surface. More carefully now, he rubbed the last fragments of plastic packing away. The high level of adrenaline already circulating left no room for further anxiety.

"Seven minutes," Parker shouted.

A shiny tubular surface five feet long emerged, with a bulge at either end.

"Just as you predicted, looks like a big metal peanut shell," Mac called out. "Where do we open it?"

"On left," the Russian voice said. "Sixty centimeters. No laser."

"Chemical explosive underneath," Ramsdell shouted to explain. "If it blows, it may prime the nuclear reaction and there isn't a damn thing we can do."

"So we have to get those packets out of there without heating them?"

"Or else."

"Jake, how many craniotome blades do we have?" Mac asked.

"Six. And that's it for the whole OR." Jacob looked anxious.

"Irrigate on this drill like crazy," Mac called. He took the diamond drill in his massive mittens and drilled an inch-wide hole in the metal casing. So different than the delicate micromanipulations of hamartoma surgery. More like orthopedics, he thought as he completed the hole.

"Your radiation badge has just flipped to the early danger level," Ramsdell said. She looked around the table. "In fact, all of ours have. We don't have much margin."

Mac gave her a look that he hoped reminded her that there was no place to go. She looked away, then at the clock.

"Give me the craniotome," Mac shouted, barely making his voice heard over the torrents of water and the fire alarm. The nurse slipped the guard over the drill bit. Mac fitted the foot of the whirling bit under the edge of the metal, hoping it would keep the device from injuring whatever was below. Although that was usually the brain, this time it was the explosive that needed to remain undamaged.

After four inches of opening, the drill bit snapped. Mac knew this would happen. The metal was soft, but still harder than the bone the instrument was designed to cut. He handed the instrument to Jacob, who replaced the blade without a word.

"Five minutes," Parker said. His voice cracked and his eyes were wide. Ramsdell turned away from the OR table.

Four more times, Jacob replaced the blade. Mac handed him the instrument for the last blade with three inches left to open.

"It's jammed," Jacob complained. "I can't get the blade out."

Mac didn't bother to touch it. "Periosteal elevator," he said, and with the sturdy instrument pried the two-foot flap up from the surface.

Below him lay a series of small packets.

"Lens array," Ramsdell said. "Every one has to go."

"Two minutes," Parker said.

No voices came from the speaker system, and Mac felt time slow down and sound fade away. He tried to remove the small packets with the massive gloves. As the seconds ticked by, he realized it was too cumbersome.

"Radiation be damned," he muttered as he slipped off gauntlets and goggles, wiped sweat from his forehead, and tore at the rest of the packets with his latex gloves.

"One minute." Parker yelled. "We're not going to make it."

"Oh yes we are," Mac could see an inner beryllium layer below him as well as the electronic trigger that would ignite the array. He scooped the last pellet away and dropped in on the floor.

"Go," he said, pushing the disabled warhead toward Ramsdell, who had closed her eyes. "Damn," she said, opening her eyes and hauling the lead coffin to a position beside the table. She and Parker rolled the defused warhead into it with a loud crash. They slid its massive cover closed as Parker counted: "four, three, two, one."

A buzz sounded from the lead-lined coffin and a small puff of smoke escaped under the lid. Then, nothing.

Mac, Ramsdell, and Parker looked at each other for a full sixty seconds. Ramsdell began to smile, the first time Mac had seen her do such a thing.

CHAPTER FIFTY-SIX

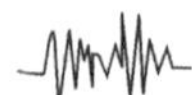

WASHINGTON, D.C.

JULY 3

Mac and his family arrived at the East Room of the White House half an hour before the official ceremony began. Other recipients of the Presidential Citizens Medal and their families gradually filled the hall. The cool air provided a welcome contrast to the ninety-degree heat outside the windows.

Lauren stared at the beautifully decorated walls, oriental rugs, crystal chandeliers, and silk window treatments.

"Don't get any ideas," Mac whispered to her. "Our living room is fine as is."

"Look at that piano," Lauren whispered. "The program book says it was bequeathed by the Steinway family more than a century ago. Wouldn't you love to play on it? This place is like a living museum."

Peter and Maggie played "guess the portrait," pointing particularly at the pictures of George Washington and Theodore Roosevelt on the walls.

As they waited, Mac considered the whirlwind that had followed the dismantling of the warhead. Relations between the DPRK and the USA improved. The Supreme Leader initiated steps to abolish his country's nuclear program. With

Mac's help, Dr. Ahn had been given permission to do a fellowship at Harbor Hospital.

At the hospital, Mac's Brain Tumor Center received approval from the Board of Trustees. Tony Whitemore had been encouraged to find another job, but was still looking. Knight continued to be a pain until he finished his residency in June. He then took a position in Florida, but vowed to return.

At home, Lauren gave Mac complete dispensation for past and future missed commitments. As she put it, "I'm not going to argue about scheduling with anyone who has disarmed a nuclear warhead." His headaches had resolved once the implant was taken from his scalp, and his hands had not suffered any side effects so far from the radiation exposure. He had dermatology visits booked every six months to check them.

Maggie kept thanking him for her visit to Korea, since she got the highest grade ever for her show-and-tell class presentation. Peter demonstrated his fancy new game system to everyone he could, emphasizing that it had not yet been released in the USA.

Mac began to rethink the Korean experience. The opportunity to make a real difference resonated with him. If he were honest with himself, resuming his neurosurgical routine bored him.

Mac felt a tap against his shoulder and turned to see a secret service agent standing beside him. "Dr. MacGregor, please come with me. The president would like to speak with you before the ceremony."

They crossed the corridor to the Oval Office. Mac felt a rush of anxiety as he stepped into the sacred space, so rich with tradition. The yellow striped wallpaper, thick rug, and hanging portraits proclaimed understated power. The president, initially silhouetted by three large windows, rose and invited Mac to sit in an overstuffed armchair across from him.

"I'm very happy that you and Mrs. MacGregor could join us today," the president said as he shook hands. "Congratulations on the award I'm about to bestow. You did a great service to your country in locating and defusing the nuclear warhead and eliminating a rogue North Korean general. To understand what I'm about to say, however, you need to know that I'm aware of the whole story."

Mac opened his mouth, but the President raised a hand to stop him. "I've had several conversations with the Supreme Leader of the DPRK. He's a new man, committed to de-escalating nuclear weapons. He wanted me to tell you he's not having any laughing spells, but he's smiling a lot. He's also finding his weight and temper easier to control. He is truly grateful to you, Dr. MacGregor."

Mac said, "But—"

Again, the president stopped him. "Your help and discretion in this matter lead me to ask if you would be willing to serve your country in a new ongoing way."

"Sir?"

"I have created a team of special citizens who act as emissaries of the United States in situations relevant to their expertise. They are vital to the country."

"Are they spies?"

"No, nothing like that. They just help when the need arises. For you, it would mean occasionally consulting on international medical situations that have political significance. James Brogan, the director of the CIA, will give you details. I would be grateful if you would accept his offer. Thank you again for your work. Now we'd better get to the big event."

Twenty minutes later, Mac smiled as the president pinned the Presidential Citizens Medal on him with the commendation, "Exemplary deeds for his country."

His smile broke into a grin when he saw the awed looks from Peter and Maggie. Lauren's eyes were moist as he marched back to his seat with the gold eagle flashing on his chest.

After all the other medals had been awarded, he shook hands with well-wishers while the family surfeited on sandwiches and scones. He felt his heart rate accelerate when a tall, silver-haired man introduced himself as James Brogan and maneuvered him to the edge of the room.

Brogan explained what would be involved in the new job occasionally working with the CIA.

"What about my responsibilities at the hospital?" Mac asked.

"Already dealt with. Your colleagues have agreed to back you up whenever you need it, and the hospital president has given us carte blanche to take you away when we need you."

"And my family?"

"I have taken the liberty of talking to Mrs. MacGregor," Brogan said.

"And she is bursting with pride at her husband's invitation," Lauren said, coming up from behind and encircling his waist with a hug.

Mac shrugged. "What can I say? I accept."

The head of the CIA reached out to shake Mac's hand. "Welcome aboard, Doctor."

THE END

ACKNOWLEDGMENTS

This book would not have been possible without Carole Holladay, who helped develop it from idea to completion. Thanks are not enough—she probably needs a vacation too!

Mayapriya Long of Bookwrights.com created the final format. Her skill and patience made collaboration a joy.

Michael Palmer got me started as an author. The writing course he and Tess Gerritsen taught for many years provided both education and inspiration, and Michael added much personal encouragement.

My writing group furnished priceless support and advice. Jay Shepherd, Shelly Dickson Carr, Cheryl Malone, Judy and Hans Copek, Carol Lynn, Stephanie McPherson, and Paula Steffen—you ignited me each week and sometimes stopped me from flaming!

Dorian Mintzer, Sal Tripple, Norm Appel, Susan and Christopher Black, and Alex and Wiera Malozemoff added feedback at many points during the book's development.

And finally, my family made it all worthwhile.

ABOUT THE AUTHOR

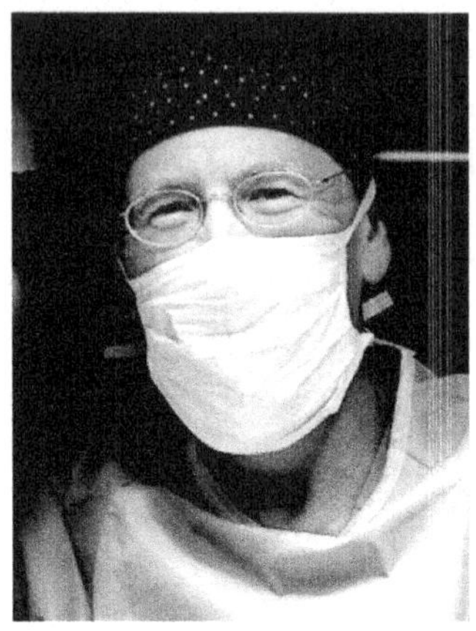

DR. PETER BLACK has served as a physician to Congress, professor of neurosurgery at Harvard Medical School, and president of the World Federation of Neurosurgical Societies. As an author, he now draws on his experiences as surgeon, scientist, teacher, and traveler to craft medical thrillers. Packed with high-tech medicine, relatable characters, exotic locations, and unexpected plot twists, Black's stories will keep you reading late into the night.

Dr. Black writes from his home in the great Boston area. You can find him on the web at peterblackbooks.com

Made in the USA
Monee, IL
10 April 2022

94494929R00203